CRIMSON CROSS SERIES

NATE DONOVAN

REVOLUTIONARY SPY

DEDICATION

To the brave Patriots, both soldiers and civilians, who were willing to give their lives in America's struggle to gain her freedom from Great Britain. And to the young Patriots of the next generation, who are prepared to sacrifice whatever it takes to keep her free.

ACKNOWLEDGMENTS

The authors want to express our grateful thanks to Bill Troppman, a Park Ranger at Valley Forge Historical Park, whose research tips were invaluable to us in learning the true story of the Continental Army's ordeal at Valley Forge.

CRIMSON CROSS SERIES

NATE DONOVAN
REVOLUTIONARY SPY

PETER MARSHALL AND DAVID MANUEL
AND SHELDON MAXWELL

B&H
PUBLISHING GROUP
Nashville, Tennessee

978-0-8054-4394-3

Published by B&H Publishing Group,
Nashville, Tennessee

Dewey Decimal Classification: F
Subject Heading: SOCIETY OF FRIENDS—FICTION \
UNITED STATES—HISTORY—1775–1783, REVOLUTION—
FICTION \ HISTORICAL FICTION

This book is a work of fiction, intended to entertain and inspire.
Although it is based on actual historical events, some of the names,
characters, places, and incidents are the products of the authors' imagina-
tion. In some cases, fictitious words or actions have been attributed
to real individuals; these, too, are imagined.

1 2 3 4 5 6 7 8 9 10   11 10 09 08 07

THE CHARACTERS

THE DONOVAN FAMILY

William: patriarch of the family, a schoolteacher and devout pacifist, is determined that his Quaker family remain neutral in the war between the British and the Americans. (This character is the only one who retains the original Quaker language.)

Lydia: William's wife is strong willed and capable. Her sympathies are clearly with the Patriots in their struggle for independence.

Charles: the elder son, defies his father and storms off to join the Continental Army on their way to winter quarters in Valley Forge.

Nate: the younger son, who at fifteen is one year too young to join the army but old enough to join General Washington's spy network.

Rachel: the daughter, sixteen, strongly attracted to the elegant British captain and gentleman, John André.

Andrew and Molly: the three-year-old twins who are the delight of their father's eyes.

THE SPY "FAMILY"

Running Fox: the Oneida Indian scout who befriends Nate and teaches him the "ways of the fox."

Major Tallmadge: General Washington's chief of intelligence and the head of the spies.

Colonel Cadwalader: the Donovans' neighbor, who recruits Nate as a member of General Washington's spy network.

Captain McLane: an important courier of messages for the spy family.

David Bushnell: the inventor of the submarine, who plans surprises for the British ships in Philadelphia's harbor.

Jacob and Odus Levering: brothers who ferry secret messages up and down the Schuylkill River for the spy network.

Pastor George Duffield: the beloved Philadelphia minister and army chaplain who is a fiery evangelical preacher of American independence.

Hyam Solomon: the wise and deeply spiritual Jewish banker who saves Nate's life in prison.

Aunt Neuss: the eccentric but patriotic Quaker who runs Rising Sun Tavern, a frequent meeting place of the spy network.

Sally Winston: a pretty young courier in the spy network.

Widow Foulke: the crusty old matron of Foulke mansion, with whom Sally is staying.

Mr. Ludwig: the baker who organizes the other Patriot bakers in Philadelphia to come to the aid of the army at Valley Forge.

AT VALLEY FORGE

General Washington: the Commander in Chief of the Continental Army.

Captain Hamilton: General Washington's aide-de-camp.

Marquis de Lafayette: the young French General who came from Europe to assist the American struggle for independence.

Tad Walker: a local farm boy who becomes Nate's closest friend.

Sarah Walker: Tad's loving mother, who tends the army's sick and becomes known as "the angel of Valley Forge."

General Wayne: Sarah's cousin, living with the Walkers at Valley Forge.

Dr. Rush: determined champion of better treatment in the hospitals at Valley Forge.

BRITISH OFFICERS

General Howe: the British Lord in command of His Majesty's Royal Army in North America.

Captain André: chief of British counter-intelligence, who commandeers the Donovan home for Lord Howe's staff meetings and becomes infatuated with Rachel Donovan.

1

NIGHT STORM

Nate Donovan, clad in a homespun muslin shirt, gray knee britches, and long white stockings, tiptoed from his bedchamber, sniffing the air as he went. Padding quietly down the hall, he descended the narrow back staircase to the bottom, where he took a step into the brick kitchen and stopped.

His older sister Rachel stood before the large fireplace, which was as wide as the room and taller than she. A chilly November wind puffed down its chimney, twisting her ankle-length skirts away from the fire, as she poked embers into flames. Two kettles, hanging from black iron hooks, simmered over the blaze, sending delicious odors curling up the stairs.

Nate snuck past her back and ducked into the larder. It had been his favorite hiding place since childhood. He loved to jump out and scare her, which irritated Rachel to no end, so he did it as often as possible. At fifteen, however, his weight caused the floorboards to creak under him, and the storage space was tighter.

Leaving the door ajar, he watched her empty sugar and dried blackberries into one of the kettles. Nate breathed in the aroma of blackberry flummery, their family's favorite pudding!

Wiping her hands on her apron, Rachel poured the pudding into a tin mold and headed toward the larder to let it cool on a shelf.

Perfect! Nate tensed, ready to pounce.

A floorboard groaned.

Rachel jumped; her wooden ladle flew through the air, splattering flummery all over the ceiling.

"*Stop hiding*!" she screamed. Tripping on her skirts, she dropped the tin mold, and it clattered over the hearthstones, coming to rest upside down in the fireplace ashes.

Sheepishly, Nate crawled out.

"Shame! Shame!" Rachel scolded. "Have you nothing better to do than spy on me?"

Looking up at the purple mess overhead, he burst out laughing.

Furious, she snapped, "Wait till Father sees the ceiling he just whitewashed!"

Nate's laughter died away.

"And look what else you have done! Ruined the flummery!"

He was sorry about the dessert, but his sister, now of marrying age, was getting too bossy these days, running the house as if it were hers.

"You'd think you're the mother!" he protested.

"Not quite," said a gentle but firm voice behind them. Lydia Donovan, their mother, slipped in from the front hall and shook snow from her garments.

Noting the tin mold in the ashes, she asked, "What happened here?"

"Nate jumped out at me!" cried Rachel. "It's all his fault! The flummery's ruined!"

"Looks like you've gotten some of it on the ceiling," observed Mother.

"Sorry, Mother," muttered Nate, as he stooped to pick up the tin mold.

"Never mind that now; you can clean it up later," said Mother, handing Nate a stack of pewter plates. "Let's get dinner on the table."

"Not soon enough for me!" declared his older brother, coming in and stomping snow from his boots. Eighteen years old and three inches taller than Nate, Charles slumped into a chair by the hearth. He had spent the afternoon helping their father dig a grave in frozen ground.

Once more the kitchen door opened. In shuffled William Donovan, grim and weary, his bearded head hung low. Before the war came to Philadelphia, Nate's father had been master of a small but well-respected school for young ladies on Society Hill. Now their families were fleeing the city ahead of the British occupation, but William Donovan stubbornly remained. Falling back on his carpentry skills, he made coffins in which the occupying Royal Army buried their dead and American prisoners.

Nate felt badly for him. His father's eternal optimism had faded in his misery over the war and the failing school.

When Nate reentered the kitchen, he maintained a safe distance from his father, hoping he wouldn't notice the ceiling.

Not a chance!

"Nathaniel Donovan, heed me: Thou hast tricked thy sister from that larder for the last time! Is *that* clear?"

"Yes, Father," responded Nate meekly. No one dared disobey Father.

"When art thou going to grow up and be useful around here, lad?" Father shook his head. "Thou must clean up the hearth and ceiling before bed tonight."

The clatter of little feet on the stairs announced the arrival of Andrew and Molly, three-year-old sandy-haired twins. Tumbling into the room, they hugged their father around the legs.

"Here are the wild beasts!" Nate teased.

The twins were the only ones who could brighten Father's dark moods. As he lifted them into his arms, delight spread across William Donovan's face.

Lydia Donovan untied her black silk bonnet, revealing gray-streaked auburn hair. After she kissed Andrew and Molly, Father put them in their little chairs and took his place at the head of the table. When all heads were bowed and clasped hands rested on the starched white linen tablecloth, Father asked God's blessing over the corned beef and boiled cabbage.

As soon as the Amen was said, plates were quickly filled.

Her fork halfway to her mouth, Rachel asked, "Whose coffin did you deliver today, Father?

William Donovan's brow furrowed. Clearly he did not want to discuss the day's activities at the dinner table. But everyone sat silent, waiting. Finally putting down his knife, he said, "We buried Sally Winston's cousin Luke today."

"Sally's cousin died?" asked Rachel, sensing her best friend's grief.

Father nodded. "He was shot through the stomach at the Battle of Germantown. His family was in agony for two months while he hovered between life and death."

"He was a good boy," sighed Mother.

"He was a soldier, a disgrace to the Friends!" Father retorted. "His Meeting has disowned him."

"What for?" Nate asked.

"For running off to fight. But the elders decided to give him a decent burial anyway."

Mother frowned. "These 'disownments' are tearing families apart. Sally's family left town yesterday for the country. They're staying with their aunt, the Widow Foulke."

"Poor Sally," sighed Rachel dramatically. "Her aunt is strict as a witch and straight as her broom! How is Sally?" she asked.

"She's withdrawn from my school." Father shook his head. "One more gone. I'm closing it."

No one spoke. Finally Mother asked, "Has it come to that?"

"Everyone's moving to the countryside till this war is over. Sally was my brightest scholar." He jabbed his knife into the butter crock. "What good is a schoolmaster without students?"

In straightforward Quaker manner, their mother replied, "William Donovan, no doubt the school will reopen. But right now people haven't an extra farthing to spend. In the meantime, you are still Philadelphia's finest carpenter, and the British need coffins for the burying of their soldiers. You will prosper, be assured of that."

William responded without looking up, "Teaching the young is nobler than burying them."

Gloom settled over the table.

Charles wolfed down his food, obviously hoping they would soon be excused.

Father announced, "Since there is no dessert, it's early to bed. We have meeting tomorrow." Fixing his elder son with his gaze, he added, "We will not be the cow's tail on the Lord's Day again. We'll *all* be on time. On the bench. Together."

Rachel groaned. Nate smirked. She and Charles never sat on the down-stairs benches anymore. When each reached sixteen, they were allowed to sit in the balcony, though last week's mishap had apparently cost them that privilege.

Rachel had absent-mindedly dropped her hand muff through the railing. It had fallen on the head of the dozing Widow Foulke, startling her awake. "Mercy sakes!" she'd cried. People bit their knuckles to keep from laughing. And when everyone looked to the balcony, there were Charles and Sally, brazenly making eyes at each other, totally smitten!

Father was now making certain *that* would not happen again.

The dining room echoed with the sound of Charles' chair scraping back on the oak planks. Jaw set firmly, he stood up without being excused, something he'd never done before.

Everyone stared at him.

Taking a deep breath, Charles declared, "Father, I'll be leaving before meeting tomorrow."

"Why?"

"I'm going to the Presbyterian church. Their pastor is standing against this British invasion!"

"Duffield?" his father exclaimed. "The rebel's chaplain?"

"The Continental Army's chaplain."

William Donovan's eyes narrowed. In a firm voice his father commanded,

"Nay, son! I forbid it! Thou shan't listen to that warmonger! That poor sap-skull we buried today was poisoned by Duffield's preaching!"

His voice shaking, Charles replied, "Colonel Cadwalader says Pastor Duffield speaks for God. He says we have a right to defend ourselves, because the British will take our houses if we don't."

"Our neighbor said that?" The veins in William Donovan's neck stood out. "Presbyterian Scots and Irish Quakers should *never* live side by side!"

"But William Donovan," said Lydia quietly, catching her husband's eye, "does not our Lord say that we are to love our neighbors as ourselves?"

"That may be so, but next thing thou knowest, he'll have our son sneaking off to join that ragtag band of farmers he put together."

No one said anything.

"That Cadwalader!" Father scoffed. "Sat with those Patriot rebels in the Blue Anchor Tavern all day, planting seeds of rebellion in young men's minds. They called themselves the Sons of Liberty," he sneered. "There's no liberty in the grave!"

Charles refused to back down. "War's in the Bible, Father. King Saul and King David fought the Philistines, and Joshua led Israel against her enemies."

"We Quakers are peacemakers!" declared William. "Our Lord said, 'Blessed are the peacemakers.'" Glancing at his wife, he added, "Thou art not supporting me. Dost thou realize that if he does this, he will almost surely be disowned by the Meeting?"

Nate stared at them. In all his years he had never seen them divided like this. Mother was the family peacemaker; why was she not quelling this storm?

Father waited for her to side with him, his expression cold as stone.

Mother would not speak, though she was trembling, and her eyes were growing moist.

Charles drew up to his full six feet and broke the silence. "*I'm eighteen! Of age! You can't stop me!*"

He strode to the front door, threw it open, and stormed out into a driving snowstorm. "Your coat!" Mother cried after him, tears welling in her eyes.

But he took no notice and disappeared into the darkness.

2

SONS OF LIBERTY

The early morning sun gave little warmth as the Donovan family headed for the Quaker meetinghouse. It was Sunday, and because of the snow Father chose to use the coffin sleigh instead of their carriage. Under his firm guidance, their matched pair of black mares, Goodness and Mercy, pulled the narrow sleigh over the newly fallen snow at a brisk pace. Beside him sat Mother, holding the twins, while Rachel sat in back, and Nate ran alongside, struggling to keep up.

Later, slumped on an old wooden bench in the meetinghouse, Nate fought drowsiness, as an elder's somber voice droned on and on about the "Inward Light" of Christ.

Talk of inward light held no interest for Nate this morning. Already he was missing his brother.

Staring at the tall bare windows, he began counting the bubbles in the glass of each handblown pane. Whatever Charles was doing now had to be more exciting than this boring meeting!

All at once he became aware of new snow being driven against the panes. Had anyone else noticed it? He glanced at his father. William Donovan's head was bowed in prayer. Though usually keen about the weather, today he seemed too concerned about his missing son to be aware of the mounting storm outside.

Nate's mother, however, was well aware. Peering out from under her bonnet, the twins nestled in her lap, Lydia Donovan observed the snow accumulating on the window sills. Would she get Father's attention? Would he alert the elders? Would they dismiss early?

Mother did nothing.

Nate looked up at Rachel in the horseshoe-shaped balcony, where she'd hastened before Father could object. The fair Irish beauty with long strawberry-blond locks perched proud as a peacock. Her entire attention was given to two young men on the other side of the modesty board that separated boys from girls in the balcony.

Mother better not catch her doing that, thought Nate, remembering her stiff lectures on the need to curb "worldly desires." Had Rachel seen the storm? No, his sister was too much of a witling to think of anything but flirting. And her friend Sally wasn't even there to encourage her!

The wind outside picked up and banged a loose shutter against the side of the meetinghouse. It reminded Nate of his father slamming the door shut behind Charles last night. He shivered, wondering how his brother was faring in this storm with no coat.

All at once the elders on the facing benches clasped hands. People were standing up, pulling on coats, hurrying past him. Meeting was over! Outside, William Donovan started to scold his daughter severely for disobeying his order to stay with the family when suddenly shouts and commotion came from the direction of Old Pine Street Presbyterian Church.

"Duffield's church!" Father exclaimed with disgust.

A young boy came running from that direction, tripping over his long red scarf. Nate stopped him. "What's happening?"

Panting to catch his breath, the boy gasped, "The British are hanging some Patriots!"

"Why?" Nate demanded.

"Pastor Duffield preached fierce today!"

Father stepped in. "What did he say, lad?" he asked quietly.

Whirling his arms like a windmill, the boy cried, "The pastor shouted, 'To arms! To arms!' and tore off his robe." He paused for breath. "Should'a seen what was underneath!"

"What?" Nate begged.

"Continental Army uniform!" The words tumbled out of the boy's mouth. "The men got up and marched right out with him. Now the Redcoats are gonna hang two of them!"

Father grabbed the boy's arm. "How old are they?"

"Don't know, sir."

Frightened, the boy pulled his arm free and ran off through the snow.

Father whirled to Nate. "Take the family home, right now! I'm going over there!"

"I'm coming with you!" Nate blurted.

"Thou wilt do as thou art told!" Father insisted, as he strode off toward the church. "Do not tell thy mother. I don't want her to see this."

Reluctantly Nate turned to the coffin sleigh, where Mother and Rachel were waiting with the twins. As Nate climbed onto the driver's seat, Mother was startled. "Where's Father?"

"He had business at Duffield's church," replied Nate. Before she could ask more, he slapped the reins on the horses' flanks. The sleigh slid forward through the new snow and over the old, as Goodness and Mercy, unbidden, turned onto Second Street.

When they reached number 177, Nate reined the horses to a halt. The driveway was fast filling with snow. Mother got down, handing Molly to Rachel and tucking Andrew under her cape.

Abruptly Nate announced, "I've got to go back for Father!" Before his mother could say anything, he was already turning the corner onto Little Dock Street.

"Hurry up, you two!" he cried to the horses, cracking the sleigh's whip above their backs. "Charles might be dead before we get there."

Nate urged the horses forward, grateful that his was the only sleigh out in the storm. Squinting through the swirling snow, he caught his first glimpse of Duffield's church up ahead.

Turning into the churchyard, he found it filled with people standing near an old sycamore tree. Beneath one of its broad limbs stood an open wagon. Two ropes hung down from the limb, a noose at the end of each.

On the wagon's bed stood two British privates and a sergeant. Behind the wagon a squad of twenty more soldiers surrounded two men whose hands were bound behind them, their heads covered with black cloth bags. One wore the uniform of a Hessian soldier; the other, in civilian clothes, appeared to be a young man.

Trembling, Nate wondered, was it Charles?

An irate William Donovan suddenly appeared at Nate's side and climbed up to take the driver's seat. He turned to his son. "I told you to take the family home!"

"I did."

"Then what are you doing here?"

Nate pointed to the younger prisoner. "Is that Charles?"

His father couldn't answer, gripped by the same dread.

Nate watched in horror as the Redcoats in the wagon reached down and hauled the Hessian and then the younger man up onto the wagon bed. The sergeant settled the noose around the neck of the Hessian and tightened it.

Turning to the crowd, he now proclaimed: "While on picket duty, this guard consorted with the enemy and accepted a bribe, allowing sixty traitors from this church to pass through our lines and join the rebel army.

For treason against the Crown, he is hereby condemned to be hanged by the neck until dead."

The sergeant moved to the younger man. Fixing the noose around his neck, he declared to one and all: "And this 'Son of Liberty' did the bribing! Spawned in that nest of sedition," he gestured toward the church, "he, too, shall forfeit his life and be hanged by the neck until dead."

Bending his head close to the younger man, he said, "You have one last chance to avoid death: Tell me who put you up to this? And where is the list of the other Sons of Liberty?"

There was no sound from beneath the black hood.

"Very well," the sergeant exclaimed, "since you will not speak, you will hang! By order of King George, on November 30, the year of our Lord, 1777."

Now the young man did speak. At the top of his lungs, he cried, *"No King but King Jesus!"*

The sergeant ordered the two soldiers off the wagon and jumped down himself, as murmurs of protest erupted in the crowd of onlookers.

Scanning the British detachment, Nate's gaze settled on the man in charge, a nervous young lieutenant who obviously realized that in another few moments he might have a full-scale riot on his hands.

"No, no!" cried Nate, fearing he was about to witness the death of his brother. But there was nothing he could do. The lieutenant gave the order, and the sergeant struck the flanks of both horses. They plunged forward, pulling the wagon out from under the two men, leaving them writhing and twisting in mid-air.

A roar of outrage went up.

"May God have mercy on their souls!" muttered William Donovan.

Shaking, Nate leaned over the side of the wagon and heaved up his breakfast. Wiping his mouth, he stammered, "Was it . . ." he couldn't finish.

His father shook his head. "Charles was taller," he whispered, "and this one had a coat."

"The British have no right!" hissed Nate.

"We've seen enough," said his father, slapping the reins on Goodness and Mercy. "Ah, William Penn," he lamented as they left the churchyard, "look what's become of your 'City of Brotherly Love!' I fear we've set you turning in your grave!"

The last phrase stuck in Nate's mind. He seemed to hear it with each creak of the sleigh's spring. *In your grave . . . in your grave . . . in your grave.*

3

WITHOUT LYING OR KILLING

Goodness and Mercy knew the way home. Without being guided, they turned into Second Street, passing familiar wrought-iron fences and white-columned brick mansions toward the Donovans' house. Nate felt numb. He pulled up his collar and closed his eyes. Charles' face flashed into his mind.

At 177 the horses turned into the long drive, now clogged by snowdrifts. Nate jumped down and took the mares' bridles by hand, attempting to lead them. When they would not budge, he looked up at his father. "Should we just leave the sleigh here?"

Father reluctantly agreed. "We'll get it out of sight as soon as we can. We don't want the British to see it's a coffin-sleigh and press us to be their undertakers."

William Donovan climbed down and unhitching Goodness and Mercy. Slowly, he and Nate coaxed them through the drifts and into the carriage house.

With the horses safely in their stalls, Nate climbed up to the hayloft and threw down several pitchforks of hay. Father separated them into two piles, one for each stall.

Scrambling down the ladder, Nate threw a woolen saddle blanket over Mercy. Father smoothed it down, loosely fastening the girth beneath her. As they did the same for Goodness, Nate, sensing the moment might be right, cautiously said, "Father, Charles believes . . ."

"Charles is too zealous for his own good! Fighting the rebels' war instead of the Lamb's war won't bring anybody peace."

William Donovan picked up a curry brush and started grooming first Mercy, then Goodness. "In Ireland," he murmured, "my family never recovered from the rebellion. It never stopped, one bloody uprising after another!" He glanced up at Nate. "That's all I could think of when Charles ran off with those Yankee Doodles."

Nate was startled. His father had never talked to him like this before. Taking the curry brush and walking around to the front of Mercy, the boy responded, "Charles doesn't believe in the Lamb's war, beating swords into plowshares, not taking up weapons."

He turned to his father. "What if the British take our house and these horses? Then what'll we do?"

Without replying, William Donovan picked up the pitchfork, looked at Nate, and flung it up into the hayloft. It clanged against an iron pulley, and a fine rain of straw dust sifted down. Taking a shovel, he stalked off to clear the drive.

When Nate started to follow, his father turned and dismissed him. "Go in the house and help your mother."

"But when can we talk about this?"

"When you're old enough."

Nate's heart sank.

Kicking his boots against the brick steps to remove the snow, Nate entered the kitchen.

"Where's your father?" asked his mother, carrying dishes to the dining room table.

"Shoveling the drive."

"We'll go ahead with dinner." She looked at him closely. "What ails you?"

"We saw a hanging."

"What?"

"Two men—a Hessian sentry and the young man who bribed him to get Duffield and his men through the lines." He paused and his voice broke. "For a moment I feared it was Charles. So did Father."

"Thank the good Lord, it wasn't!" his mother exclaimed. Then she added gently, "You saw something today that no one your age—no one, any age—should see."

Rachel emerged from the larder, with cold leftovers, since Father forbade cooking on the Lord's Day. She'd been listening. "Sally was right," she said grimly. "We should have left town with them!"

Lydia Donovan ignored her, motioning them to the dining room.

Nate slid into a straight-back chair at the long walnut table as Mother bowed her head to ask the blessing, concluding, "Help us to love our enemies."

Frowning, Nate studied her face. "That's Father's position. But what do *you* think?"

Lydia Donovan smiled. "Your father and I do not agree on this matter of the war. But as you know, in our faith Quaker women may take initiative when necessary. I am one who does. Pennsylvania is God's province, and we must do all that we can, without lying or killing, to preserve the freedom that William Penn intended."

"Father said that what happened this morning has set William Penn turning in his grave."

Mother's eyes caught his. She thought a moment, then said, "God has blessed Pennsylvania for a century, and good William Penn would not agree with King George oppressing it, though he would have us resist by peaceful means."

Nate smiled, surprised at the depth of her conviction.

"And," she added, "there's much we can do by peaceful means."

"What are you going to do, Mother?" Rachel scoffed. "Become a spy? Get yourself hanged like those two?"

"That will be enough!" Lydia rebuked her. Looking out the window at the diminishing snowstorm, she mused half to herself, "Each one must do what they must do."

They finished eating Saturday's leftovers in silence. As Rachel got up to clear the table, Mother leaned close to Nate and said softly, "Nathaniel, you are worried about Charles, aren't you."

"I'm worried about how I'm going to do all his chores—mucking stables, chopping wood—on top of my own."

His mother looked at him tenderly. "But you *are* worried."

Nate nodded.

After lunch Mother sat in the parlor reading the leather-bound family Bible, as she did every Sunday afternoon. Next to her on a table rested an inkwell, into which she was dipping a goose-quill pen and writing in the Bible.

Nate was careful not to disturb the only time she had to herself all week. In stormy times she had always been a pillar of strength.

But they had never encountered a storm like this.

4

THE WORLD TURNED UPSIDE DOWN

Nate hesitated at the entrance to the parlor until his mother looked up. Seeing his expression, she put down the pen and beckoned him to come in. As he sat down on the braided rug next to her, she smoothed down a tuft of his light brown hair.

He looked up at her. "Will the Quakers disown Charles?"

"I pray not, but if he's disowned, he'll become a Free Quaker, as some have already. They hold to Quaker customs but choose to take up arms to defend our land."

Nate's eye fell upon what she'd just written in the margin. "May I read it?"

She turned it for him to read.

Father in Heaven, bless General Washington, our Moses, delivering us from Pharaoh. And may the angels protect our Charles who has gone to help him.

Nate raised his head. Their eyes met. Neither spoke.

Lydia Donovan closed the Bible and locked its silver clasp with a tiny key on a red silk ribbon.

Getting up, she walked over to the tall cherrywood desk her husband had made for her. Carefully she folded down its front, revealing the hand-tooled leather writing surface. At the back of the desk was a row of open cubicles containing letters, bills, and other papers. In the center of these was a tiny door. She opened it. Fascinated, Nate watched over her shoulder as she slid the compartment's bottom to one side, revealing a narrow space containing two gold coins and two letters with broken wax seals. Placing the Bible's silver key in it, she returned the bottom to its original position.

Nate stared at her, wide-eyed. "Mother! I never knew that was there!"

"You must tell no one," she said softly, closing the desk. "What you have seen today—what I've written, and what has been written to me—can get us hanged."

Her son looked at her in amazement and wondered if there were other things about his mother that he didn't know.

"So what *do* we say about Charles?"

"He's in Germantown, helping Aunt Neuss. You and I know she doesn't need any help, but the British don't. To them she's an elderly widow who needs a farmhand to get along."

A floorboard in the hallway creaked. Had Father returned?

It was only Rachel, coming in from the kitchen.

"You were listening again!" Nate exclaimed.

"We keep no secrets in this house," his sister retorted, "do we, Mother?"

"No, young lady. And we don't eavesdrop, either."

Rachel, growing bolder at sixteen, spoke her mind. "I think Charles was brave to join the army!" She turned to Nate. "Too bad they wouldn't take you, but mere boys of fifteen aren't allowed."

He glared at her. "They'll take me next year! But they'd *never* take a girl!"

"Well, if they would, I'd go," she declared, her nose in the air, "disownment or no disownment."

"Yes," her brother shot back, "go to find yourself a soldier boy! Or in your case, a whole army of them! You and Sally would have your pick!"

"That will be enough! From both of you!" declared Lydia Donovan, replacing the Bible on its shelf. "You'd be better off praying than bickering. I've heard the British are now seizing houses in this part of the city."

"Sally says Lord Howe has his eye on *our* house!"

"She's crazy as a bedbug!" Nate spat out. "This is Society Hill; things like that don't happen here."

"Sally says Father ought to move us and the school to the country."

Nate ignored her, but something in Sally Winston's warning made him uneasy.

Standing by the bay window, Mother announced, "The sun's coming out." Going to the armoire in the front foyer, she added, "Aunt Barrington's son's wife Prudence gave birth yesterday, a block away. I'm going to go call on her."

Pulling out her black nursing bag and her heavy felt cape, she opened the front door. Blinding diamonds of sun sparkled off the snow. Squinting through them, Nate suddenly gasped, "Redcoats!"

Down Second Street toward the corner of Little Dock, led by three officers on elegant horses, came a column of Grenadiers marching to the beat of a field drum. The King's finest, he thought with sarcasm, as the sun reflected off their polished silver helmets with their golden silk pompadours.

Nate frowned. People were cheering! Some of their neighbors were obviously British sympathizers—Tories! Women were waving handkerchiefs from upstairs windows.

Just before the column reached the corner, they came to a halt, directly in front of their house. The officers dismounted.

Nate froze. Was Sally right?

He held his breath. Accompanied by a detail of soldiers, the officers went up the drive across the street.

He breathed a sigh of relief. They were investigating the Cadwaladers' house, stables, and grounds that extended all the way to the banks of Little Dock Creek. Mrs. Cadwalader, a frail aristocratic lady, stood shivering outside. Did the British know her husband commanded a regiment of American militia?

Mother grimaced. "Dear God, what is to become of her?"

Mrs. Cadwalader escorted the officers inside.

Three soldiers now came up their own driveway. As they stopped to examine the coffin sleigh, Nate whispered, "Where's father?"

Mother pulled them away from the door. "He's probably in the barn getting the horses to pull the sleigh into the carriage house. Pray he sees them before he comes out."

Nate's scalp tightened. Sally was right! The war had just come to their front door.

Mother slammed the door shut.

Rachel collapsed into her arms, whimpering, "They've found out about Charles! They're coming to hang us!"

"Get hold of yourself!" her mother snapped. "They're only here to see if our house is of any use to them. They won't harm Quakers. They think Friends are Tory in sympathy."

Through a glass panel on the side of the front door, Nate watched the street. "Wait!" he whispered. "They're leaving!"

Indeed, the soldiers had turned and were now going back down the drive to rejoin the column. They watched the British resume their march up Little Dock toward the harbor.

"Cheer up!" Nate cried to his sister. "We've just slipped the noose!"

But his mother was not smiling. "They'll be back," she said under her breath.

The kitchen door opened, and William Donovan came in. Seeing his wife in her cape, holding her bag, he asked, "Where are you going?"

"Prudence Barrington's, to make sure she's doing alright with her newborn."

"I'd better escort you. I saw our unwelcome visitors."

She slipped her arm through his. As they were about to leave, William Donovan instructed his son, "Finish your chores, and don't forget to grease the sleigh's springs. Nothing's more bothersome at a burial than a creaking spring."

The first chore Nate had inherited from Charles was to replenish the firewood by the hearth. At the woodpile he selected a log for splitting and picked up his axe. Everything *seemed* calm, but there was no question that their world had turned upside down in a single day.

Shaking the snow off the log, he could not shake the uneasy feeling that worse was yet to come.

5

UNWELCOME GUESTS

Nate gathered up the wood he'd split and carried it inside. Carefully stacking it by the hearth, he stirred the fire into a blaze.

There was a knock from the brass clapper at the front door.

As Nate opened it, Rachel came up behind him. Outside there stood a finely uniformed British officer. Though he was only in his mid-twenties, the gold brocade on his scarlet sleeves indicated that he was at least a captain. He was backed by two lieutenants. "Captain John André, in the service of the King," he announced with a slight bow.

"Nathaniel Donovan," replied Nate formally, bidding them enter.

In the foyer the captain bowed to Rachel with an exaggerated flourish, as if she were a lady of the royal court.

She paused, then smiled and nodded.

Nate was shocked. How could she forget her loathing of the British so quickly?

Wrinkling his nose at the scent of the pomade on the captain's white wig, he led the officers into the parlor. Nate stepped in front of Rachel and took charge. "Would you bring our guests some hot cider?" he asked her.

His sister's green eyes flashed. Speechless, she retreated to the kitchen, not appreciating his attempt to protect her.

Captain André's steel-gray eyes caught Nate's and held them. His gaze was almost bewitching. "I'm informed you are Quakers. Lord Howe trusts the Friends. My business is with your father. Is he here?"

Nate shook his head.

"When may I expect him?"

"I've no idea," he replied. Then he heard the kitchen door open. Father!

The captain heard it, too. Without asking, he motioned the junior officers to open the large oak doors that separated the parlor from the dining room. They did, and he strode into the dining room.

William Donovan greeted him civilly as Rachel appeared with three steaming pewter tankards.

"I'm home!" called Lydia Donovan cheerily from the front hall, back from her errand of mercy. Upstairs, the twins heard her and started fussing. Rachel, who obviously would have preferred to stay in the presence of this handsome officer, hurried upstairs to tend to them.

Taking advantage of the distraction, Nate slipped into the foyer. Helping Mother off with her cape, he whispered, "British officers are here! Father needs you!"

In the dining room Father offered Captain André his own place at the head of the table. Settling into the high-backed Windsor chair, André took a sip of cider and smiled. "We noticed the coffin sleigh in your drive. I've made inquiries. Apparently you are the finest coffin maker in Philadelphia." Father said nothing. "His excellency, Lord Howe, has need of your services to bury our dead. We will require caskets of good quality for the burials, and we will need boxes for the dead from the Walnut Street Prison. Nothing fancy for them; rough pine will do."

William Donovan considered it. "If I undertake to do this, shall I be compensated?"

"Of course. A crown for a British soldier; two shillings for a prisoner."

Father shook his head. "That would not begin to cover my expenses, to say nothing of my time."

André's eyes narrowed. "You would be advised to accept what the crown is prepared to pay and be grateful for it."

William Donovan's jaw firmed; and his wife, before he could say something they might all regret, chose that moment to enter.

Following their captain's lead, the other officers rose and bowed, as her husband introduced her. She gave them a curt nod.

"Madam," said André, offering her a chair, "do join us."

Nate noted that while he was well mannered with his mother, he was not nearly as extravagant in his gestures as he'd been with Rachel.

Lydia Donovan preferred to remain standing.

With a shrug the captain resumed his place at the head of their table. "I have informed your husband of the crown's need of his undertaking skills. Now I have more news, which I trust will be good news, as I assume you are loyal subjects of the crown who desire to see peace restored as quickly as possible."

He smiled.

Lydia Donovan smiled back.

Nate realized that neither of them meant it.

"As Lord Howe will be billeted across the street, for the sake of convenience his General staff will hold our meetings here." He looked at the long walnut table and nodded. "Yes, this will serve quite well."

Lydia Donovan did not share his delight. "Will you force us to leave our home?"

"Heavens, no! As I said, we assume you are loyal subjects," he paused and added, "unlike your neighbors across the street. We are well aware of the activities of Mr. Cadwalader—or should I say, Colonel Cadwalader—who has been behaving in an exceedingly *dis*loyal fashion."

Captain André looked at Lydia Donovan carefully. "Madam, I suspect your views may be somewhat sharper than your husband's. Perhaps you had better clarify for me exactly where you stand."

Lydia drew up to her full height. "Sir, I am a Quaker. We are taught by Scripture to regard all men as Friends. We detest your shedding of blood on our soil and your hanging of two poor souls this morning without benefit of trial." She paused. "Yet we must privately regard you as a Friend and wish you well in your personal interest and safety."

André tapped the tips of his fingers together thoughtfully. "Madam, I respect your forthright honesty. You may remain in this house."

She frowned. "How shall we live here with British officers trooping in and out?"

"You will respect our need for privacy," replied André, smiling, "and we shall endeavor to respect yours."

Their conversation was cut short by a piercing wail from Molly that reverberated through the house.

André's brow furrowed. "But," he added, "you *will* have to quarter your little ones elsewhere before sundown today. We cannot have that disturbance during our meetings." He tapped the table. "For those sessions this room must be off-limits, and the parlor, and the kitchen—anywhere else we might be overheard." His smile returned.

Now William Donovan spoke. "We Quakers are peacemakers. A war council presiding here would violate our religious conscience." He sighed. "Nevertheless, there is obviously little I can do about it."

Captain André stood up, their business concluded. "Friend Donovan, it depends on how you choose to regard it. If you accept the temporary inconvenience as necessary for the quelling of the rebellion, it will go well. If you resent our presence, it will go ill. It is your choice."

"We shall make the best of it," Lydia Donovan stated calmly, before her husband could reply.

"Good," responded André. He looked out the window, "You've only a little daylight left, madam. There is a curfew at sundown. Therefore, I suggest you prepare your little ones for immediate departure."

"I ask one favor, sir—a pass through British lines. Our only relative who could take them lives outside the city. My children must be delivered safely and visited often," Lydia boldly insisted.

Nate watched Captain André weigh his response. At length he sighed, "Very well." He signaled a lieutenant who produced a paper from his leather dispatch case. The captain wrote on it and signed it for her.

André turned to William Donovan, whose face was downcast. The twins, his last joy in life, had just been banished. "Now we shall examine your grounds. I understand that you have several natural springs?"

William Donovan said nothing.

"I should think we'll be able to water our horses there," André continued. "We shall go and see."

Father turned to Nate. "We've got to get the twins resettled by sundown. I'll take thee to the British lines; from there thou canst take them by the shortcut over the fields. That will get all of us indoors by curfew. Use the wood sled. Tie it to the back of the sleigh, and *don't* forget to bring it home!"

"Yes, sir," responded Nate meekly.

The captain had one more question. "Are there any firearms on the premises?"

"No!" replied William Donovan hotly. "We are *Quakers!*"

As Nate watched the officers leave, he wondered which of their Tory neighbors had told the British about their stables and springs.

Mother headed up the stairs to get the twins bundled up, calling Nate to come and help her and telling Rachel to gather the clothes they would need.

She tried to convince Andrew and Molly that going to stay with their Great Aunt Neuss would be a great adventure, but they were close to tears.

Holding his younger brother close, Nate soothingly said, "It's going to be alright," but he wondered if it really was.

After they had dressed the twins, Mother handed Nate the coat that Charles had left behind. "Put this on under your own. You are slight of frame; none will guess you are wearing two coats. When you leave the twins at Aunt Neuss's, give her Charles' coat. She will deliver it to the army's camp at White Marsh."

Nate struggled to put on both coats as they came back downstairs with the twins. His mother brought two blankets with her to keep the twins snug on the cold ride.

"Be sure to tuck these around them, and don't mention Charles' coat to a soul." She turned to Rachel. "Go up and latch the door at the top of the stairs."

Nate saw why. Mother was hoping that upstairs the door to the kitchen stairs would be taken as a door to an unused closet. If someone didn't know about the kitchen stairwell, they would think that the front stairway was the only one in the house.

When Rachel came back down, Mother latched the kitchen staircase door and placed a small table and cane-bottomed chair in front of it. Now it, too, gave the appearance of an unused closet.

Nate hoped it would fool Captain André. They needed at least one secret passage in the house that escaped his attention.

Nate's second coat was nearly fastened when he heard his father and the British returning. "Hurry!" he whispered to his sister, who was helping him with the last button.

Oh, no! The button popped off! It bounced across the floor, and Captain André's keen eye saw it.

Nate held his breath.

6

RISING SUN TAVERN

Nate clutched the jacket shut, concealing Charles' coat, as all eyes followed the button.

"Horrors!" exclaimed Rachel. "I've lost my button!"

"Dear lady," responded Captain André, stepping into the room with a smile, "why such fuss over a mere button? It's hardly the end of the world."

If you only knew, mused Nate, crawling on his knees to retrieve the button, while André's attention was on Rachel. If you find out about Charles, it *will* be the end of *our* world!

Rachel started to help Nate search for the button, but the captain caught her elbow and raised her up. "Gracious lady," he murmured, kissing her hand, "I don't believe I caught your name."

She blushed.

Lydia Donovan pulled her daughter's hand away, clasping it tightly.

Andrew now squirmed in his heavy woolen coat and called to his sister, "Rachel, I'm hot!"

The Captain smirked. "Ah, Miss *Rachel*, it will be my pleasure to see you again. Tonight. At eight."

"At eight?" she stammered.

"When our first staff meeting convenes. Perhaps you would serve us some more of your excellent cider."

Lydia Donovan frowned. "I thought you said your councils were private."

"And so they are!" retorted the captain. "Very well, madam. Off to bed with the whole family at a quarter to eight! Understood?"

With a curt nod he and his officers departed.

Nate stared after them, his resentment deepening. The war had come into their home, and now it was entering his heart.

Crying now, the twins clung to their mother. With difficulty she loosened their grips, and Nate loaded them into the sleigh, tucking the blankets tightly around them.

As Father drove the sleigh through the snowy streets of Philadelphia, Nate noted how many houses now had British guards posted in front. So many had been confiscated! Their city was becoming a prison!

As they reached the British picket line outside of town, Father's expression was sad. He warned Nate, "Say nothing. Move quickly. Thou canst still beat the setting sun."

William Donovan set his two youngest in the small firewood sled, wrapped them tight, and kissed them good-bye. As he stood up and turned the pull rope over to his son, he quickly turned away, but not before Nate saw the tears in his eyes.

Nate pulled the sled along Nice Town Lane, past Indian Council Rock. In school Father had taught them that the Indians didn't believe in owning land and could not understand why the white men were fighting a war over it. Nate had not understood either.

But he did now, what with the arrogant Captain André ordering them around in their own house!

He paused to get his bearings. The twins, hungry and cold, began to snivel. As the sun sank lower and the shadows lengthened, they arrived at the crest of the long rolling hill down to Germantown. Nate could see the whale-oil lanterns in the windows of Rising Sun Tavern. The last rays of sun had turned the snow on the hillside to a rosy gold.

All at once he grinned. He knew how to turn the whining behind him into shouts of glee.

Aiming the firewood sled down the hill, he gave it a push and jumped on its flat wooden runners from behind.

"*Whee-e-e-e!*" cried Andrew and Molly as they flew down the hill, the new snow swirling up behind them. Down and down they went, faster and faster! By shifting his weight, Nate was able to guide the sled and steered them all the way to the inn's front gate. The twins were laughing hysterically.

Out came Aunt Neuss to see what all the commotion was about, her grey hair loosely tied back in a bun. "Land o' Goshen! What are you all doing here?"

While she ushered the twins inside, Nate recapped the most bizarre day of his life—Charles off to war, the hangings, and now British officers seizing their house. He finished as she spooned warm potato soup into little mouths.

She listened with growing indignation. "The British threw these babies out into this cold? For shame!"

Their supper finished, Aunt Neuss nestled the twins into bed under a goose-feather comforter. Then she turned to Nate. "Go downstairs, boy, and tell Cassie, the serving girl, that I said to give you some supper."

Nate whispered to his sister and brother, "I'll come back for you," and, hoping it was true, went down the steps to the tavern.

Odors of whiskey, ale, and tobacco assailed his nose, as his eyes became accustomed to the light from the flames dancing in the hearth. There were officers there in *blue* uniforms! Continentals!

Nate was surprised. Hadn't the Americans *lost* the Battle of Germantown? Then he realized the British had already withdrawn their forces to Philadelphia for the winter. Except for occasional patrols, they left the outlying towns alone and were obviously not a threat to these officers.

One of them, dressed in the buff-colored riding breeches of the Light Horse Cavalry with the insignia of a colonel, motioned Nate to come over. The boy's eyes widened. It was John Cadwalader, their neighbor!

"Nathaniel? What are you doing here?"

"It's a long story, sir."

"Well, sit down, lad, and tell it. Have you eaten?"

He shook his head, and the colonel waved for the serving girl to come over. "Cassie, this is the son of Widow Neuss's niece and my neighbor. Can you bring him something to eat?"

Cassie smiled at Nate. "Would you like some fried scrapple and barley bread?"

"That would be wonderful, ma'am!"

While the colonel waited for Nate to finish devouring what was put before him, he patiently sipped ale from a leather mug.

"What news, lad, from Philadelphia?"

"The British are taking houses for their officers to live in."

"So we've heard."

"Yes. Captain André took our house for Lord Howe's staff meetings."

"He's one of their best spies!"

Nate frowned. "What do you mean?"

"André is heavily involved in their secret intelligence service."

"What is that?"

The colonel carefully filled his long-stemmed clay pipe with tobacco. "Each side tries to discover what the other side is planning to do." He paused, lighting his pipe with a long match from the fireplace. "They do it. We do it."

When he had it going, he asked, "What else can you tell me?"

"Lord Howe himself is living in your house."

Colonel Cadwalader choked on a mouthful of ale. "*What?*" His eyes flashed. "Be they cursed o' the devil if those Redcoats touch my wife! If only I could get there," he muttered.

"I'd run them off for you if I was old enough to be a soldier," Nate volunteered.

Colonel Cadwalader studied Nate's freckled face. "I thought Quakers didn't fight."

"My parents won't. But yesterday my brother joined Duffield's militia."

"Charles did?"

Nate nodded and looking around, carefully unbuttoned his outer jacket, revealing Charles's coat. "Mother sent his coat," he whispered. "Can you help me get it to him?"

"Certainly."

Nate studied his neighbor's brooding face and realized that unlike Father, had Colonel Cadwalader been home that morning, he would have been willing to sacrifice himself defending his property.

Suddenly a shadow fell across their table—whose? Had they heard anything?

7

A PATRIOT SPY

Alarmed, Nate looked up. It was only Aunt Neuss, bringing him a bowl of cornmeal pudding drizzled with molasses for dessert. "How's my niece's boy getting along?"

The colonel looked up at her. "We're old friends, neighbors, in fact. He wishes he were old enough to be a soldier." He paused. "But he may not have to wait."

The colonel looked at the innkeeper, who returned his gaze. "He's family," she murmured. "He can be trusted."

The colonel turned to Nate. "There *is* a way the army can use you now, lad. You can be a special kind of soldier."

The lad's eyes widened. "How, sir?"

"General Howe would never suspect a Quaker living right under his nose, especially a young fellow. The strength of intelligence-gathering often rests upon unlikely sources."

Widow Neuss winked at Nate and left.

Colonel Cadwalader slid his chair closer, making sure no one could overhear. "Before I reveal any more, I need to tell you about another Nathaniel—Nathan Hale."

"Who's he?"

"He was a schoolteacher, like your father, a good one, Yale educated. At the beginning of the war, he became a spy in New York. He was caught crossing Long Island Sound by Rogers' Rangers and brought before General Howe. Howe didn't bother with a trial; they'd found secret messages in the heel of his boot. When they questioned him, he remained faithful to the cause. His last words were, "I regret that I have but one life to give for my country.""

"What did they do?"

"Howe hanged him, like the men who swung at Old Pine Street Presbyterian this morning."

Nate shuddered. "I . . . I was there."

"You saw them?"

The boy nodded. "We feared one of them was Charles."

Then the colonel surprised him. "I'm glad you saw it!"

"You are?"

"Yes. You need to be absolutely clear about what could happen to you." He looked closely at Nate. "What I'm about to tell you could cost you your life if you're caught. Shall I go on?"

The fire crackled in the hearth. Nate stared into the flames. When he turned back, he was trembling. "I'm ready."

"Very well, as of this moment you're a member of 'The Committee.' Our secret society is a spy network of soldiers and civilians, established by General Washington himself, and commissioned by the Continental Congress before they escaped to York. We're like a family; we look out for one another."

He glanced about. "This tavern is one of our bases of operation. Your Aunt Neuss is one of us." He drew on his pipe. "As are others known to you."

"Who?"

"The less you know for now, the better. You'll be briefed before each assignment. But the fewer family members you know personally, the fewer you can betray if you're caught."

Nate squared his shoulders. "I would die before I betrayed family!"

The colonel sadly shook his head. "You've no idea how persuasive the enemy can be. What if they threatened to hang your mother in front of you?"

Nate's jaw fell open. "They wouldn't—"

"They've done worse than that. We're at war, Nate. The information we're dealing in can save hundreds of lives and could affect the outcome of the entire war. With stakes that high even gentlemen can lose their principles."

Nate's dry tongue clung to the roof of his mouth.

"The Patriot spymaster for Philadelphia will have to approve of you. If he does, you'll report to him."

"Who is he?"

"When you need to know, you'll be told." He put his pipe away. "The first thing a spy learns is to listen. Don't speak, listen. And practice remembering accurately what you've heard. Now repeat back to me the first sentence I just told you."

Nate gulped. What had he said? "Um, alright . . ." He sat up straighter, "A spy learns to listen."

"Not exact, but good enough for now," replied Colonel Cadwalader. "You've got a good ear. Now remember this: The quieter you are in the company of men, the more they will relax and speak their mind in front of you. Just stay quiet and listen."

Nate mouthed the word back to himself: listen.

The colonel leaned a little closer. "One last thing: not a word of this to anyone. Not to a living soul. Do I have your word on that?"

"You do," Nate declared.

"Good. Because you already know enough to get you hanged. And mark me well, lad. You won't be shot. They hang spies—choked to death with a broken neck and left to rot on a public gallows as an example to others."

The bodies of the two men dangling in their nooses at Pastor Duffield's church flashed through Nate's mind. He rubbed his throat.

"And should you ever say anything to anyone, we'll know it." The colonel looked him in the eye. "Are you ready to do this, son?"

"Yes, sir," Nate assured him. "When Captain André took over our house this afternoon, I wished I could fight him. Now there's a way."

"How will your parents feel about your helping us if they find out?"

"My father would disapprove."

"And your mother?"

Nate chuckled. "To tell you the truth, sir, I think she'd help us."

The colonel said nothing. He paid his bill and prepared to leave. "Meet me at the inn's stable tomorrow at dawn. As it happens, I already have an assignment for you."

8

FIRST ASSIGNMENT

Nate woke up battling the dark thoughts that had haunted him all night. Spying wasn't fighting, he told himself, and Mother had said it was right to defend America. The Quaker rule was: no killing or lying. Spying was not lying; it was merely reporting the truth. But what would he tell Father? Nothing, he finally decided. He would just have to be careful to keep Father from suspecting.

As the sun rose, Nate crawled out of bed and flung open the shutters. Over by the stable he saw Colonel Cadwalader walking a fine chestnut stallion. Smiling, he beckoned to the boy to join him. In no time Nate was beside him.

The colonel looked up from cleaning his stirrups. "A good day it is, lad."

"Why is that, sir?"

"We're going to deliver your brother's coat to White Marsh and report on the house seizures at the same time."

"How can we do that?"

"Widow Neuss will sew a message into the coat's lining. In the remote chance you encounter a British patrol and they search you, they'll never think of looking in the lining."

The colonel looped his horse's reins around the hitching post by the inn's front door. "General Washington will be expecting a report from Philadelphia. The British have not yet caught on to our methods. When they do, we'll change them."

Removing a leather-bound book from his saddlebag, he tucked it under his arm, leaving Nate even more curious.

Inside they found Aunt Neuss emptying brass spittoons. The colonel told her what they needed, and she immediately got out a writing case. Nate wracked his brain to remember each house where he'd seen a British sentry guarding the entrance. Carefully he gave the old woman the street address and owner's name if he knew it.

Aunt Neuss recorded each piece of information, putting the Donovan and Cadwalader homes at the top. Then, on a fresh piece of paper, she prepared to encode the message.

The colonel handed her the volume under his arm. "We change the source book for our code frequently; this week we're using the Watts Hymnal of 1715. "

Now Nate was *really* curious! He looked up at the colonel, puzzled.

"It's a simple book code. As long as the sender and the receiver have the same book and the British don't know which book it is, it works. With our army at White Marsh, Chaplain Duffield has this same hymnal."

Nate watched, fascinated, as she encoded his family name. For the 'D' in Donovan, she turned to a well-known favorite, "Jesus Shall Reign" and circled the 'D' in "does." Then she put the page number (3), the musical measure number (20), and the first letter of the lyrics in that measure (1). The letter 'D', then, was 3-20-1.

On she went, spelling out his name.

$$D = 3\text{-}20\text{-}1$$

$$O = 4\text{-}30\text{-}5$$

$$N = 8\text{-}72\text{-}1$$

$$O = 23\text{-}4\text{-}24$$

$$V = 12\text{-}8\text{-}14$$

$$A = 6\text{-}35\text{-}23$$

$$N = 1\text{-}13\text{-}12$$

The process took nearly an hour while Nate fed Andrew and Molly their breakfast. When Aunt Neuss was finished, she pulled a needle case and scissors from her apron, opened the lining of Charles' coat, inserted the message, and stitched it in place.

Inspecting her seam, Nate marveled at her handiwork. "No one will ever know!"

Donning Charles' coat over his own, he turned to the colonel. "How will this get to Charles?"

"What did I tell you last night?"

Nate thought a moment. "That I'd be told only what I needed to know, and only when I needed to know it?"

"Exactly."

Aunt Neuss smiled and ducked into her pantry, returning with an egg basket covered with a red gingham napkin. "On your way, you can return the favor by delivering these eggs to my neighbor. They're special eggs. Treat them like glass."

Nate agreed.

"Ride in back of me," said Colonel Cadwalader, "and I'll explain as we go. You ever meet an Indian?"

"No, sir, but I did help send Quaker mission baskets to the Oneidas in the Susquehanna Valley."

"So, no bad feelings about Indians?" Colonel Cadwalader prodded, as Nate hoisted himself up behind him.

"None," the boy replied, holding the colonel's waist with one arm and the egg basket with the other, as they trotted off.

After a ride of several miles, Colonel Cadwalader halted at the gates of a brick mansion overlooking the valley where the creek known as Wissahickon joined the Schuylkill River. He dismounted and kept a wary eye for the British as Nate handed him the eggs and jumped down.

"King George keeps his Indians loyal with money and whiskey, whereas Congress can't even pay our army, let alone Indians. None would side with us, if it weren't for Duffield's missionaries. They've befriended one of the Oneida tribes, and the British will never suspect them of being spies. They assume all Indians are Tories."

"And all Quakers, too."

"Now you're catching on!" He grew more serious. "Listen, lad, you've four miles to hike in the snow. You'll be lucky to deliver that coat before sundown."

Nate wondered where but said nothing.

"Hike yonder lane. Ask for Sally Winston. She's staying with her aunt. Give her these eggs." He returned the basket to Nate. "She'll take them to the next person."

"So *that's* where they moved!"

"You know Sally?"

"She's my sister's best friend."

"Good," declared Colonel Cadwalader. "Just be sure *no one* sees these. After you give her the eggs, follow her aunt's fence line down the hill to the creek. At the bottom you'll find an abandoned track that leads to Foulke's Mill. The British won't patrol it like they do the main roads. Head west on it for a good three hours till it brings you to a spring behind a large, rose-colored granite boulder."

The colonel paused and looked at Nate to make sure he was taking it all in.

Nate nodded. "And that's where . . ."

"We have a courier who regularly takes messages from Philadelphia to General Washington. Give him the jacket and get home, quick as you can. You may not reach the British lines before curfew. But there'll be a full moon tonight to show you home." He pointed at Nate. "Whatever you do, *don't* get caught out after curfew."

The colonel put his foot in the stirrup to remount, then paused and said kindly, "Son, you do understand that if you tell anyone of this conversation, people could die?"

"I do, sir," answered Nate gravely.

"Godspeed on your first assignment, lad. I'll see you soon." And with that he swung into the saddle and galloped down the road, never looking back, his blue cape streaming out behind him.

Cradling the egg basket, Nate fought to keep his balance on the lane. The snow was melting, making it more slippery than with the sled yesterday.

The sled! He'd left it at Aunt Neuss's, and now there was no time to retrieve it! Father will be furious!

But what was looming ahead worried him more. The Foulke mansion was gray stone with high-peaked, ivy-covered gables. It looked like a castle!

Go on, he told himself, and went hesitantly forward. He climbed the slate steps until he stood before a massive paneled door. In the middle of the door was a brass lion's head with a big ring in its mouth. Gathering his courage, he reached out, grabbed the ring, and knocked it against its plate.

The sound echoed within the house and died away. Nothing happened. Then slowly the great door, creaking on its hinges, opened just a crack.

Nate held his breath.

Suddenly a stick came out and poked him.

Her broom, he thought, jumping backwards. She really had one!

He turned to run, when a bony, hollow-cheeked woman peered out.

Too late!

9

THE WAYS OF THE FOX

Peering at Nate through the lens of a single spectacle attached to a silver chain, the Widow Foulke scowled.

"Don't need any hired hands!" she declared and started to close the door.

"Wait, ma'am!" yelped Nate. "Is Sally Winston here? I need to see her for just a minute."

The door opened a little wider. The old woman stuck her whiskered chin out and looked him over from head to toe. "Do I know you, sonny?" she croaked.

"Nate Donovan, from Philadelphia. My father was a schoolmaster. Now he's . . ."

"Don't waste my time! Sally attends there. Come in. One minute is all you've asked for, and one minute is all you'll get. Then be gone with you."

Muttering under her breath, she tottered away on the ivory-handled cane that she had thrust at him.

Alone in the front hall, Nate stared at the elaborate oriental rug and the silver wall sconces. Shaking his head, he thought, she's richer than Solomon! Is she a *Tory*?

The only sound was the ticktock of the grandfather clock.

All at once down the winding staircase waltzed a beautiful girl, her blond hair swept back and held in place by a red satin ribbon. She wore a bright chintz dress that flattered a well-formed figure. There was a twinkle in her eyes.

He gasped. "Sally?"

"Nate! What a surprise! Is Rachel with you?"

"No, I'm alone. I, um," he stammered, "I brought you something."

"You brought *me* something?" she replied softly in a tone he'd never heard from her before.

"Uh, yes . . . well, no, actually. Aunt Neuss, she sent these eggs." He thrust the basket at Sally, its fragile contents nearly spilling, as the two of them broke into nervous laughter.

Nate blushed. "I've got to go."

Smiling an un-Quakerly smile, Sally looked at him through half-lowered lashes. "You'll bring me more eggs?" she murmured, resting a hand on his arm.

Nate stumbled backward, reaching behind him for the doorknob. "Maybe." His heart fluttered as he backed out the door. "Gotta go."

Running from the mansion, he wondered why he'd acted that way. No girl had ever affected him like that. Besides, Sally was *Charles'* girl, wasn't she? But why hadn't she mentioned him?

Taking a deep breath, Nate climbed the stake-and-rider fence into Widow Foulke's field. His instructions were to follow the fence line down to the creek.

Hiking along the road that was almost bare in places but so drifted with snow in others that he could hardly get through it, he wondered if he was going the right way.

Finally, at dusk he came upon a frozen swamp. Was it fed by the spring the colonel had told him about?

He looked around. Where was the granite boulder? In the gloomy shadows of twilight, the whole place seemed eerie. A nearby bird whistled hauntingly, startling him. It sounded almost human.

There! He'd almost missed the boulder in the last of the fading light. He strained to see it.

It moved.

Nate jumped, his heart racing.

A deep voice greeted him. "Spring Manatawana."

Atop the boulder sat an Indian, clad in buckskin, perfectly still. So still that had he not spoken, Nate would've never known he was there.

What should he do now, he wondered. "Colonel Cadwalader sent me," he announced.

Slowly the Indian climbed down. He was tall, with long black hair streaked with gray, but still agile, Nate noted. Leathery lines etched the dark skin of his face, and his dark eyes seemed to see the meaning of things. From his waist hung a pouch made of skunk fur, with the stem of a clay pipe poking through the top. A leather sheath containing a large steel knife was fastened to his thigh by rawhide strips.

Nate backed away, watching him carefully.

"Place where we drink," the Indian declared.

"I'm not thirsty," replied Nate, puzzled.

"*Manatawana* means 'place where we drink.' You bring a message?"

Nate nodded.

"My name, *Skuhanaksa*. Oneida. Means 'Running Fox,' like white father, Washington. Enemy Cornwallis calls him 'Fox.' Oneida chief says he's very smart and brave. Great Spirit watches over him. Enemies can't kill him, can't catch him."

"I'd like to meet him someday," said Nate.

For a long time Running Fox studied him. Then he tapped his cheekbone. "To be spy like us, you must be like a fox. Learn ways of the fox. Sharp eyes, light feet, good ears. Hide in woods."

Nate was intrigued. Then he remembered. Taking off Charles' jacket, he handed it to him. "Running Fox, Colonel Cadwalader sends this for my brother Charles Donovan at White Marsh."

Taking it, the Indian started into the dark swamp. "You follow."

Nate hesitated, recalling stories of hunters who'd gone into the swamp and never come out.

Running Fox stopped and turned. Was he coming?

Sucking in a deep breath, Nate followed.

10

MOONLIGHT CAPER

A full moon was rising, but under the canopy of giant poplars the dark-ness in the swamp was dense and creepy. Nate struggled to keep up with Running Fox.

At night the swamp came alive—crickets chirped, an owl hooted, and in the distance a wolf howled. Glowing eyes darted about. Nate froze at the piercing cry of a bobcat. It sounded like a woman screaming.

But there was no time to stop. He forced himself to take the next step into oozing layers of marsh. Five steps later, it sucked off his right shoe. Stooping, he felt around in the mire until he found it and pulled it back on over a wet sock.

Where was Running Fox? Seeing a moving shadow ahead of him, he hurried to catch up.

Finally they arrived at Wissahickon Creek, half a mile above its junction with the Schuylkill River. Running Fox paused, raising his hand for silence. In the stillness Nate could hear the roar of distant rapids. Fox led the way to a bluff above a quiet inlet.

Below them, the creek ran smooth and silvery in the moonlight.

"Where are we?"

"Devil's Pool," Running Fox answered, his voice dropping to a whisper. "Bad medicine for Oneidas. No one comes here. Spirits of dead men gather here."

Nate shuddered. "You don't believe that, do you?"

"Not afraid," Running Fox stated. "Great Spirit protects me."

His simple faith amazed Nate.

Sniffing the air, the Indian listened intently. Satisfied they were alone, he led Nate down the steep bluff to the edge of the creek. Under a limestone outcropping, he laid Charles' coat next to three small rawhide-bound par-cels. He sat down cross-legged and gestured for Nate to join him.

Silently they waited a long time.

At last Fox, responding to something only he could hear, whistled a birdcall. Nate recognized it as the same haunting one he'd heard before.

In a moment two men in a small flatboat shipped their oars and glided up to the bank. They dragged the boat ashore.

Nate looked at Running Fox, who did . . . nothing. The ways of the Fox were baffling.

Gathering up Charles' coat and the parcels, the men shoved off from the bank and rowed back upstream. Not a word had been said.

Nate wanted to ask who those men were and what was in the parcels, but Running Fox got up and went to the river. There he took out his clay pipe and lit it with the flint he carried in his pouch. Sucking on its stem, he slowly exhaled a white cloud. Eyeing his young friend, he explained. "Levering brothers. Spies, like us." And that was all he said.

Suddenly Nate was anxious to get back to Second Street. "How do I get home?"

The Indian nodded to the top of the bluff.

"What? Climb back up there? My pants are already ripped. That'll be the end of them."

"Need buckskin," Fox commented, as he started up the cliff. Nate had to scramble after him. At the path's steepest point, they had to climb hand over hand.

At the summit Nate hoped they could rest long enough for him to catch his breath. But his guide immediately turned downstream and strode off into the moonlight. In a few minutes they arrived at the ruins of Foulke's Mill. Its shadowy outline and the creaking of the old waterwheel raised hackles on the back of Nate's neck.

Fox raised his hand. He whispered in Nate's ear, "Danger! You stay here!"

The Indian slipped away into the night. In a few moments he returned. "No soldiers. We go now."

"Where?"

"Me show you the way home."

Nate followed him along the bank until the creek emptied into the Schuylkill River. In a thicket of cattails, Fox uncovered a concealed canoe. Motioning Nate to the bow seat, Fox slipped into the stern and pushed off. A few powerful strokes took them into the swift downriver current. Soon Fox guided them back to shore and pointed into the woods.

"Go to the broken tree killed by sky fire. Find Coocaconoon. Follow this way." He held up his right hand.

"Coocaconoon?"

"White men call it Little Dock Creek. Runs past Cadwalader house."
Nate grinned in relief. "And past ours, too!"
Turning to leave, the Indian made a strange request.
"Next time you bring gingerbread."
"You like gingerbread?"
"Missionaries bring. Me like!"
"What missionaries?"
"Duffield. He's a friend."
Fox jumped into his canoe. In a few seconds, he had disappeared.
Alone, Nate started into the woods. But the Indian had not told him how far to go or how long it would take. Only that he would come to a broken tree, struck by lightning.
And he hadn't come to one. Fear clutched his heart. Which way now?
The dark and foreboding woods gave no answer.
Shivering, Nate squinted in the pale moonlight. On the top branch of a tree up ahead, something moved. An owl? No, too large.
All at once the bird, bigger than any he had ever seen, left the tree and glided down toward him. Just before reaching him, it banked right and soared away. Gleaming in the moonlight, its pure white wings were broader than both his arms outstretched!
Nate had the strangest feeling it wanted him to follow.
So he did.
The bird waited, then flew off again. Nate pursued. Once more, the bird paused for Nate to catch up.
Were they going toward the broken tree? Or away from it?
He didn't know, but there seemed to be more moonlight on the path now. He kept going.
Suddenly, up ahead, there was the broken tree! And below it Little Dock Creek!
He was saved! Thanks to . . . he looked around, but the ghostly bird had vanished.

11

EARS TO THE WALL

Arriving home, Nate peeked in the dining room window. Good, no Redcoats! Bursting in through the door, he made straight for the hearth fire in the kitchen and stood as close as he could. There his mother found him shivering when she came in with an armload of his bedding and belongings.

"Mother! What are you doing?"

"Captain André's guard took your room. You will be sleeping on a pallet by the hearth."

Nate couldn't believe his ears. Kicked out of his bedchamber? No!

"Sorry," said his mother with a grimace, "all of us must endure suffering these days. More important, are my babies safe? And what of Charles' coat?"

"The twins are safe, and the coat is on its way to Charles. But there's something I need to talk to you about."

"Not now, Nate. Captain André returns at any moment." Wearily she wiped her brow and straightened her organdy cap on neatly pinned hair.

Then, seeing the expression on her younger son's face, she sat down on the chair in front of the door to the back stairs. Quietly she asked, "What is it?"

Nate described his adventures in the vaguest terms, taking care not to reveal anything of a sensitive nature, and only in general what they might entail.

His mother astonished him. "So John Cadwalader would recruit you, too, as a spy for General Washington?"

His jaw fell open, but before he could say anything, she put a forefinger to her lips, her brow furrowed in thought. Then Lydia Donovan stood up and looked him in the eye. "Are you *sure*," she asked slowly, "you want to do this?"

"Aye!" he declared, remembering to keep his voice down, as he rose to his full height. "In another year I'll be old enough to join the army, like Charles! Until then . . ."

There was a long silence.

"Alright," she said at length. "I'll help you."

"You will?"

She nodded. "The larder has thin walls. In the evenings we'll be unseen guests at Lord Howe's staff meetings, hearing all their plans. We'll have much to report."

Nate stared at his mother in amazement.

"What about Father?"

"Leave him to me. Now run along and change."

He was just congratulating himself on his ripped pants escaping her notice, when she added, "And leave those torn britches on my sewing table. I shall mend them this time, but since you think you are a man now, you must learn to mend them for yourself."

Feigning sleep on his pallet in the kitchen, Nate listened intently, as the British staff officers gathered in the dining room. He could make out Captain André's voice, ordering a sergeant to make sure the household had all gone to bed as instructed.

In a moment the kitchen door opened, and a silhouette appeared. Nate lay motionless. The door closed, and their meeting began.

There was a barely audible creak on the back stairs. A faint light glowed under the door. Nate jumped out of his makeshift bed, silently moved the chair, and opened the door to the stairs. There was his mother in her flannel nightclothes, holding a pewter candlestick.

She leaned close and whispered, "A presence of evil weighs heavily on my heart this night. We must listen as carefully as we can. We may well hear matters of life and death for Charles, and many others."

As she crept into the larder, she withdrew a goose quill from her hair-bun and a sheet of rice paper hidden under her night cap.

Next, she pulled a crystal goblet from the shelf, and placing its mouth against the wall, beckoned Nate to listen through it.

His eyes widened at how easily he could hear the sounds from the next room. Where had she learned that?

Mother tapped him on the shoulder, bringing him back to the task at hand. Holding a tiny porcelain cup of black walnut ink out to him, she raised the candle higher and whispered, "Write down *everything*."

Nate nodded, listening intently.

The voices had stopped.

Oh no! We're too late.

On the other side of the thin wall, he could hear pens scratching, punctuated by a cough. A chair scraped across the floor; someone had apparently stood up, for what came next was a summary of their meeting.

Nate scribbled furiously: *British plan to attack Patriots at White Marsh. First units will march at Midnight, Friday, December 5. Possibly 12,000 regulars.*

Lydia Donovan stifled a gasp. "That's two nights from now!" she whispered. "We must move quickly!" She frowned. "We have nowhere near that many men!"

Nate looked at her amazed. How did she know that?

"Do you see now how important this is?" she asked, barely audibly.

Nodding, he bent to the glass again. Someone was saying something else.

An officer laughed. "Lord Howe is right. This engagement will destroy the rebel army. After our victory we can enjoy the ladies of Philadelphia this winter while the Continental Army disintegrates."

André spoke now. "Indeed, Colonel Percy, I plan to enjoy the company of the lovely young filly of this very house, who has never been broken to the bridle."

There were muted chuckles cut short by Percy. "Captain, I should remind you of the order forbidding fraternization with civilians not loyal to the crown."

"Never fear," responded André, "I shall not jeopardize our security."

As Nate made notes of this last, the pen trembled in his hand. He whispered, "André has designs on Rachel, Mother."

Lydia Donovan's jaw tightened. "Not so long as there is breath in this body!" she hissed in a voice only he could hear.

Many chairs scraped, the front door opened, and voices bade farewell.

In a flash Nate hid everything, and Mother slipped upstairs as delicately as an Irish faerie, leaving only a thin trail of candle smoke behind. Nate put the chair back against the door and crept back to his pallet. To all appearances the household was fast asleep.

Abruptly there was a sharp rap at the door of his parents' bedchamber. Nate jumped as another rap echoed through the house.

We've been caught, he silently screamed, unable to breathe. Why didn't Mother answer?

Finally, she responded sleepily, "Yes?" And Nate breathed again.

The voice of Captain André announced, "Mrs. Donovan, we're leaving. Trim the candles. See to your fire. Good night."

He left, and Nate lay staring up at the dark ceiling, his eyes wide as saucers. What would happen if Captain André ever found them out?

12

SOLDIERS & SANDWICHES

Awakening at morning's first light, Nate rolled off his bumpy pallet just as Mother greeted him with a bowl of hot porridge sprinkled with molasses. "We've got work to do, sleepyhead."

"Has Father given permission?"

"I'll choose the time to talk to him," she assured him. "He's in his wood shop now."

While Nate spooned down his porridge, Mother carefully copied their report onto two separate pieces of paper. As she did, Nate gasped. The letters were disappearing!

"Invisible ink," his mother said, smiling as she wrote. "This can't be read until heated, and the reader must be careful not to burn the paper trying." She demonstrated, holding it over a candle. The 'invisible' handwriting reappeared!

"Where did you get the ink?"

"I boiled it from recipes in your father's science papers."

Nate just shook his head in wonder.

His mother now took the original copy and carefully burned it in the hearth, making sure the flames consumed every bit.

Then, retrieving a cloth bag from the larder, she instructed him, "Take this empty flour sack with your pass to the British lines. Tell them you're going to visit the twins in Germantown and to Frankford Mill to buy flour. On Tuesdays the miller grinds wheat instead of corn. Baking flour is so needed by our army that there will be soldiers there to guard the mill from British raiding parties. It's the perfect place to pass one copy of our message to their officers. Be careful not to tell them where we live."

She tucked two peppermint sugar sticks in his pocket. "Give these to my babies at Rising Sun Tavern. Give Aunt Neuss the other copy. Tell her it's urgent. Surely, one of the two will get through. I'm going to hide them inside sandwiches."

Curious, he watched her open a wooden cupboard, pull out cold slices of boiled beef and lay them on rye bread. She placed their messages between the layers.

"The British won't suspect," she murmured, wrapping both sandwiches in cheesecloth and tucking them in his coat pockets.

When Nate showed his pass to the British pickets, he was waved through with no questions asked. Dropping his empty flour sack off at Frankford Mill to be filled, he saw two American officers in royal blue and buff, sporting Continental cockades on their hats. One now trotted toward him on a handsome gray mare.

Nate hesitated. Could he be trusted? If he missed this chance, he might not get another.

As the officer drew near, Nate held up a sandwich. "You must get hungry patrolling out here."

The officer frowned. "What's your name, son?"

"Nate Donovan."

"Why are you giving me this?"

"I was told to."

"By whom?"

"Colonel Cadwalader."

The officer unwrapped the sandwich, and took it apart. The secret ingredient was discovered!

He looked hard at Nate. "Where'd you get this?"

"It's for General Washington, sir. It tells what I overheard last night at the meeting of Lord Howe's staff."

The officer relaxed and smiled. "I will make sure it gets to the General directly." Tipping his tricornered hat, he trotted toward White Marsh.

Was he sincere? Nate wanted to trust him, but he wasn't sure. He would not be able to rest until the other message was on its way, too.

After trudging through two hours of snow flurries, Nate arrived at Rising Sun Tavern. Andrew and Molly raced to hug him. Laughing, Nate reached down and surprised them with Mother's peppermint sticks. Delighted, they ran off to play.

In Aunt Neuss's parlor, he said, "I've an urgent message for General Washington. I just gave the other copy to a major at Frankford Mill."

"Describe him."

When Nate mentioned his gray mare, she smiled. "Major Tallmadge." She looked at him. "What's so urgent?"

"The British plan to attack White Marsh tomorrow night. We've got to get word to the General. A second copy's in here, in invisible ink." He held up the second sandwich.

"Wait here till I get Colonel Cadwalader. He's downstairs."

Promptly they both returned. After hearing Nate's message, the colonel clapped the boy's shoulder. "This confirms what we've suspected. Well done, lad!"

Nate beamed.

"I'll sign your message with my secret signature. General Washington will know it's from me." He stood up. "We've got to deliver it before nightfall. I can't go; you'll have to carry this to Running Fox yourself."

Aunt Neuss interrupted. "Colonel, if spies are watching, they'll notice a boy arriving and then leaving so quickly. They'll suspect he's a messenger. I can't put Lydia's child at such risk."

Colonel Cadwalader smiled. He had a plan.

"Widow, Nate's about your height. Have you any old clothes he might wear?"

Nate shook his head stubbornly. "Me? Dress like a girl? Aw, no!"

The colonel replied coolly, "Did your parents give their permission?"

"My mother did."

"Well, consider yourself in the army now. In the army we do as we're told, not as we please. We must mislead the British, in case they're watching. A boy arrived. A girl departs. They won't realize how often you come or how long you stay."

Aunt Neuss agreed. "Anyone watching will just think she's one of our guests boarding here."

The colonel nodded. "Hurry and get dressed, lad. Lives are at stake."

Scowling, Nate consented.

Aunt Neuss pulled a dusty trunk from under her bed. Lifting its lid, she bent over and rummaged through it.

"Ah!" she cried, and brought out an old gray skirt that she'd worn when her plump waist was thin. Next she produced a tattered wool cape, dyed cranberry red, and straightened up, rubbing a crick in her back.

She held out the same needle case she'd used to sew Charles' coat. "There! Your message goes into my needle case. Running Fox will recognize it; he saw it last week when I mended his moccasin."

Aunt Neuss took apart the sandwich Nate had brought, handing the hidden piece of paper to Colonel Cadwalader, who signed it with a curious scribble. He gave it back to the widow. Twisting it now into a tight roll, she tucked it into the needle case and tied a ribbon around its worn leather flaps. As she did, Nate hungrily consumed the beef and bread sandwich pieces she'd discarded.

Now she gave Nate his orders. "Wait at the ferry landing on Wissahickon Creek. If Running Fox is watching, the color of that cape will get his attention. Give him this. Then hide my clothes in the grain bins of Foulke's Mill. Be sure no one's watching."

Nate tugged on the ill-fitting garments over his own clothes. "Aw, Aunt Neuss, I look like a doodle! This is ridiculous! Can't I just. . . " he stopped when her eyes shot a warning of stern Quaker discipline.

"General Washington never started out like this!" Nate grumbled.

"Maybe not, lad, but he'd be proud of you for a job few would do," Colonel Cadwalader added, clearing his throat to hide a smile. "Might even thank you himself someday."

Nate brightened up. "I'd sure like to meet him, sir!"

Aunt Nuess fastened the bonnet on his head and pecked his cheek good-bye. "Keep an eye over your shoulder, boy. You'd better be hurrying along. Godspeed!"

Stepping off the porch in Aunt Neuss's old clothes, Nate never felt so foolish. He grumbled to himself, scratching at the wooly cape, and was halfway across the yard when an unexpected visitor approached, carrying Widow Foulke's empty egg basket.

Oh, *no!* Sally!

Pulling the bonnet low over his face, he dashed back to the tavern to keep from being seen.

He never made it to the steps. Down them clattered three American soldiers, led by Colonel Cadwalader. They almost bowled Nate over as they ran for their horses in the barn.

Looking down the road towards White Marsh, the boy could see the reason for their hasty exit. A large patrol of British light horse was trotting toward them, less than a quarter mile away!

The Americans, whipping up their horses, exploded out of the barn! Seeing them, the British spurred in hot pursuit.

And Sally was directly in their path!

"Sally!" cried Nate, "Look out!"

She turned to see the source of the danger and froze.

At Nate's shout, Colonel Cadwalader looked back. Spotting her, he wheeled his mount and galloped back. Leaning out of the saddle, he stretched out his arm and he scooped her up, basket and all. Then he pounded hard up the road after his friends.

Nate stood, transfixed. What—

"*Boy!*" Aunt Neuss cried from an upper window. "Get back in here! Quick!"

Coming to his senses, Nate hurried up the steps and into the inn, just as the first British horsemen arrived.

Aunt Neuss flew downstairs. "Go into the kitchen! Pretend you're washing dishes. Stay there until they leave."

Nate did as he was told.

In a moment the kitchen door opened, and a sergeant stuck his head in.

Nate kept his head turned to the dishes and held his breath.

"You the only one in here, miss?"

Nate nodded but said nothing.

The sergeant backed out and closed the door, muttering an unflattering comment about the ugliness of American kitchen maids.

In a few minutes the British, disgusted that the rebels had eluded them, and gathering no useful information from Aunt Neuss, rode away.

Nate emerged from hiding, still shaking. His aunt's presence of mind had saved his life.

She smiled at him. "Only a spy would wear women's clothes."

"Thanks, Aunt Neuss!"

She gave him a hug. "Hurry now to Running Fox. But don't forget your father's sled. It's in the barn. Oh," she added with a mischievous smile, "you'd better stay in those charming clothes a little longer, just in case you encounter any more British."

As she'd anticipated, Running Fox was scouting the Wissahickon ferry landing. Nate handed him the needle case. "Widow Nuess sends this message for General Washington. He must see it right away."

Fox looked him up and down and shuddered. "Ugly squaw," he chuckled.

Nate blushed and could hardly wait to leave the borrowed clothes at the ruins of Foulke's Mill. He looked up the path to the old ruin. From there he would go all the way back to Frankford Mill for the flour and then home. The thought of being in his own bed, even if it was now a pallet on the kitchen floor, never seemed so good.

He turned to say good-bye to Running Fox, but his friend had already disappeared into the woods.

13

SPYMASTER OUTWITTED

Two mornings later Nate reluctantly tackled the chores he'd inherited from his older brother. As he dug ashes from the hearth and poured them into a tin bucket, he wondered what Charles was doing. Had there been a battle? Had their news reached White Marsh in time? Two days had passed since he had delivered his messages, and they'd heard exactly nothing.

Coming back indoors from scattering the ashes on his mother's little rose garden, he mindlessly swung open the kitchen door and hit Rachel!

"You *dolt!*" she screamed.

"It was an accident," he shrugged gloomily. "Sorry."

"Where've you been sneaking off to, anyway? You're hardly ever around."

At that moment their mother appeared. "Young lady, who do you think fetched the flour you bake with?"

As she approached them, she held up a book. Rachel blanched. Her diary!

"Better to mind your own business, daughter. It is not very pretty."

Rachel tried to summon indignation. "Mother! You read my . . ."

"If you have anything you do not desire others to see, do not leave it open on your nightstand." Mother shooed Nate away. "Finish your chores in the parlor."

Relieved to escape, he quickly shut the parlor door behind him and stooped to stoke the embers of its fireplace. Long ago he'd discovered voices from the kitchen always traveled through its twin chimneys. He paused and listened; their argument was a welcome distraction from worrying about Charles.

"Your flirtations will get you into serious trouble, along with everyone else in this family," Mother lectured Rachel.

"I have no idea what you are talking about!" his sister countered.

Their mother apparently quoted from her diary: "The most eligible bachelor in town flirts with you every night? Is that right?"

Rachel was unrepentant. "Not exactly. I simply described his debonair manners and elegant clothes."

Nate stifled a guffaw at his sister's verbal maneuverings, and listened more intently.

"That is *not* the whole truth. You have no idea how dangerous is the game you are playing. I hope you never have to find out!"

Rachel refused to be cowed. "Mother, I am not a child. Becky Winston was married two weeks ago. She's only three months older than I."

Mother continued lecturing to a deaf ear. "I know you're not a child. Unfortunately, so does Captain André. That, my dear, is the problem. You are only sixteen, and he flatters you as if you were at least eighteen. You think he is charmed with you, as do some other maidens of Society Hill. I've watched him. He's a heartbreaker. You shall see."

Rachel had no answer. But mother was not finished. "And who says he's eligible? He probably has a wife in England and a girl in every port. He's the enemy, not our friend."

"But Father says we are neutral, neither Tory nor Rebel. Captain André thinks we're his friends!"

Nate peeked in from the hall.

Mother searched Rachel's eyes, but her words had made little impression. "For you to welcome the attentions of a British officer is nothing less than treason to Charles!" She glared at her daughter. "See you don't betray your own brother to his grave."

An abrupt hush fell as Father entered from his workshop, requesting a hot drink.

Mother poured him a mug from the kettle of cider simmering on the back of the hearth.

Rachel fled into the parlor sulking, her face white.

Nate ignored her, busy at his chores, as if he'd heard nothing. He pumped air from a black leather bellows into the flickering fire until it grew into a proper blaze. He could still hear his mother through the chimney.

"William Donovan, I've something to tell you."

Before she could go further, the front door was flung open, and in strode Captain André as if he owned the house. His face was livid with anger. "I am sure you will be interested to know what happened last night at White Marsh!"

Nate stepped back with alarm.

William Donovan's jaw set, but before he could express his resentment at André's entering without knocking, Lydia threw him a glance.

Calmly but firmly, William Donovan ushered the captain into their parlor while Lydia Donovan took André's cloak and tricornered hat. "Please, Captain, have a seat. You seem disturbed."

Seeing his parents pulling together in this crisis, Nate whispered to Rachel, "Give him some apple cider again. He likes it."

André chose Father's favorite horsehair chair. Everyone else positioned themselves nervously around the room.

When Rachel returned with the cider, Nate was disgusted at how she promenaded in. He'd never seen her walk that way before. She leaned down to serve the captain, flirtatiously batting her eyelashes. "I wish we could serve you tea, Captain, but, alas, the tea tax has made that a luxury a modest Quaker family can no longer enjoy." She handed him the mug of cider. "This homely potion will have to suffice."

Her voice amazed Nate; she didn't sound like herself at all. She was *cooing!* Like Sally had cooed at him.

Captain André seemed completely charmed. He responded in kind. "Served by your hands, it will be as nectar from Mount Olympus, I assure you."

Mother looked on, disgusted. But as Captain André lowered his head to sip, Rachel winked at her. A quick smile crossed her mother's face, and she gave an imperceptible nod.

André wiped his mustache with an aristocratic flourish of his lace-edged handkerchief. He always made himself the center of attention, Nate thought, even without his overpowering cologne.

The captain set down the mug. "You'll be interested to know what happened last night. We had intended to surprise the rebel forces encamped at White Marsh."

Nate's hands grew clammy. He bent over the fireplace to jab its embers with a poker.

"One thing is certain," the captain went on. "The enemy knew our plans. We marched back here like an army of fools."

Nervous silence filled the room, broken by the drumming of André's manicured fingernails on the wooden armrest.

Nate peeked over his shoulder. Father, his back to the captain, facing Mother, mouthed silently, *What hast thou done?*

Nate wanted to blurt out something in her defense. Instead, he watched a quiet courage rise in her. Lydia Donovan stared back at André, her backbone as straight as a board.

Then she spoke. "My household was sleeping, sir," she answered truthfully, for during the attack indeed they were. Now she smiled; a lie had been avoided.

Captain André pursed his lips and searched her face. Would he pry deeper?

The captain arose. He walked over to the fireplace and looked up the chimney, then circled to the kitchen through the hall, stopping where Nate's pallet lay each night. "These walls have ears then, Madam. Yes, it was difficult to rouse you from sleep, as I recall."

Looking at each one of them in turn, he finally said, "Good day to you, Donovans." And retrieving his cloak and hat, he went to the front door.

As he opened it, he held out a British crown to Nate. "Here, lad, fetch as many gingerbread cookies as this will buy. My staff meeting convenes tonight at eight."

As Nate extended his hand, the captain added, "Hike fast. Perhaps you'll wear yourself out and sleep more soundly tonight."

And with that he marched out the door.

Avoiding Father's questioning look, Mother sighed, "God be thanked!"

She'd outwitted a British spy, Nate thought. Never had he been so proud of her!

14

THE GINGERBREAD SHOP

Captain André now began regularly sending Nate on personal errands all over the city, and he loathed them. "I'll help the Patriots overthrow that strutting peacock and the rest of the Lobsterbacks," he fumed, "if it's the last thing I do!"

The only bright spot was Ludwig's Bakery. Even with the British occupation, it was always full of customers who loved Christopher Ludwig's gingerbread. One afternoon twelve days later, Nate pushed the door open, its tinkling bell announcing his arrival. The aroma of fresh gingerbread drew him straight to the samples basket of broken gingersnap cookies.

A robust Christopher Ludwig in his baker's apron greeted him. "Back again, eh, lad? You're getting to be a regular."

Nate nodded, and waited in line until only one customer was left, a man buying mints. Nate overheard him whisper to Mr. Ludwig: "May I have your ear a moment?"

Curious, the baker leaned closer.

The man eyed the room and stared at Nate before continuing. Nate shuffled away to the jars of peppermint sticks in the window display at the far end of the shop. The man lowered his voice.

Ducking below a counter, Nate crept back toward the two men—and listened.

"Congress may be out of money," the visitor whispered, "but General Washington's army needs bread."

"I wish there were some way to help," replied Ludwig earnestly.

"Perhaps there is."

"What?"

"I'll pay for the flour," the stranger said, "if you'll bake it and find other bakers sympathetic to our cause."

"How many bakers?"

"At least seventy."

"Seventy!" Ludwig exclaimed, barely remembering to keep his voice down.

"We've a large army to feed."

"There aren't that many of us in all of Philadelphia."

"The outlying towns around have bakers. I'll pay you enough to hire help."

Nate peeked from behind the display case, as Ludwig leaned over the counter and shook the visitor's hand. "Done."

Then he smiled proudly. "The General likes gingerbread cookies. I'll include some for him." Both men laughed.

At that moment the back room curtain rustled and a gentleman of military bearing, though dressed in civilian attire, emerged. "Are you aware you have a spy in your midst?"

Ludwig and the stranger stared at him, astonished. "What do you mean?"

The gentleman grabbed Nate by the arm and pulled him out from behind the counter, where he'd been crouching. "This is what I mean!"

"I thought he'd left," stammered Ludwig.

"Next time make certain before you reveal anything you don't want the world to know," he said severely. Turning to the stranger, he said, "Would you excuse us, sir?"

The stranger nodded and abruptly left the shop.

As soon as they were alone, the gentleman relaxed and smiled. "As it happens, I am acquainted with this particular spy. His work saved our army at White Marsh."

Only then did Nate recognize him. He was the officer who had been with Major Tallmadge at Frankford Mill!

"I'm Captain McLane," he said with a Scottish accent, shaking Nate's hand.

The captain turned to Ludwig. "He's one of us. Nathanial Donovan is the newest member of our little club." He chuckled. "Stick in a few gingerbread cookies for Running Fox, too."

Seeing a movement outside the bakery, the captain ducked back behind the curtain into the back room just as the bell over the door rang again.

In came an elderly woman, her face completely covered in a cloak. Nate wondered if she was just cold or hiding.

Buying all the day-old bread she could fit into her basket, she turned to leave, hobbling slowly on her cane. Ludwig followed her to the door, locked it after her, and hung up a "Closed" sign.

Something about that woman seemed familiar to Nate, but he couldn't place her.

Nate left for home, proud of his new mission. He tucked the parcel of cookies for the General and Fox in his jacket and carried André's sack of gingerbread cookies under his arm.

He passed Fourth and Pine just as the sun was slipping behind the spire of Pastor Duffield's church. Cutting through the church's graveyard, he was surprised to discover Hessian soldiers digging mass graves. While one dug, two others dumped bloated bodies into the pit and covered them with lime.

That was hardly the way his father did it. What had they died of? A plague?

Keeping out of sight, he ran along behind a boxwood hedge. Nate realized there must be a deadly disease among the Hessians. He'd tell Running Fox about that, too.

At the other side of the property he stopped in shock. Hessian soldiers were hauling pews out of the sanctuary and throwing them on a bonfire built to warm sentries on duty. And cavalrymen were leading horses into the church! Nate could not believe his eyes! The church was being used as a livery stable!

Nate knew Father blamed Duffield for leading Charles astray, but would he not be upset about Hessian soldiers vandalizing the church? It wasn't right!

Nate took a shortcut home. Now he had another reason to see Running Fox. He'd want to know about Pastor Duffield's trouble.

15

TOO CLOSE FOR COMFORT

As soon as Nate got home, he hurried to the kitchen to share his discovery with Mother. But Captain André intercepted him. "You're late! My guests are here, and there are *no* cookies to serve!"

Nate held out the bag.

"Disappear!" barked Captain André, grabbing the bag.

Nate headed for the front hallway stairs.

"Wait, boy." André eyed him shrewdly. "Have you no other way upstairs than to disturb my meeting?"

Nate stopped cold. Did he know about the back kitchen staircase? Mother had concealed it well, and the captain had never questioned it.

"Only the hallway stairs, sir."

"That's not what I asked you." André's gaze swept the room, focusing on the larder, the staircase door, and a recessed cupboard near the fireplace. "This house certainly has more than enough storage spaces, doesn't it?"

"No, captain," responded Nate truthfully. "There's never enough room for everything."

Unsatisfied, André fingered the latch to the larder, watching Nate to see if he would react. "I will not have this family sneaking around behind my back or entertaining any secret visitors."

Suddenly he yanked open the larder door. Out tumbled a pile of iron cooking pots, one of which marred the shine of his boots. "Pick them up!" he commanded, and stormed off into the dining room.

Relieved, Nate replaced the pots and waited until the parlor doors slid shut. Then he clomped noisily up the main staircase to assure André he'd used the "only" staircase in the house. But General Howe's officers were talking too loudly to notice.

Upstairs Nate knocked softly on his parents' door.

Mother greeted him, finger to her lips. Father was napping.

Nate whispered, "Mother, I think Captain André suspects me! He seems to know about the larder and the kitchen staircase!"

Mother waved the anxiety away calmly. "What if he does? He suspects us all. We'll just have to be more careful than ever."

She led him to her sewing room. There Nate's heaviest jacket was laid out. The customary Quaker cloth coverings on its five buttons had been removed.

Before he could ask her why, Mother whispered, "Your buttons will carry messages of what we hear tonight."

"Buttons?" he asked. "Aunt Neuss used Charles' coat lining."

"The British may suspect that trick by now; we can't risk it."

She nudged him into a cold fireplace chimney. "Safer for us to listen here than downstairs—and almost as clear through the chimney's flu."

Listening, Nate heard an officer's voice he didn't recognize.

"One of our ships is due to arrive from the Canaries this week. She is carrying enough of the King's gold and sterling to meet the army's needs for the entire winter. And as we offer the local farmers hard currency and not worthless scrip, they sell to us rather than to the rebels. By spring the rebel army will be too weak from hunger to fight—if it still exists."

"Gentlemen, I propose a toast! To Lord Howe's victory and a restful winter in Philadelphia!"

"Hear, hear!" replied the other officers, goblets clinking.

Percy closed the proceedings with a final toast. "Gentlemen, I give you the King!"

Chairs scraped, as all rose to their feet. "The King!" they responded in unison.

The meeting was breaking up. Nate quickly but quietly slipped downstairs and into his pallet. Lying there, he suddenly remembered that he had not yet had a chance to tell Mother about the Hessians' mass grave and the vandalizing of the church. That should go into their report!

As soon as the last sounds of the British departure died away, he tiptoed back upstairs to tell her what he had seen. He was careful to keep his voice down, to avoid alerting the guard in his room. Nate found her preparing to write out their message. After sharpening her quill pen with a razor, she once again dipped its tip into her homemade "invisible" ink.

"This time," she informed him, "we will use cryptology."

"Cryptology?"

"The language of coded abbreviation. Father taught it to Charles and me for fun, but it shall serve a more serious purpose today."

Nate frowned. "How come he didn't teach me?"

"You were only four, too little to understand." She smiled. "I've not thought of it in years."

First, she wrote out all the letters of the alphabet. Then she gave each an ascending numerical value. But, she explained, instead of "A" equaling "1," she would use the Donovan family code. "Our street address, 177, adds up to 15, so A is 15, B is 16, and so on."

Nate just stared at her.

"You'll have to take this to Charles," she went on, "because only he will know the Donovan code. He can translate it for General Washington."

Nate watched Mother write the message on five tiny paper strips. Folding them tightly, she put each on a bare button, then sewed its cloth covering back in place.

Before sending Nate back to bed, she said, "Tomorrow, you can go to Widow Neuss. To visit your siblings, if anyone asks."

Downstairs Nate transferred the parcel of cookies to his backpack.

A chill wind swept the road to Germantown. Nate's feet were feeling the effects of the miles he'd traveled recently, but he felt guilty grumbling, knowing that Charles and most of his fellow soldiers were marching through the snow without boots.

Nate missed his brother. Passing Sally's mansion, he stopped, wondering if she were home. Just then he saw her walking toward him, a hundred yards away.

Nate slowed his pace to reach her gate exactly when she did.

She approached, lovelier than ever in a wintergreen cloak with a white fox fur muff on her hands, the egg basket over her arm. Nate instantly felt warmer, forgetting all about Charles.

"Good day, Sally."

She cocked her head. "You appear different from the last time I laid eyes on you," she teased.

"Oh, yes," he blushed, "my disguise."

Softly she spoke. "Thank you for warning me the other day. You helped save my life."

Nate beamed and, noting her creamy cheeks and rosy lips, could feel his heart beating.

Sally lifted her chin and dreamily lowered her eyelids, pursing her lips. Nate closed his eyes, too, and leaned forward.

A shrill whistle from the mansion startled them. Widow Foulke, at her front door, was summoning her niece with a stern look of disapproval.

Nate jerked back, as if stung by a bee. But Sally's eyes danced with merriment, in spite of her aunt's rebuke. "Nate, you know what they say about he who hesitates," she murmured sweetly, walking away.

"What *do* they say?" he called after her.

Before she could reply, Widow Foulke announced, "Your minute's up, young man. Now shoo!"

Crestfallen, he turned away.

16

RUNNING AWAY

Daydreaming of Sally, Nate entered the yard of Rising Sun Tavern, glad to be in his own clothes this time. The twins were playing in the snow and squealed with delight at the sight of him. He hugged each in turn and mounted the steps to the porch, wondering if there were any British spies about. With all the woods around, it was impossible to tell.

In the tavern he found Aunt Neuss serving lunch. She waved him toward Cadwalader's table, where the colonel was enjoying roasted goose with plum sauce.

"Good day, lad. What news from your house?"

Nate sat down and related what he had overheard, concluding, "My mother and I put it all in coded messages under my button covers." He tapped his jacket. "My brother Charles knows the code and can translate it for the General."

Pleased, the colonel smiled. "You've got a sharp mind for this, lad. I knew I could count on you."

Nate's heart swelled. Praise was something he rarely heard—never from his father and hardly ever from Mother.

Colonel Cadwalader patted Nate's shoulder. "Clever woman, your mother." He stood up. "We need to get these messages to your brother."

Pulling on his cape, the colonel paused. He drew his flintlock pistol from its holster and offered it to Nate. "You know how to use one of these?"

Nate recoiled. "No. Firearms are not permitted in our household."

Cadwalader returned the pistol to its holster. "You're probably better off without it, then."

He started upstairs with Nate hurrying after him. "I'll take you to Running Fox, but then I must return here. Running Fox can take your buttons up the Schuylkill to the army's camp at Gulph Mills."

To Nate's dismay Aunt Nuess once again fitted her cape and bonnet on him, having retrieved them from the mill. He would again leave them at the mill, this time *before* he reached the swamp, so as to avoid Running Fox's laughter.

Colonel Cadwalader stopped a short distance before the swamp. Cupping his hands to his mouth, he made a birdcall, not unlike the one that Nate had heard before. In a moment there was a reply from Running Fox.

"It's clear," the colonel said, proceeding forward.

Fox greeted them from atop the boulder at Manatawana Spring.

When Nate finished relating the news concealed under the button covers, Running Fox pulled his English hunting knife from its sheath. Before Nate could flinch, with one swift stroke he sliced all five buttons off his jacket.

Fox retrieved them. He removed the covers, giving the buttons back to Nate and carefully secreting the messages on his person. Then Nate pulled the parcel with the cookies from his backpack. Opening it, he gave Fox two gingerbread cookies, then gave him the parcel. "This must go to General Washington."

The Indian nodded and sniffed the cookies. "You saw Duffield!"

"No, Captain McLane," he said with a laugh. "Seems like *everyone* knows your fondness for gingerbread!"

Then he grew sober. "There's bad news about Duffield's church." He told him what he'd witnessed. When he got to the bloated bodies, Fox muttered, "Smallpox. They bury at night. No one knows how many die."

The colonel nodded. "My thoughts, exactly." Gazing into the swamp, he added, "If the pox is widespread, it could seriously weaken the enemy's forces. General Washington needs to hear this directly from the one who saw it." He turned to Nate. "You'll have to go to Gulph Mills yourself." He paused. "You do have your parents' assent to be involved with us, don't you?"

Nate hesitated. "Not exactly."

"What does that mean?"

"My mother knows and approves. She has not told my father yet."

Colonel Cadwalader straightened. "You're a mere fifteen years, boy. I cannot be responsible for your further involvement without the approval of your parents. *Both* parents."

Nate said nothing.

"Then you'll have to go home at once, lad, and gain your father's approval." He turned to Running Fox. "As soon as you've delivered the messages and the parcel for the General to his brother, return to the city, meet Nate, and take him to the General."

Running Fox looked at Nate. "Midnight. Duffield church boneyard. You be there." Without another word, he slipped away into the swamp.

Cadwalader shook his head. "They're desecrating Duffield's church and hanging his men to discourage any other pastors from preaching liberty. I hear the British have put a higher bounty on his head than even the General's."

Nate raced home, holding his buttonless jacket flapping in the cold night air. A short way up the road he hopped on the back of a hay wagon traveling Nice Town Road. The driver, hunkered down against the cold, never even noticed him.

Arriving home shortly after dark, he saw candlelight in the dining room—another staff meeting. Ducking low, he ran behind a stone wall to the elm tree next to the balcony of his parents' bedroom.

Stealthily climbing up from limb to limb, he swung over the balcony railing and rapped softly on the door to his parents' bedroom. In a moment it swung open, and Father abruptly waved his son inside.

Closing the door, he whispered sternly, "Art thou out of thy mind climbing up here? And where hast thou been?"

Nate took a deep breath. "Father, Colonel Cadwalader has asked me to come to the American camp, to make a report in person to General Washington. May I go?"

"Colonel Cadwalader had best mind his own business, rather than mine!"

Nate glanced at his mother, which infuriated his father. "Do not look to thy mother for support! She and I do not at all agree about this spying business. It is completely against Quaker principles!"

"William Donovan," she firmly interjected, "you know I have long favored the Patriot cause. But I have even more reason now, with our son Charles in our army. If I can do anything that might preserve his life and the lives of other beloved sons, I will do it!"

William Donovan said nothing.

Nate heard the grandfather clock in the dining room strike the half hour: 11:30! Running Fox would soon be expecting him!

In the silence Mother pointed to Nate's buttonless jacket, and he produced the five naked buttons. Deftly she recovered them and reattached
them.

Nate tried again. "An Indian guide will show me the way, Father. It's
urgent!"

"No!" declared his father. "I have already lost one son to this rebel
army. I'll not lose another!"

"But I've given my word!"

"It wasn't thy word to give! Thou livest in my house. Thou shalt do as
I say!"

"Then I'll stay with Charles!" And before his father could restrain him,
Nate swung open the window and jumped for the tree.

Scrambling down and nearly falling, he hoped there were no sentries
about. Seeing none, he dashed down the snowy drive to the street and ran
to meet Running Fox. It was almost midnight.

17

A TASTE OF WAR

Rounding the corner of Pine Street, Nate slowed his pace. At night the church's fog-enshrouded graveyard seemed more foreboding than he remembered. Why couldn't Running Fox have chosen another place to meet? And where was he, anyway?

Nate approached the wrought-iron entrance gate in the stone wall. It was ajar. Squeezing through, he accidentally let it slam shut behind him; and now trying to reopen it, he discovered it had locked. They'd have to find another way out.

Where *was* Running Fox? He surveyed the dark graveyard with its ancient black slate markers, tilted in all directions.

Through the swirling fog, a glow of lantern light came toward him. Sentries! He ducked out of sight behind a cluster of tall tombstones. As the light came nearer, it cast eerie shadows. He fought down the fear that was closing over his heart like an icy fist.

"Boy!" hissed a deep, familiar voice, startling him. "You must learn the ways of the fox."

His Indian friend materialized out of the fog beside him.

Nate's heart leaped. "I was looking for you!" he whispered.

"Not in right place." Fox pulled him into the shadows. "Get down!"

Nate ducked behind a granite tomb. They waited until the lantern light moved away.

"Your father agrees?" The Indian's eyes searched his.

"Not exactly."

"Then why did you come?"

"I had to. You heard the colonel. General Washington must hear from me what I saw here. Besides, this might help save my brother Charles' life someday."

Fox did not reply. He pulled open the moss-covered marble slab over a vault.

As its musty fumes arose, Nate grimaced. "We can't rob the dead!"

"Down!" Fox commanded, as the lantern light approached again. Then without warning, he jumped into the open vault, landing with a soft thud.

The sentries slowly passed. There was no sound from the grave.

Clammy sweat rolled down Nate's back as he crept to the edge of the hole. "Fox?"

No answer. Only a faint scratching noise came from the vault's icy walls.

In an instant Running Fox sprang out.

Nate yelped in surprise.

Immediately the lantern light turned in their direction. "Hessians!" murmured Fox, quickly stuffing the object of his search, a black cloth bag, into a buckskin haversack slung over his shoulder.

Then he rose and ran toward the spiked iron gate, not realizing that Nate had accidentally locked it. Finding it shut, he leaped onto the gate and quickly scaled it.

Nate arrived, panting and out of breath, just as Fox landed lightly on the other side.

"Climb!" the Indian insisted.

Nate tried but couldn't.

"Quick!" urged Fox, as the sentries, lanterns held high, appeared out of the fog.

Reaching through the bars of the gate, Fox joined his hands, making a step for Nate. With this boost from Fox, Nate was able to grab the top of the gate, avoid the spikes, and haul himself over.

As he jumped down, one of the sentries raised his musket and took aim while the other held the lanterns.

Ahead, Fox waited for him just inside the wood. The Indian hand-signaled the boy to crouch, and Nate did, running doubled over.

Behind him a musket exploded, and he heard the hiss of a musket ball passing his ear. He ran harder.

As Nate reached Fox, the Indian took off again. Gasping, Nate followed. A second shot rang out, sending a ball into the trunk of the tree next to him. Nate lurched after Fox, who seemed to be heading for Little Dock Creek. As he ran, he could hear the cries of more guards being called out. A whole squad was coming after them!

Ahead, Fox was racing up Fifth Street toward the creek. Nate stumbled after him, as the Indian leaped down the creek's muddy bank.

"Halt!" cried the nearest sentry.

Nate plunged down the bank after Fox, while his friend swept away the bulrushes that concealed a canoe.

More shots rang out!

The Indian held the canoe and quickly waved Nate to the bow. But the boy caught his foot in a tangle of vines and fell. Another musket ball whistled past Nate, splatting into the creek. Frantically he struggled to free his trapped foot.

Like lightning, Fox was at his side, cutting him free. Then the Indian practically tossed him into the canoe and shoved them off. Fox's paddle dug deeply into the creek, moving them quickly to its middle, just as their pursuers arrived at the bank and fired two more wild shots past them. They had made it!

After some minutes of paddling the Indian turned into an inlet near the broken tree where Nate had first seen the great white bird.

"We rest," Fox announced, driving the bow up on shore. Nate nodded, too tired to speak, as his friend got out and held the canoe for him.

As soon as they were both sitting on the bank, Nate was overwhelmed by curiosity. "What *is* in that bag?" He wanted to add, that nearly cost them their lives.

Reaching into his haversack, the Indian pulled out the bag and withdrew three parcels, each carefully wrapped in oiled otter skin, to protect it from the damp. Fox unwrapped them. The first was an overstuffed folio of papers with handwriting on them. "Duffield's sermons," he explained. "We take them to him."

"Is he with the army?"

Fox nodded. Next came a leather-bound ledger. "Members of his church."

Nate's eyes widened. "The pew roster! The British hanged a man for not telling them where it was!" He looked at Running Fox, his head tilted. How had he known where it was?

The Indian just shook his head. "You keep these," he said, handing the oilskin parcel of sermons to Nate.

Nate wanted to ask why, but the Indian was saying little. Nervously the boy stored it in his backpack.

Now came the last item in the bag, a fragile red-leather pouch; and from the way Running Fox handled it, it was the most valuable of all.

"It looks old," observed Nate, reaching for it. "May I see it?"

Instead of handing it to him, the Indian moved it out of reach. "Secret. Very old." And with that he tucked it and the pew roster into his haversack. "We go."

As they glided down the creek, Nate asked, "Why are you helping us?"

"Dr. Duffield."

"Why?"

"My father was a chief. Many moons ago, missionaries came. David Brainerd was one of them, a friend of Dr. Duffield. My father became a Christian. But I didn't; at least, not then."

"Why not?"

"No sign." Running Fox pointed to the sky.

"Sign?"

"Everything have sign. Sun, moon, star, fox, bear, hawk. I see them." He made a hand signal for each. "If the Christian Great Spirit is up there," he gestured to the night sky, "he will give a sign."

"*Did* God gave you a sign?"

Fox nodded. "Through Duffield."

"When?"

"Many moons ago. I was very sick . . . smallpox. Many Oneida died."

Nate remembered hearing about the dreaded plagues that often ravaged tribes as well as towns.

"Dr. Duffield come. He prayed for me, and I got well." The Indian pushed back his sleeve, revealing a scarred and pocked forearm. "The Great Spirit healed me." He shrugged and smiled. "A sign."

Nate marveled.

"One day the Redcoats will leave," Fox predicted. "Americans will triumph. Till then, we must have courage, like Duffield."

Impressed at his friend's certainty, Nate made no reply.

Arriving at a quiet inlet, they saw the lights of a small farmhouse. Fox led them to the door and knocked.

At Nate's questioning glance, Fox said, "Mr. Woods. Makes shoes. Friend."

A cobbler in a leather apron appeared and ushered them in.

The Indian gave Woods a deerskin from his haversack; and he, in turn, presented Fox with a pair of new moccasins. "Running Fox," exclaimed the cobbler smiling, "you always keep your word!"

The Indian turned to Nate and held them out. "These for you. British will not hear you walking now. I'll teach you."

Nate tried them on. They fit perfectly!

Fox nodded in the direction of the cobbler's barn. "We sleep there?"

Woods shook his head. "A patrol of Continentals is bivouacked there for the night." He thought a moment. "You could use the tobacco shed." He gestured to a small structure used for curing tobacco.

As Nate and Fox turned to leave, he said, "Wait."

He went to a cupboard and returned with two large hunks of dried venison and a jug of cider. "Supper," he said to Fox, laughing. "Your deer pelts are the best around."

In the middle of the night, Nate was awakened by Running Fox shaking him. Before he could speak, the Indian put a hand over his mouth. Then bending close, he whispered, "Many British around the barn! Make no sound!"

He moved silently over to the cracked door, motioning Nate to join him.

Nate looked out but could see only darkness. Frowning, he glanced at his friend.

Fox pointed to two shadows on the edge of the woods to their left that were not still, like the trees. He then pointed to their right—more moving shadows.

Nate was barely able to hear his friend's whisper. "I go out while you sleep. Many American horses, there." He indicated a horse line to the left of the barn. "Americans inside, sleep." He shook his head sadly. "Their two sentries, there and there, also sleep."

As Nate strained to see, the clouds that had obscured the moon parted. Now Nate could see that the shadows were British soldiers. By the horse line next to the barn, he could make out a Continental leaning up against a tree, his head bowed in fatigue. And in front of the barn, sitting on a wood-splitting stump, was another, also doubled over in sleep.

As Nate watched, two sets of British soldiers crept toward each sleeping sentry. Nate opened his mouth to warn them, but Fox again clamped a hand over his mouth so hard that it hurt. The Indian vehemently shook his head and directed Nate's attention to the edge of the clearing. There were British soldiers *everywhere,* a whole platoon of them!

"Too many!" Fox hissed. "If you make noise, we die!"

Nate couldn't breathe. Everything in him wanted to shout, to stop what was about to happen. He started to tremble as the British on the left signaled to those on the right. Abruptly they rushed forward and slit the throats of their sleeping victims.

Nate gagged in horror. He had just watched helplessly as two men were murdered in cold blood!

Now the British moved quickly to surround the barn. Four of them came forward with blazing torches and set fire to the barn in many places. The wood was tinder dry and caught quickly.

As the flames leaped up and began to consume the barn, there were muffled cries of alarm from inside. The large door flew open and five half-dressed Continentals ran out. They were instantly cut down by a volley of shots from the waiting British.

Nate started to cry. Silently.

Now from the barn came two well-aimed shots, and two British soldiers fell. The last Americans were determined to sell their lives dearly.

But there was no time to reload. The barn had become a blazing inferno. All at once several Americans burst out of it, straight into the leveled bayonets and muskets of the Redcoats, who were taking no prisoners.

From inside the barn a ragged scream tore the night air. And another, and another. The Americans were burning alive!

Running Fox grabbed Nate. "We go! Now!" And he half-dragged him out of the shed, while the attention of the British was fixed on the burning barn.

Sobbing silently, Nate stumbled after the Indian into the woods. Behind him he could still hear cry upon piercing cry . . . until they finally stopped.

But he could not get them to stop in his mind.

18

BACK FROM THE DEAD

Nate's new moccasins felt strange but soothing on his feet as he ran along after Fox. But nothing could soothe the agony in his heart as he struggled to understand the horror he had just witnessed.

Running Fox said nothing. Nate feared they were heading toward Devil's Pool again, and he was right. At the ruin of the old mill, he watched from the doorway as the Indian slipped inside and poked awake the two sleeping youths huddled together on a pile of old feed sacks.

"We need a boat," he told them.

As they scrambled up, the older one queried, "Who's this with you?"

"Nate Donovan," replied Running Fox. Turning to Nate, he pointed to the older one. "Odus Levering," he said by way of introduction, "and Jacob. Brothers."

That Levering name, where had Nate heard it before? Yes, the scruffy pair of swamp rats who'd retrieved Charles's jacket under the bluff!

They clumsily tipped their tricornered hats, freckled faces framed in dirty dark hair falling freely down their backs. *Whew!* They smelled as bad as they looked!

Jacob, tall and thin, motioned for Nate to help tug their flat-bottomed boat from its hiding place behind the ruins of the mill. "We've got to get going up the Schuylkill. The British are out tonight. They'll be on the old Hog's Head Road that leads here. And," he shivered, "it's cold enough to ice us in if we tarry."

What did that mean? Nate puzzled. He found out soon enough, as Odus pushed their boat into water that was already turning to icy slush.

"Where are we going?" asked Nate.

"Meet Duffield," responded the Indian. "We'll go with him to the Great Fox."

"General Washington?"

His friend nodded and jumped nimbly into the boat. Nate followed, rocking the boat.

Jacob looked over his shoulder. "Where to, Running Fox?"

"Duffield's cave."

Jacob nodded. "We'll leave the boat there and go to Valley Forge to see what's left of Papa's mill." He spat. "The British burned it last week."

After an hour of rowing steadily upriver, the Levering brothers began using their oars as poles.

As they reached the point where the Schuylkill was joined by Wissahickon Creek, the river suddenly quickened, running between boulders. "Help us!" cried Jacob. Fox snatched up one of the two spare paddles lying in the bottom of the boat, but before Nate could grab the other, the boat suddenly rocked hard to one side and stopped. They were hung up on a submerged boulder!

As the river came in over the submerged gunwale, carrying away the other paddle and the stern line, all four of them jumped to the high side of the boat.

Muttering an oath, Jacob pushed hard against the boulder with his oar. "Come on, you lazy lout!" he cried to his younger brother, who joined his efforts to Jacob's.

With a lurch the boat suddenly came free and pitched in the opposite direction. The Levering brothers and Running Fox were expecting this and were agile enough to shift their weight in time.

But Nate wasn't. Thrown over the side, he was swept downriver, sucked under the dark surface of the turbulent water. The shock of the cold river hit him in the chest like the kick of a mule, paralyzing him.

Scenes of his life passed before him like phantoms: Mother waving her Bible; Father shaking a finger, forbidding him to join the war.

God save me!

More faces flashed by. Charles. Sally kissing him good-bye.

He struggled for the surface, but his water-logged jacket held him down. If only he could get his head above water! He had to breathe! Finally he had to gasp for air, and icy water flooded his lungs.

The last thing he remembered was grabbing something that passed across his arm.

"He's gone!" cried Odus, resting on his oar. "He's been under too long!"

Running Fox ignored him. The stern line was taut, and with all his strength, the Indian began hauling it in, hand over hand.

The lad had it in a death grip, and as soon as Fox could reach him, he hauled his limp form over the stern and into the boat.

Nate's face was cold, white, and still in the moonlight.

"Dead!" pronounced Jacob.

"It's our fault!" moaned his brother.

Fox silenced them with a wave of his hand. Bending over the still form, he declared, "No. Great Spirit will give back wind."

Opening Nate's mouth, he blew three times into it and pleaded to the dark heavens above, "Give back wind."

Nothing stirred in the skies. Clouds had again obscured the moon.

The Indian yanked Nate's feet up and had Odus hold him upside down. Then Fox thumped Nate repeatedly between the shoulder blades.

Finally, water gurgled from the boy's mouth. Choking, Nate sputtered and started breathing.

"Back from the dead!" Jacob exclaimed in awe.

"Indian magic," muttered Odus, wide-eyed.

"No!" retorted Running Fox. Looking up, he murmured, "Thank you."

Quickly removing Nate's wet clothes, he asked the Levering brothers for their coats, which they readily offered, and put them on Nate. Then Fox removed Nate's soaked moccasins and carefully folded his wet jacket with its precious buttons.

In spite of the two coats, Nate shook uncontrollably. He started slipping into unconsciousness again, this time from the extreme cold.

The last thing Nate heard, as his eyes closed, was Fox urging the Levering brothers to row faster. "Boy needs a cave and fire, or he will die."

"We're going as fast as we can," Jacob assured him. "But the ice is thickening. We'll be lucky to reach that cave before the river freezes solid."

19

THE HAWK RETURNS

Nate's eyes fluttered open as dawn's first light spread over the stark white terrain. Lying in the bottom of the flatboat, he was alive—barely. Chills wracked his body, and he could no longer feel his fingers or toes. Worse, an icy wind made it impossible to get warm.

Even if he tucked his chin into his chest, he could not stop his teeth from chattering. He strained to focus on Running Fox. His friend was pointing to a thin curl of smoke apparently rising from the ground near the place a tree had fallen into the river.

Jacob rowed up to the trunk, allowing Running Fox to hop onto it.

"Dr. Duffield?" called the Indian.

Nate saw no one.

"Cave," Fox muttered, dragging the boat alongside the log. The Leverings lifted Nate up to Fox. Nate's bare feet were too numb to walk on, so Fox supported him until Jacob and Odus had hauled the boat out of the grip of the thickening ice. Then he ran ahead to find Duffield while the Leverings carried Nate, still wrapped in their coats, toward the cave. Soon Fox emerged with the pastor, who greeted everyone and led them through the cramped cave opening to a crackling fire inside.

Quickly noting that Nate was chilled to the bone, Duffield helped him out of the Leverings' coats and put around Nate's shoulders the bearskin coat he slept on. "This will warm you up soon enough, lad."

An iron kettle of steaming vegetable soup was suspended over the flames. "I'll get some of this into all of you straightaway," said the pastor with a smile. Fox took a second, smaller pot and filled it with water and winterberry leaves and put it over the fire, as well.

The Levering brothers gratefully sat down by the fire. When they were warmed, they got up to leave and inspect what was left of their father's mill.

"Thanks for your coats," Nate managed from the folds of the bearskin.

Odus grinned and spat tobacco juice into the fire. "We spies have to stick together!"

As he ate the pastor's hot soup, Nate's shivering finally subsided. The numbness in his toes gave way to burning as they began to thaw. Gradually the pain subsided, but his feet still throbbed relentlessly.

To get his mind off the cold, he studied this man so admired by his brother and Running Fox. Duffield's white hair was parted in the middle and framed his long, thin face. His expression was serious, but when he smiled, it seemed to radiate warmth. Nate sensed he did not use words unnecessarily.

"Had you been in that river much longer, you would have developed some frostbite," sighed Duffield. "The army is losing a lot of toes that way."

Running Fox emptied Nate's backpack and handed Duffield the two oilskin parcels he had been carrying, the pew roster and the sermons.

Duffield received them with delight. "How did you rescue these, my friend?"

The Indian explained that he'd been listening to Duffield's sermon in the back of the church on the day he'd marched to war. In the excitement the sermon was left behind, open on the pulpit. Its title, "To Arms!" would have enraged the British. After Duffield and his new recruits left, Fox had snuck back inside and snatched it.

Just then he heard British soldiers running into the church yard and up the front steps. Darting through the door behind the pulpit, Fox entered the pastor's study. On the other side of Duffield's desk was the back door. But standing at the desk was Robert, the young man whom the pastor was training for the ministry. Seeing Fox and knowing he could be trusted, the young man held out three items to him.

"These are Dr. Duffield's. The British must not get them! You keep them for him; I'll go delay them." And with that he went into the church.

Fox told how he'd run through the graveyard behind the church. Seeing a marble slab slightly off its pedestal vault, he slid it open further. He put the precious items in his haversack and dropped it into the vault, closing the cover. Then he ran for it. A day later he returned and wrapped each in oilskin for protection, putting the three parcels in a black cloth bag.

Duffield interrupted him. "What happened to Robert?"

The Indian shook his head. "Last thing I saw: they were taking him out of the church."

"I was there when they hanged him, sir. It was horrible!"

Duffield winced and buried his head in his hands. "Robert was like a son to me," he groaned.

Fox looked at Nate. "You tell the rest."

As Nate cautiously told of the pew burnings and mass graves, Duffield never raised his head, though his lips were moving. *What is he doing?* Nate wondered, bending closer to hear.

He was astonished: the preacher of fiery resistance to British tyranny was praying for his enemies! "May God have mercy on their wretched souls," the pastor whispered.

"If you pray for them," Nate asked, "why do you fight them?"

"A tyrant will not yield to reason," responded Duffield. "Only to force. Yet if he is defeated, he may repent."

Intrigued, Nate rubbed his cold feet.

Then Fox handed Duffield the ancient red-leather pouch, the sight of which brought tears to the pastor's eyes.

Something of sentimental value? Nate hoped he'd open it, but he didn't. Instead, he laid it on top of a Watt's Hymnal.

Nate looked more closely; it was a 1715 hymnal! The one Cadwalader had used for the spy code. Was Duffield part of the ring?

Fox got up and went to the back of the cave, returning in a moment with a bow and six arrows. "I go hunt," he said and, without waiting for a reply, left the cave.

In the silence that followed, Nate said haltingly, "Sir, this cave . . . and the fire . . . and the bearskin—without them I would have frozen."

The pastor smiled. "God provides what we need, lad. After all, we're fighting for His cause."

"Yes, sir," the boy replied thoughtfully and then added, "One more thing: Was Charles Donovan among the men you brought with you?"

Duffield looked at him. "You know him?"

"He's my brother."

"Your brother's in good hands," the pastor assured Nate with a smile. "He assists me when I minister to the sick and dying; you can be proud of him."

"I *am* proud, sir. And his health?"

"He is, I fear, suffering with the rest of the soldiers. Barefoot, half naked—the whole army appears forsaken. They've little bread and less meat. They're coming this way, to make winter camp at Valley Forge. They must make a permanent encampment soon, or sickness will be filling more graves than Lord Howe's bullets."

Nate frowned. "Are things that bad?"

"I fear so," the pastor replied. "Some curse God, disobey their General, desert us. As one of his chaplains, I do my best to encourage His Excellency against the overwhelming odds we face." He sighed. "Only God can save this army from falling apart before spring." With that, he excused himself and went outside to check the weather.

Nate looked around the cave. How could a once prosperous man now live here, like an animal in a lair?

In a moment Duffield returned. As if he were reading Nate's mind, he smiled and said, "My hideout's not much to brag about, is it? The British have put a price on my head. But I should be grateful. As our Savior said, 'The birds of the air have nests, the foxes holes, but the Son of Man has nowhere to lay his head.'" He shrugged. "So who am I to complain?"

Nate nodded sleepily and dozed off.

He was awakened by murmurs of greeting. Fox had returned with breakfast—two fat rabbits in his haversack.

When the rabbits had been roasted, Pastor Duffield blessed their meager meal, and they ate ravenously.

Breakfast over, Running Fox and Duffield took turns watching for the approach of the army from Gulph Mills while Nate slept soundly.

When Duffield gently shook him awake again, the cave had grown darker. "Come, lad," urged the pastor, "we must be going."

Nate crawled out of the bearskin, donned his now dry clothing, and joined Fox and Duffield outside the cave. He was stunned to realize he'd slept away most of the day. As they started walking, he discovered that much of his strength had returned, even though his toes were still tender inside the moccasins. He was grateful to be alive and walking at all! Running Fox had saved his life; he'd follow him wherever he led.

Running Fox led the way to the massive bluff known as Gulph Rock, the level top of which afforded a magnificent view of Gulph Road winding below, from Philadelphia to Valley Forge. There they awaited the army's arrival while heavy, gathering clouds threatened to unleash a snowstorm.

The Indian kept scanning the skies, and Nate wondered what he was looking for.

Then, holding one hand over the other and putting them to his mouth, the Indian made the sound of an injured rabbit. No one but a hunter would have paid it any mind.

Suddenly Running Fox pointed to a huge white bird circling the distant ruins of the burned-out mill. Nate's eyes widened. It was as big as the hawk he'd seen when he was lost in the woods!

Running Fox made the sound again.

Now the bird flew toward them. It circled so close Nate could see its markings and white wings. His heart leapt. "The hawk of *Manatawana*?"

"She guardian of journey," proclaimed the Indian. "Good omen."

"You believe in omens?"

Fox nodded.

"So do I," added the pastor.

Fox's gaze remained fixed on the hawk as she gracefully circled higher. "Snow hawk not from here. Someone captured her, but she got free."

Squinting, Nate could see a broken strap dangling from her right leg. "Does she have a name?"

"Oneida call her White Ghost. I call her America," said Fox quietly. "Must be free."

"But she's already free," Nate observed.

Pastor Duffield contradicted him. "She's prisoner to the British sport of falconry. Falcons and snow hawks are cousins. And I'd say she's not too far from her captors. It may mean the British are around here somewhere. Their scouts follow our army."

"This one is very wise," Fox mused, not taking his eyes off the hawk.

"You know her?" asked Nate, incredulous.

"Meet her many moons ago, far from here."

"Where?"

"Canada. The place where British and French fight."

"The last war?"

Fox nodded. "She followed me. Then the British snared her."

Running Fox watched her fly away. "They steal birds. Steal homelands. Steal freedom."

Nate sensed his sadness. Like Duffield, Running Fox's emotions ran deep. "Could we not recapture her?"

"Possible," Fox murmured. "She's a good omen."

The boy nodded emphatically. "Then we want her with us all the time! I saw her at the broken tree that night I was lost. She led me home. But how . . . ?"

Running Fox was still following her flight. "Great Spirit sent her."

20

THE GENERAL

As Nate waited with Running Fox and Pastor Duffield atop Gulph Rock, the first flakes of snow began to fall. There was no sign of the army anywhere—or was there? Without a word Fox suddenly climbed down from the bluff and disappeared.

Shading his eyes with his hand, Nate peered intently to the east. Sure enough, between flecks of white, tiny black silhouettes began appearing on the pale horizon. A steady column of soldiers, wagons, and horses, stretching as far as the eye could see, trudged over the frozen ground.

After a while, the column reached them. Marching four abreast, forlorn men began to pass by the rock, heads down, bent into the wind.

Nate searched for Charles among the downcast faces until daylight faded and images blurred in the swirling snow. To see better he jumped down from Gulph Rock, and Duffield followed. It was only a few feet to the ground, but he landed off balance and tumbled into the snow.

As he stood up, brushing the snow from his hands, he noticed something odd. His fingers were stained with fresh blood. Where had *that* come from? Nate looked at the ground and made a shocking discovery. Some of the barefoot soldiers tramping by were leaving a trail of bloody footprints in the snow!

Nate was shaken. He'd suffered only one night's agony; how many days had these men marched on frostbitten feet? And without complaint—their dedication amazed him.

Nate's musing was interrupted by the snort of a horse. Turning, he found an imposing gray stallion, measuring a good two hands taller than Goodness and Mercy. The horse was pawing at the frozen ground, snorting misty breath.

Astride this magnificent animal sat an erect, well-built man, with a calm demeanor and steady blue eyes under the brim of his tricornered officer's hat. He was tall—Nate estimated at least a head taller than most of the soldiers passing in front of him.

Duffield came up beside him and addressed the horseman. "Good day, Your Excellency."

Nate stared at the statuesque figure, realizing it was the Commander in Chief. His quiet confidence seemed to instill strength in the weak soldiers marching past. They believed in him.

"Greetings, Chaplain Duffield," the General welcomed him in his well-mannered Virginian accent.

Duffield saluted.

The General saluted back. "And this is Nathaniel Donovan?" Nate was shocked; how did he know his name?

"It is, sir, and a brave lad he is. Too young for a Continental but not too young to risk his life for our cause."

"True words," concurred Running Fox, now emerging from behind the General's horse.

Leaning slightly forward in his saddle, Washington inspected Nate with penetrating eyes. All at once, the General smiled. "It seems you and I have something in common: we share a taste for gingerbread."

Running Fox chuckled and Nate laughed, realizing now where Fox had gone: to deliver Ludwig's package.

"Tell me, lad, has Mr. Ludwig sent any other information from his excellent bakery?"

"No, sir. But our house has ears to Lord Howe's secrets. His staff meets there, and Captain André—"

"On General Howe's staff?" General Washington's eyebrows rose.

"Yes, sir. They hold their war councils in our dining room. To him we are peaceable Quakers. He does not yet know we are listening."

"So I've been informed," responded the General with a smile. "It has come to my attention, Master Donovan, that you have already served your country well; indeed, your efforts saved many lives at White Marsh." He paused. "It would seem we are in your debt, young sir." He gave a slight bow.

Nate was speechless.

The Commander in Chief was not finished. "While you may yet have some growing up to do, you are already doing the work of a grown man. "

Nate could hardly believe what he was hearing: praise for a job well done. His father had never done that.

The General straightened in his saddle. "And your brother is Corporal Donovan, Chaplain Duffield's assistant?"

Nate nodded. "Yes, sir."

General Washington turned to his aide-de-camp. "Colonel Hamilton, it seems we now have fighting Quakers on our rolls!"

"We have indeed, sir!" the young officer replied.

"While he's with us, have him assigned to his brother's company. That would be the 2nd Pennsylvania, I believe."

"Done, Your Excellency."

"Oh, and Colonel? Have him join my campfire tonight. Colonel Cadwalader tells me he has a report on conditions in Philadelphia."

He turned to Duffield. "Chaplain, join me as I move these troops along. I need you to lift their morale and give them some hope."

"It would be my privilege, sir, as soon as the lad's brother brings my horse."

Nodding, the General wheeled his horse and patted his neck. "Come, Nelson, we've work to do." He trotted down the column to encourage the stragglers.

In a moment Fox said to Duffield, "I go to Oneida scouts," and departed.

Finally Nate spotted his brother, dressed in a fine blue uniform and leading a bay mare toward them. "Charles!" he cried for joy.

His brother stared at him in disbelief. "Nate? What in the—?"

Instead of bothering to explain, Nate ran to Charles and threw his arms around him.

Smiling at their reunion, Duffield swung into his saddle. "You're not strong enough yet to march the rest of the way to Valley Forge, lad. Wait here till I come back for you," and with that he spurred after the General.

Charles fired questions at Nate. "How burn the home fires without me?"

"I've been doing all your chores."

"Not too happily, I'll wager," Charles teased. "You ought to try army chores sometime!"

Nate had worried about never seeing him alive again, and now here he was! He studied Charles. A full beard covered his gaunt face, and his cheekbones protruded sharply under hollow eyes. Had he slept at all? Eaten?

"Anyone miss me?" asked Charles hopefully.

"Mother, of course." Nate avoided mentioning Father.

"And Sally Winston?" Charles beamed.

Nate's heart skipped a beat. He turned away to avoid his brother's eager eyes. Yet *was* she still Charles' girl? Had he not left her? And now quite innocently, she had become part of Nate's life.

Charles shook his shoulder. "Nate?"

"Why should Sally care about you? You never even told her good-bye," Nate snapped. "Or any of us, for that matter."

Charles' joy faded to an expression of anxiety. "Well, if I die, Nate, do you suppose they'll forgive me?"

Instantly Nate regretted his meanness. He'd been so happy to see Charles. Why on earth had he turned on him? Just because of a girl?

He searched the ground for something to say. But instead of finding an apology, he saw more of his brother's woes. "Charles, look at your feet! Your stockings are showing through your shoes!"

"I've gotten used to it," replied Charles. "It's nothing compared to those of us who have no shoes at all."

"Here!" exclaimed Nate, pulling his own boots from his backpack, "Take these!"

"They're yours."

"I don't need them. Running Fox gave me these moccasins. Besides, you're marching every day in the snow."

"You get used to it, when you can't feel your feet anymore," his brother replied with a rueful smile. "We march in all weather. Afterwards, campfire feels so good, we get too close. The shoe leather dries faster than we realize and splits."

Charles stooped to measure the boots against his feet. They were an inch too short.

Nate groaned.

Charles grabbed a passing soldier whose feet were bound in bloody rags. He slapped the boots into his hands and bent down to unwrap the suffering man's feet and help put on the boots. They were a perfect fit.

"Charles," Nate whispered, "they were for you!"

His brother shook his head. "He needed them more."

Nate marveled at his brother's kindness. No longer was Charles the boy who had fought with him over every little thing. Watching the soldier shake Charles' hand in gratitude, Nate felt ashamed and realized that indeed he did have some growing up to do.

Soon the Commander in Chief rode by again, urging his troops onward. "Keep moving, men; we're almost there."

"I'd better find my company," Charles announced. "Why don't you fall in with me? Brothers must stick together."

"Thanks, but I should stay here. Chaplain Duffield told me to wait for him."

"I'm glad you two met," Charles called back, fading into the gathering darkness, becoming just one of the mass of soldiers.

Daylight was gone. Nate's limbs ached from the bitter cold invading them again, and his toes throbbed. Last night's ordeal in the river had left him weak, and climbing up to Gulph Rock had sapped what little strength he'd regained.

21

"I CAN DO IT, SIR"

Just when Nate thought he could not stand there another minute, Chaplain Duffield returned. He took a blanket from his saddlebag and put it around Nate's shoulders, then got him up on the horse behind him. They rode for a half an hour until the chaplain pointed ahead to Valley Forge, a small quiet village nestled among rolling hills along the banks of the Schuylkill River. Warm candlelight twinkled from the windows of its scattered stone farmhouses. But there would be no warmth for the army tonight. They would camp in open snow-covered fields with nothing to break the wind but the hills themselves.

When they finally located the bivouac of the 2nd Pennsylvania Regiment, Nate found Charles and told him, "Come with us. We need you to translate a coded message for General Washington."

"Me? What are you talking about?"

"Mother put it in our family code. You know it; I don't."

Mystified, Charles followed as Duffield led them to the General's campfire.

When they arrived, orderlies were gathering wood for the fire and by lantern light were erecting a tent for their commander. Nate saw that the canvas structure was hardly big enough for a child, let alone a tall man. "What kind of tent is that?"

"A Bell of Arms tent," Charles explained. "It was only meant to cover stacks of muskets and rifles, but it will shield the General until they can get his headquarters tent up."

Nate's stomach grumbled. "Um, anything to eat around here?"

"Not until the commissary wagons show up," replied Charles. "And tonight they might not."

Everything had taken hours longer than expected, causing many units to forego raising tents at all. Men were lighting fires and lying down with no bedding in the still-falling snow—even the sick ones.

A gray horse appeared at the edge of the firelight. The General had arrived. Dismounting, he returned his officers' salutes. Nate noticed how his presence suddenly lifted everyone's spirits.

A commissary cook arrived, apologizing for the delay, and set to work fixing what dinner he could. Nate watched him mix flour and water, slap it onto a rock in the fire and serve the scorched patty with a weak beef broth.

"What am I eating?" he whispered to Charles.

"Firecake and stew," his brother whispered back. "And it doesn't get any better than this, I'm afraid."

Nate gulped it down but could hardly keep from spitting it out.

Charles grimaced. "Cook must have dropped his ladle; I can't find the meat for the dirt in this concoction!"

General Washington's manners were, as always, impeccable. If he thought the stew bordered on being inedible, he didn't mention it. Tasting one bite, he simply laid down his spoon, cleared his throat, and addressed his officers. Turning to a handsome young cavalry officer, he asked, "Major Lee, what exactly happened last night?"

Henry Lee, known affectionately to his men as "Light Horse Harry," waved toward Cadwalader who was just walking up with Captain McLane and a boy. "The Colonel was in charge of the operation last night, sir."

Cadwalader reported solemnly, "In accordance with our orders, sir, we sent out cavalry patrols, to ensure there would be no nasty surprises awaiting us as we marched here. One unit of forty men spent the night in the barn of a Patriot named Woods. Two hours after midnight the barn was surrounded by a much larger British force and put to the torch. Thirty-two of our men perished in the fire, or were shot or bayoneted, as they attempted to flee the barn. Four others were taken prisoner. Only four of our men escaped to tell us what happened." Cadwalader's voice caught. "It was butchery!"

Nate covered his face with his hands, trying to blot out the cries of the burning men, the bayonets plunging into fallen American soldiers. He gave a strangled cry.

Around the fire the men stopped eating and talking.

Captain McLane came over to Nate and asked, "Are you alright, lad?"

"Burned alive," groaned Nate. "I saw it."

Cadwalader looked up, surprised. "You were there? How? I didn't send you with the cavalry."

Nate struggled to answer. "Fox . . . Mr. Woods . . . moccasins . . . we got away." He fell silent.

Now General Washington walked over to the boy and with fatherly concern put an arm around his shoulder. "I hope that's the worst your eyes will see," he said with a sigh. "But I fear not. Was this the first time you have seen death?"

Nate wiped his nose on his cuff. "No, sir. I saw the two men hanged at Pastor Duffield's church. But I've never seen men burned alive."

The General gave an understanding nod. "It's never easy to see men die. But I believe you have the makings of a good soldier."

Now the commander turned to Cadwalader. "Where did they take the prisoners, Colonel?"

"To Walnut Street Prison; it's the one under Hessian guard, sir."

Nate listened intently. Walnut Street Prison? That was only five blocks from his house!

The General shook his head. "I fear our men in there are being treated far worse than we treat their prisoners. I want to know how many of our men are there and how they are getting along."

McLane frowned. "I'm not sure we can find that out, sir. The only way would be from a prisoner, and no one's ever escaped."

"I can do it, sir."

Surprised eyes fell upon Nate.

"Are you out of your mind?" Charles whispered to his younger brother. "Nobody comes out of there except in a coffin!"

Nate nodded. "That's the point." He turned to the General. "My father makes the coffins for their dead. Once a week he goes to pick up the bodies at that prison. I could sneak inside with his coffin sleigh."

Charles shot him an alarmed glance, mouthing, *Are you crazy?* But Nate ignored him.

The General's eyes searched Nate's. "Go ahead, lad," he said at length. "But if you're caught, you know you'll be hanged as a spy."

Fear crept up Nate's spine, but it was too late to back down on his offer.

General Washington turned to Charles. "I'm glad to have another Donovan in this army."

Before the latter could reply, a young major carrying a lantern came up. "General, your tent's ready. Please, sir, get some sleep. You've been up since before dawn."

Reluctantly the Commander in Chief stood. All present came to immediate attention, Nate imitating how Charles did it.

As the General left, he settled back down near the fire.

Sitting nearby, Colonel Hamilton confided to Cadwalader, "Usually he doesn't listen to us. We need Mrs. Washington here. He'll listen to her."

The colonel grimaced. "We've got to keep him healthy. If he goes down, we're finished."

The boy with Cadwalader, whom the colonel now introduced, was about Nate's age. "This is Tad Walker. Sarah Walker's oldest."

Tad was shorter than Nate but older, as the stubble on his chin indicated. He was stocky and thick through the shoulders—a farm boy, Nate decided. And he detected a hint of mischief in his green eyes.

Walking back to their campsite, Charles scolded Nate, "Wait till Father discovers you've volunteered his coffin-making business and our wagon for a Patriot spy mission!"

Sitting next to Charles at his campfire, Nate discovered that Tad Walker was attached to Charles' company.

"Think they'll hang ya?" Tad taunted from across the fire.

"Me?" Nate blinked.

"Aye. Ya can't spy inside that prison. Nobody can."

"We'll see."

"Not without my help," came a baritone voice behind them. Nate turned to see the tall, sandy-haired officer Nate had given the sandwich to at Frankford Mill. Captain McLane and Chaplain Duffield were walking up behind him.

"Major Tallmadge!" Tad scrambled to attention, as did the others.

"At ease, men. We'll discuss prison later. Right now I need those special buttons." He pointed to Nate's jacket. "Running Fox told me about them before I sent him out scouting tonight."

Standing next to Tallmadge, Captain McLane handed the farm boy a pair of mustache scissors from his pocket. "Snip 'em."

Tad grabbed Nate's jacket. The silver scissors flashed in the firelight as he cut off the buttons.

McLane handed the buttons to Charles, who put them inside a metal foot warmer, which he thrust briefly into the campfire.

Tallmadge looked over McLane's shoulder. "You've tried this before? Burning intelligence before we've read it?"

"Don't worry, sir," responded Charles, "I've watched my father do this. The invisible ink will heat up, so we can read it."

Nate hoped falling in the river hadn't washed that ink away. Best not to mention that. He waited with the others.

In a moment McLane removed the foot warmer and opened it. Tossing the buttons back and forth in his hands until they cooled, he removed their fabric covers.

Nate sighed in relief; water had indeed blurred the messages, yet they were still legible.

Charles now set to work, decoding his mother's shorthand.

Then it dawned on Nate. "This is crazy! Mother only wrote what I told her. And I could tell it again without all this fuss!"

"Bear with us, lad," said McLane calmly, "we could not be sure of your being here. Your jacket might well have outlasted your life."

Nate swallowed hard, not wishing to be reminded of it.

Looking Nate in the eye, McLane said, "I need you here in Valley Forge with Tad for a few days. You two will scout out the farmers in this area. It's been our experience that some farmers will sell us provisions, some will hold back, and more than a few will trade with the British, who pay with silver and gold instead of paper Continental dollars. We need to know who we can count on around here, and we can't go ourselves; they wouldn't be honest with us. But they'll probably tell you two the truth."

Tad spoke up. "That'll be easy, sir. Our farm's here. The neighbors all know me; I used to play in their barns. And my mother takes care of them when they're sick."

"Perfect!" exclaimed Captain McLane, taking his leave. "Good evening, gentlemen."

"My mother's also handy with a needle," Tad reassured Nate. "Tomorrow she'll have those buttons back on your jacket in no time."

22

SARAH WALKER

In the morning Nate awoke stiff, sore, and sniffling from sleeping in the snow. His empty stomach grumbled as he and Tad walked toward the Walker farm.

"Where's your family from?" Nate asked.

"Ireland. My grandparents came over," responded Tad.

"We came from there, too. They didn't much like Quakers."

Tad scoffed. "You're religious, eh?"

"My parents are. Not me," Nate assured him, having never declared such a thing before.

"Good! Because I'm not pairing up with any ninny. In war ya figure out pretty quick that religion's a waste of good sense. Use your head and don't waste good time prayin', I say."

Tad talked bigger than his age, thought Nate, as he rambled on. "Ain't no miracles in this place!" Tad concluded bitterly.

"Maybe you only get a miracle when you need one," Nate offered.

"Nope! It's all just luck," Tad declared with a scowl.

Nate followed Tad over stubbles of cornstalks while blackbirds scavenged in the snow-covered fields. In the distance Nate could see a sprawling farm with tobacco drying barns, a dairy barn, chicken coops, and a grain silo. At its center was a large white-washed stone house. Grazing cattle dotted the fields nearby.

"You've got a lot of cows," Nate commented.

"Dairy cattle," replied Tad. "I figure my father will slaughter most of them now to feed the army. He's already nearly emptied our silo to feed men instead of animals. Mama will be sad to lose the cows, but she'll accept it because the men are mostly starved. She never met a stranger she didn't like, or a soldier she wouldn't feed."

As they came up to the house, Sarah Walker was sweeping snow from the porch steps. Playfully she swished clumps of it over two of Tad's six younger brothers, who ran about her feet, giggling with glee.

Willowy and fair, she had silky golden tresses that curled down her long neck. As the sun shone on her homespun cape billowing in the breeze, she looked like a young and beautiful angel, Nate thought.

Delighted to see Tad, she kissed him on the cheek and pinched Nate's, too, before they were even introduced! As the two cold boys eagerly devoured her fried meat patties in front of the cheery kitchen hearth, Tad told his mother about their assignment and Nate's buttons.

Pulling a needle and thread from her wicker sewing basket, Sarah Walker said, "Bring me those buttons." She smiled at Nate. "You need looking after, so consider me your mother away from home. That'll make your own mother feel better."

Sarah sewed and rocked, helping the boys plot their cover story. "You'll carry eggs and milk from here to the troops. Each time you go, you'll call on different farmers, asking them if they'll make a contribution from their stores." Nate nodded readily. She was as intelligent as she was pretty!

"These mercy missions will shield your spy work," she concluded.

Now Mr. Walker came in, kicking off his boots and affectionately hugging his wife. He was robust in the shoulders and blond like her, but he limped with a deformed foot, which had prevented him from serving in the army. He was a strong Patriot, nonetheless.

Mr. Walker shook Nate's hand. "And who are you?"

Tad jumped up to introduce him. "Nate Donovan, this is my father, Joseph Walker."

Mr. Walker welcomed Nate and shared with the boys the burden on his heart. "I've just found out that when our neighbors learned the army was coming here, many doubled or even tripled the prices on their produce. They hid their horses and wagons, too, to keep the army from taking them." His eyes narrowed. "The worst of it is, this very week some of them stood back and watched the British burn a mill, where Colonel Hamilton had stored a food supply gathered from local farmers. Those rascals are the devil's kin. They'll starve this army if they don't get paid for their goods in hard currency."

"Are they Tories?" Nate asked.

"Some are. But most are greedy cowards, caring more about lining their pockets than the future of this country." He pounded the table in disgust. "They don't deserve this army's sacrifice!"

Using scraps of cloth to cover the buttons, Sarah finished attaching them and handed Nate his jacket. He donned it and thanked her.

As it turned out, Sarah Walker's idea worked better than they'd dared hope. People would offer them cider and cookies, and the boys would ask for contributions of food for the army. Those who donated were profusely thanked, and those who refused were asked, "Will you be able to make it through the winter without the British or the Americans stealing your harvest?"

And then they would tell the two worried-looking lads not to worry, that their feed and grain and livestock were safely hidden in the woods.

When the boys had sipped all the tea and hot cider they could hold and nibbled all the cookies, they would head back to camp with their food stores and information.

Late one afternoon, as they were crossing a pasture near the camp, Nate looked up and saw her again.

"There she is!"

23

THE WHITE GHOST

Tad stared at him. "There *who* is?"

"The snow hawk!" Nate exclaimed, pointing to the great white bird gliding toward them with its wings outspread.

Tad was awestruck. "I've never seen a bird like *that* before!"

"You might not ever again."

"How do ya know?" gasped Tad.

"The British captured her in Canada and started to train her for falconry."

"What's falconry?"

"Nobles train falcons to hunt small animals. Running Fox says she's partly trained."

"Who'd believe that ol' Injun anyway?" Tad sneered.

"I do. He's a woodsman, knows things about every creature in these parts."

The snow hawk swooped down, and both boys paused to watch her.

"What else does that redskin know about her?" asked Tad, genuinely interested.

"She likes her freedom, like us Americans. So does Running Fox. He wants the Continentals to win, 'cause he's not Tory, like some Indians. Takes good care of me."

Tad walked on ahead across the field. "How d'ya know he's not Tory? Injuns can lie."

"Colonel Cadwalader, Major McLane, and His Excellency all trust him."

Unable to argue against the weight of that, Tad shrugged his shoulders. Then he ran off down the field after the snow hawk, yelling over his shoulder, "She's beautiful!"

"That she is!" Nate gasped, running to catch up. "And someday she's gonna be mine."

"How are you going to make friends with her?"

Nate considered. "I don't know yet."

Tad headed straight for the burned-out mill Nate had seen from Gulph Rock. Far above the snow hawk circled.

Only the stone chimney was still intact. The rest was in charred ruins. A hanging rafter creaked in the wind. "This place is spooky!" Nate muttered.

"I saw her burn!" Tad boasted. "Night before last. You could see it for miles! We tried to help the Leverings and Colonel Hamilton rescue some of the supplies stored there, but the British and their torches got here first. And then they set an ambush in case anyone tried to put out the fire. We had to make a run for it!"

"So that's why your father's silo is empty and your cows are starving!"

"Yup. The miller and his wife died in the fire. I ain't been back here since it happened; too many British around. But since the army arrived, they're long gone."

Nate shivered. "Come on, we'd better get out of here; it's getting late!"

Now the hawk glided down, and with a great flap of her wings came to rest on the top of the chimney. Nate was thrilled. "The White Ghost," he murmured.

Both boys gazed up at her, in awe.

"You believe in ghosts?" Tad asked, laughing.

"Naw, but the Oneida call her that. Must be an Indian thing."

"You believe all those stories, city boy?"

Suddenly the snow hawk spread her wings and dove toward them. They ducked. As she passed over them, Nate noticed that she was carrying something shiny in her beak. The hawk wheeled back and perched once more atop the chimney. Up close the hawk was even larger than he had thought, almost as big as an eagle!

As he admired her, she dropped the shiny object down the chimney, as if she wanted them to find it. Nate went over to the fireplace to see what it was. Blowing off the soot, he discovered it was a bright metal button with an inscribed design on it, a uniform button.

Tad came up to look. He pointed out the lion rampant embossed on the minting.

"Whoever burned the mill must have lost it," Nate mused. "And I don't think it's brass. It looks more like gold."

"How can you be so sure? Maybe the bird brought it here from somewhere else. Heaps of British been around these parts."

"Just a hunch," Nate insisted. He looked at the darkening sky. "We have to get back to camp before a British patrol finds us."

Tad agreed. As they started walking away from the ruins in the gathering twilight, Nate looked up at the snow hawk, wondering if she would follow. But she remained perched atop the chimney, watching them.

He hurried to keep up with Tad. "You think that hawk likes us?"

"Naw," scoffed Tad. "Don't go thinkin' you can make a friend out of her that easy. Besides, she wasn't interested."

"How could you tell?"

"I just know about these things," Tad insisted. "Believe me."

But Nate didn't believe him, and he wasn't going to give up that easily.

About a mile from the camp, they noticed shadowy figures lurking in the cover of the trees bordering the riverbank. Nate and Tad broke into a dead run toward the encampment. Had they been seen?

Nate looked back again. Nobody behind them. He began to wonder if he had imagined the figures.

Finally, within sight of camp, the boys slowed their pace as the last rays of light faded. Darkness shrouded their way. The stars didn't twinkle, and the moon was momentarily obscured by clouds slowly thickening into a solid overcast. Nate figured it was fixing to snow again. What a long, cold winter it was getting to be!

"Think we're being followed?" He wondered aloud.

"Hope not. Just crossing this field without sentries coverin' ya is risky." Tad frowned and held up his hand. Then he whispered, "Did ya hear something?"

Both boys stood motionless, listening and peering into the dark.

Briefly the moon peeked through the clouds, casting shadows on the ground. Something *was* moving behind them! Hair raised on the back of Nate's neck.

All at once they heard horses galloping!

"Run!" cried Tad. The boys raced toward the lights of Valley Forge. Sprinting through the dark, they tore through brambles and corn stubble, Tad outrunning Nate. Suddenly he disappeared!

A scream of pain alerted Nate, and he was barely able to stop in time, at the edge of a deep ditch.

Nate could not see Tad, but he could hear him. The boy was hollering with fear, as well as agony. "I'm bleeding to death!"

Nate stumbled down the steep side of the ditch, to find his friend with a sharpened stake protruding through the calf of his right leg.

"Help me! Do something! I'm gonna die here!"

At the sight of the blood oozing from his friend's wound, Nate started to grow light-headed. Then, getting a grip on himself, he said, "Don't worry, I'll get you out of here!" But he wasn't sure he could.

Taking a deep breath, he knew that the first thing he had to do was to free the leg from the stake. With both hands he firmly gripped Tad's leg, and quickly pulled it off.

Tad screamed.

Now blood gushed from the wound, and Tad passed out. Nate was frantic. He had to get him out of the ditch and fast! He had to stop that flow of blood!

Grabbing Tad under the shoulders, he tried to haul him upward, but the fresh earth on the sides of the ditch would not support them both. What to do?

It came to him to use their two belts. He removed Tad's and looped it under his friend's shoulders. Then he took off his own, and tied it to Tad's. By himself, he was able to get out of the ditch. Then he squatted and, using his legs, hauled Tad up with the belts.

When he finally had Tad on the ground beside him, he put his own belt back on and used Tad's to make a tourniquet just above the wound, as his mother had shown him. His friend had lost a lot of blood, and he tightened the belt to make sure he didn't lose any more.

Now he had to get Tad to the army's doctors. He couldn't drag him that far, but his father had shown him how to carry someone. Grabbing Tad's left wrist and his good leg by the ankle, he wrestled him up on his back. Then, doubled over, he staggered toward the nearest campfire.

"Halt!" cried a sentry. "Who goes there?"

24

FRIENDS FOREVER

H elp me!" Nate begged.

"Advance and be recognized!"

"I'm Nate Donovan," he called out, "with the 2nd Pennsylvania. And I've got Tad Walker here; he's hurt bad!"

Holding up a lantern, the sentry called for the sergeant in charge. Soon hands were lifting Tad off Nate's back and laying him over a horse.

"We'll take him to the hospital tents," the sergeant assured him.

"Which one?"

"The main one. Follow me."

Nate walked beside the horse to keep Tad from falling off. When at last they reached the main medical tent, he was shocked at Tad's rapidly worsening condition. He was unconscious, and his face was pale. The wound, aggravated by the bouncing on horseback, was oozing again, despite the tourniquet.

In the hospital tent Nate could not believe his ears. The attending physicians in their blood-stained smocks started arguing about whether they could spare the silk thread it would take to stitch up Tad's leg!

The older doctor, spectacles on his nose, protested that the precious little thread they had was needed for soldiers wounded in battle, not in accidents.

The younger doctor exploded. "Dr. Shippen, this is madness! How can we run a field hospital with no supplies?"

"Congress knows we need more of everything!" the older man fired back. "And their solution? Print more money! To buy supplies that don't exist! And if they did exist, Continental paper wouldn't buy them, only British coin!"

"Then bring Congress *here!*" cried Dr. Rush.

"*No!*" Shippen shouted. "Their meddling only makes things worse!"

At that moment a senior officer entered. "Stop fretting, Dr. Rush. You cure this cough, and I'll go convince Congress myself," he wheezed, overcome by a spasm of coughing.

"It's not that easy, sir," retorted Dr. Shippen. "They made me Director General of all our military hospitals, but they won't even listen to me."

Nate looked at the senior officer gasping for air and spitting a great glob of phlegm into a handkerchief. Except for his illness, he was a formidable fellow, dressed in a uniform with gold braid on the epaulettes. A General! Someone who could help!

"Please, sir!" Nate pleaded, as the officer's coughing subsided, "*Do* something! My friend here's bleeding to death!"

The General came over to where Tad lay. He looked closely at him. "That's Cousin Sarah's boy! You, two!" he exclaimed, turning to the doctors, "What are you waiting for? Sew him up!"

"On your order, General Wayne, we will proceed."

Dr. Shippen called for a lantern and undid the belt tourniquet. Tad, regaining consciousness, moaned.

Dr. Rush pushed Nate out of their light, and as he backed away, he looked at the tent full of sick men. One soldier's amputated knee stank of rotting flesh. Next to him was a patient covered with blisters. Nate recoiled. The pox! The most dreaded of all diseases! He bolted to the other side of the big tent.

There he found a comforting sight. Chaplain Duffield was there, praying over a shivering man. Nate went up to him. "Chaplain, could you come and help Tad?"

"Nate? What are you doing here?"

"It's Tad, sir. He fell into a ditch and got a stake through his leg." He led the chaplain to Tad, at whose side Pastor Duffield bowed his head, expecting others to do the same.

Nate was glad the pastor couldn't see Tad's face, as his friend was scowling in mockery.

But the chaplain seemed to know Tad's mind. "Don't worry, son. This won't hurt a bit."

Nate closed his eyes, hoping God was real enough to stop the bleeding since the doctors hadn't yet.

He didn't know whether it was Chaplain Duffield's prayer or General Wayne's order that did the trick, but immediately everything changed. Thread for stitching was located, and Tad underwent surgery, biting on a stick wrapped with brandy-soaked rags to endure the pain. His leg stopped bleeding but was swollen to three times its size.

Into the tent hurried Captain McLane, a look of deep concern on his face. "Nate! I just heard what happened on the sentry line! How is he?"

"He's doing fairly well. They're tending to him right now. They say he's going to recover."

"Thank God," sighed McLane. "And you're alright?"

"Yes, sir."

The captain smiled. "Tell me, are you ready and able to give me a report? Were you two successful?"

And as the doctors dressed Tad's wound and bandaged it, Nate told the captain all they'd learned from the farmers they'd visited.

"Well done, both of you!" exclaimed McLane. "I knew you had the makings of first-class agents."

When the surgeons had finished their work and Tad's leg was swathed in cotton rags, he raised up on one elbow and weakly said, "Nate, you saved my life!"

"The doctors saved you."

"No, son," affirmed General Wayne, "your courage, Nate, in applying that belt tourniquet and carrying your friend into camp did."

"I'm just glad that I was able to carry him," Nate responded.

Chaplain Duffield was concerned. "Tad, that's a nasty wound, and we can't have it getting infected. Normally I'd insist on keeping you here under observation. But as you see, we have no extra cots here."

General Wayne answered, "Sarah Walker will nurse us both to health. I'm quartered there. Nate can hold Tad in the saddle, while I lead my horse home."

"Well," said Dr. Rush, "in that case, I will release him into your care, General."

General Wayne hoisted Tad's shoulders up, as Nate carefully lifted his legs. Then with Tad slumped over in the General's saddle, and Nate riding behind him to hold him on, the General led the little party home.

Sarah Walker gasped when she saw Tad's leg. She put him straight to bed.

In the kitchen Joseph Walker thanked General Wayne, and to Nate he said, "I'll always be obliged to you, lad. I just pray our Tad doesn't stay lame like me."

"I think Dr. Rush did a good job sewing him up, sir."

"I hope so. We need him on his feet around here. His mother couldn't get along without him."

Joseph Walker served Nate and the General some stew from a kettle Sarah had simmering on the hearth. "She's the best wife a man could ask for, a truly good woman who loves everybody."

After Tad had fallen asleep, Sarah came in. "What is it like in that hospital?"

Nate described the hospital tent in all its horrifying detail, as Sarah sat in her rocking chair, searching through a tin box of buttons to mend a pile of little shirts. "We've got to do something to make that place better," she sighed.

Her wish was Anthony Wayne's command. "For my favorite cousin," he vowed, "I'll petition Congress to get that medical unit better supplied."

Her merry laugh filled the kitchen, but then she set her jaw. "Indeed, gentlemen, we *are* going to help those doctors. They'll need hospital laundry washed. . . ."

"A good idea, my dear," beamed Joseph Walker, delighted with another opportunity for his family to help the army.

Nate crawled under a warm comforter of goose feathers on the bunk above Tad's, grateful not to be enduring another sleepless freezing night in camp.

The next morning Nate woke up at first light. And then he remembered it was First Day. He didn't know what the Walkers did on Sunday, if they were religious or not. He hoped he could sleep in. He turned over and dozed off until a crow call awoke them.

Nate looked out the window. "It's Running Fox," he cried with a laugh. He lifted the window and called back like a crow.

"He's come to take me back to camp, Tad. But I won't forget you."

Tad extended his hand. "Friends forever."

Nate shook it. "Forever."

In the kitchen Mrs. Walker was preparing breakfast. The aroma of fluffy buttermilk biscuits filled the room as she brought them out of the brick oven. With the clotted cream and apple-butter she spread on top, they were delicious! Remembering Fox was outside waiting, Nate asked if he might have an extra one for each of them.

Joseph Walker came in from milking and addressed Nate. "You've got a visitor outside, an Indian."

"Yes, sir," Nate replied. "He's going to take me to camp."

"Cousin Wayne's going there," Mr. Walker added. "You can all go together."

Handing him the biscuits, Sarah said, "Tad can't thank you enough, Nate. You're part of our family now," she added fondly. As she shooed him out the door, the General was saddling his horse and coughing. To Nate he seemed worse than the night before.

"Anthony Wayne!" Sarah called. "Promise me, you'll stop by that medical tent and see Dr. Rush! Then fetch their dirty blankets and bring them to me, you hear?"

"Yes, ma'am," he agreed, saluting her and smiling.

Running Fox, hearing this as he munched on the biscuit Nate had given him, shook his head. "Not good."

"What'd you say?" asked Sarah.

"Sick men's blankets kill," said Fox, raising his voice. "Last war British gave them to enemy Iroquois. Everyone in the tribe got the pox. Many died."

"Then that's why they have to be washed," announced Sarah stubbornly, waving good-bye.

"Why are you here so early?" Nate asked his Indian friend, as they got underway.

"Great Fox have meeting. You are missing it. Hurry."

25

VACCINATION

Nate followed General Wayne into the headquarters tent. Next to a small potbellied stove on muddy ground covered with sawdust sat General Washington in a green folding canvas chair. He was pulling on his black leather cavalry boots. Captain McLane stood beside him, briefing him on the subject of the supply wagons the British had ambushed.

The General turned to the new arrivals and raised his eyebrows. "General Wayne, what would you recommend?"

"Recapture them, sir. Quick as we can!" But his enthusiasm brought on a new round of coughing so severe that it left Wayne gasping for breath.

The commander wore an expression of grave concern. "General, I fear you are ill. Normally I would order you home on furlough until you recover. But these are not normal times. I'm afraid I cannot spare you."

"I don't want to be spared, Excellency, especially when there's the possibility of seeing action!" And with another coughing spasm, he settled into a vacant seat.

An orderly came in. "Sir, there's an Indian outside. He calls himself Running Fox."

"Have him come in," the General said.

When Running Fox entered, Captain McLane asked, "How many of your Indian friends arrived to scout for us?"

Running Fox held up five fingers.

"Where?"

"Fairview Hill."

"You know about the supply wagons we lost?" asked McLane.

The Indian nodded. "Wagons full of food from farmers. Hessians took them."

"We cannot afford any losses like this," General Washington observed. "We don't have enough food to feed this army as it is."

There was silence, then Running Fox spoke. "Oneidas bring corn."

"Corn?" asked the General.

The Indian nodded. "Many wagons. They come a long way. From Oneida country, New York."

"Good! And you know how critical our situation is. We can't wait long."

He turned to his aide. "Colonel Hamilton, keep me informed." And he thanked Fox and dismissed him.

More officers came in. Captain McLane identified them for Nate. He already knew Anthony Wayne; the other two Generals were Muhlenberg and Knox. Two of the colonels were also known to him, Cadwalader and Chaplain Duffield. The other was Benedict Arnold. Major Tallmadge he knew, and he'd seen Light Horse Harry Lee. The other major was Clark. Nate hoped he could remember all their names and ranks.

General Washington called the meeting to order. "Major Clark, may I have the report on New York."

Clark arose and cleared his throat. "Bad news, I'm afraid, sir. It seems that one more has been removed from our family of spies. Hyam Solomon, traveling here from New York, has disappeared."

Murmurs of dismay arose.

"Hyam Solomon?" General Washington pounded his knee. "Losing such a loyal Patriot sorely grieves me! And," he added gravely, "we must assume the information he was carrying has fallen into enemy hands."

That set the tone for a long discussion about all the army's woes. Nate fidgeted as topics of digging latrines, burying dead horses, securing medical supplies, building huts, and feeding the army and its mounts were covered.

He looked at the yellowed tent sides growing brighter as the sun rose higher. Was it any warmer outside?

At last the meeting concluded, and everyone filed out.

Captain McLane tapped Nate's shoulder. "Wait a moment, lad. I want to have a word with you and Colonel Cadwalader."

Hearing his name, Cadwalader paused and joined them.

McLane turned to Nate. "We have it on good authority that a shipload of winter clothing, enough for four British regiments, is arriving on one of their sloops at the end of this month. We need that gear more than they do. Go immediately to Philadelphia's waterfront. Find the master shipwright. He will be posing as an ordinary seaman or dockhand. When you locate him, speak this password: 'Turtle.' If it's him, he'll reply, 'Turtle Soup.' And if it's safe to talk, he'll say, 'Cold turtle soup.' If he says, 'Hot,' give him the message as quickly as possible and leave. Do you understand?"

"Yes, sir."

"Repeat it back to me."

Nate did so, and the captain said, "Good luck, lad. We're counting on you. Now be on your way."

Nate's heart raced. He was going home!

But watching everyone leave, he wondered who would guide him back down the Schuylkill and when?

"Are you in a hurry, young Nate?" asked a deep voice behind him. It was General Washington, walking in the same direction he was.

"I'm on assignment, sir."

"Can it wait until we've talked?"

"Of course!" Nate fell in beside him.

"What happened at the sentry line last night?"

Nate blinked. How did he know? "My friend Tad fell in one of the ditches. A stake went through his leg."

The General pursed his lips. "What did you think of our 'flying hospitals'?" Nate looked puzzled. "Our movable medical tents. Their mobility saves lives, but they're the hardest places I visit."

Nate hoped they weren't going back.

General Washington pointed to his own face. "You see this?"

Nate saw round scars pitting his forehead.

"I caught pox at your age, so now I'm immune. Otherwise I could not visit my men stricken with that plague." He looked at Nate. "Have you ever had the pox or been vaccinated?"

"No, sir."

"I thought not. You'd best be vaccinated before leaving here today," the General ordered with fatherly concern. "In fact, I'll take you myself."

Nate's knees felt wobbly as he followed him. They walked through camp past row upon row of twelve-man log huts going up. The sound of axes could be heard all around them. From atop the roof of a new hut, a sergeant hailed the Commander in Chief. "What do ya think, Excellency? How do ya like our new accommodations?"

The General smiled. "I like them fine, sergeant. And I'll like them even better when they're finished."

Leaving the noise behind them, Nate tried to keep stride with the General's long legs. "Where are they building your cabin, sir?"

"I will not leave my field tent until every last one of my men is under shelter."

Nate was impressed; the Commander in Chief wasn't requiring anyone to do something he wouldn't do. "That's not the way Lord Howe does it," he commented.

"Oh? How is that?"

"He took over Colonel Cadwalader's house. And now he lives in it like a king. They took over our house, too, and many other Patriots' houses, as well. Their men are comfortable in our city while our army suffers out here."

The General's lips compressed in a thin smile. "That's why we'll win. We're willing to pay any price for freedom."

Soon they arrived at the medical tent where Nate was to be vaccinated. He dreaded it, but there was no getting out of it. He was a soldier, even if he wasn't in uniform, and the Commander in Chief himself had ordered it.

Slowly he entered behind the General and saw Dr. Rush operating on a man who had passed out from the pain. The doctor looked at General Washington sourly, plunking a bloody amputated foot into a bucket.

Nate swallowed. He hoped Tad's leg would never end up that way.

Dr. Rush spoke coldly. "Sir, I don't suppose you've seen my last request for supplies."

"I did see it, Doctor," General Washington replied. "I forwarded it to Congress with the most urgent appeal I could make. But they are not responding."

The tent flap opened again. It was Albigence Waldo, one of the doctors.

The General placed both hands on Nate's shoulders and propelled him forward. "Can you vaccinate our young friend?"

Dr. Waldo nodded. Picking up a needle and thread, he said, "We're going to vaccinate many of the men. You'll be one of the first."

Nate said nothing. Suddenly he started. Next to them he noticed the form of a fresh corpse under a sheet.

"Died of pox this morning," Dr. Waldo informed him matter-of-factly.

Nate turned white. He wanted to run—and would have if the General hadn't been standing there.

The doctor unfolded a napkin on a table, revealing a row of threaded needles—*big* needles, the biggest needles Nate had ever seen!

Choosing one, Dr. Waldo drew back the sheet from the dead man's head, stabbed the needle into an oozing pustule on the man's forehead, and drew the thread through it.

Then he turned to Nate. With his free hand he patted a camp stool for the boy to sit on.

Nate froze. He looked at General Washington, who nodded.

Trembling, Nate sat down on the stool, as the doctor pushed up his sleeve. The boy gritted his teeth and turned his head away. The doctor pinched his shoulder and jabbed the needle into his skin.

Nate flinched, holding his breath as the thread was drawn all the way through.

"You'll have a blister," said Dr. Waldo cheerily. "Don't scratch it because this must not spread. And don't get it wet, either. It will dry up in a week."

Looking at the corpse, Nate asked, "Sir, does anyone die from the vaccination?"

"Oh, yes," replied the doctor, still smiling. "Quite a few, actually. But you're a strong boy; you'll be fine. If you have more than a mild fever, come back."

"I'll be in Philadelphia."

"Well, don't visit Tory doctors; they might suspect where you got this." Then seeing the boy's expression, he quipped, "Don't worry; it saves far more than it kills."

Nate hoped he was right.

26

CLOSE CALL

That afternoon Running Fox took Nate back to Duffield's cave. As the daylight faded, Nate squeezed through the now familiar cave entrance. The Levering brothers were there, roasting squirrels on a stick and nibbling walnuts.

"Eh! Our new swamp rat has returned!" teased Odus, as Jacob served Nate a roasted squirrel.

Nate took a few chewy bites of the greasy meat, and then they all went out to uncover the flat-bottomed boat from its hiding place. The river was still coated with ice along the shore, but in the middle it had thawed and was running clear again. Nate was glad of that, but after his ordeal of a few nights before, he felt a bit nervous about getting back into the boat.

It was late at night by the time the Levering brothers had finished rowing them down the Schuylkill, nearly to Philadelphia. Rounding a bend, they received a shock. Ahead were lanterns and Redcoats—a new picket outpost! Fox said quietly, "British have shut off river. Not good."

Nate thought for a moment. "I'll get by; I have a pass." He fished in his pocket for it. It was still there, and so was the snow hawk's gold button. Better hide that, but where?

Nate tucked it in his hair, at the cinch of his pigtail under the knotted ribbon. Would it stay in place? Shaking his head to test it, he suddenly grew dizzy. It was the vaccination!

He groaned. "I've to get home. Fast."

The Leverings rowed quietly over to the bank and let Nate out, after which they and Fox rowed back up the Schuylkill.

Climbing out of the brush, Nate walked boldly up to the picket line and presented his pass. "Nathaniel Donovan," he announced.

The nearest sentry looked at it. "Permission for Donovan to pass."

Nate sighed with relief and started quickly through the picket.

"Wait!" called the Sergeant of the Guard after him. "That family's on the suspicion list!"

Nate's heart raced.

The sergeant came over and scrutinized him. "What's your business out so late at night?"

"Visiting my little brother and sister staying with family out in Germantown."

"Are they quarantined out there?"

Nate shook his head. Forcing himself to keep his voice calm and casual, he said, "No, just staying with an aunt."

The sergeant was not convinced. "Search him!" he barked to two of the sentries. "Drop your britches, boy! Now! And give me your jacket!"

Reluctantly, Nate obeyed. They laughed at his shivers, and grabbing his pants and jacket they searched the linings and pockets.

Pulling his britches back on, Nate remembered Mother's caution; the British would quickly figure out that messages could be smuggled in coat linings. But if they removed his shirt, how would he explain his fresh vaccination?

The wait for his jacket seemed like an eternity. And he kept hearing the words of General Washington: "Captured spies are hanged."

Disappointed at having found nothing incriminating, the sergeant returned Nate's jacket and was about to dismiss him when his eyes fell on the moccasins.

Nate froze. He'd forgotten about them!

The sergeant grabbed Nate's shoulder in a viselike grip, right over the vaccination, and spun him around. "What are you doing in Indian moccasins?"

His grip tightened, and the pain was more than Nate could endure. He cried out.

"Take them off!" the Sergeant ordered.

Nate did so, shuffling from one bare foot to the other, until the sergeant inspected them, then finally pitched them in the snow in front of him.

"You may go."

Nate pulled on his moccasins and hurriedly left. Though shaken and thoroughly chilled, he counted himself fortunate. He could still deliver his message. And they had not found the gold button hidden in his hair.

It was almost two o'clock in the morning when he finished hiking the three miles to Second Street. Nate knocked at the darkened house, wondering if Father would admit him. No answer. Stepping off the porch, he spied one hopeful candle flickering in the window of a stair landing upstairs.

Presently Mother opened the door and was astonished to see him. Taking him into her arms, she clasped him tightly, looked up, and whispered, "Thank you, Father."

Rachel came up behind her, holding a candle, as Nate plucked the gold button from his pigtail. He handed it to Mother. "This will interest you. The pickets searched me, but they didn't find it."

Lydia Donovan was surprised. "They searched you? You had a pass."

"We're now on their suspicion list."

His mother said nothing, but fear flashed across her face.

"May I see that?" Rachel asked, pointing to the button. Her mother handed it to her, and she fingered the ornate object thoughtfully. "Why, it's pure gold!" She hesitated. "And I do believe I've seen the like of it before."

"The whole Redcoat army wears them," said Mother.

"Not gold ones," insisted Rachel, "The Redcoats have brass. Only a few officers have gold ones." She frowned, perplexed. "I've seen this design somewhere before. . . ."

She handed the button back to her brother and went back up to her bed.

"Did you see Charles?" Mother asked.

"Yes! And good news: he's Chaplain Duffield's assistant."

Lydia Donovan sighed. "That *is* good news! I pray our army will return to free Philadelphia before much longer. Captain André exhausts our hospitality; he treats us like slaves."

"George Washington does not run his army that way," Nate declared. "He sleeps in a tent right alongside his men."

"A wise leader inspires loyalty," Mother commented, ushering him into the kitchen where she spread his bedding for him.

As he gratefully took off his outer garments and crawled into it, he said, "General Washington won't let us down." He yawned. Thinking about Charles sleeping on the hard cold ground, he murmured, "I have to tell you about Valley Forge, what it's like there."

She smiled at him. "We'll catch up after you've had some rest, young man." Her nose wrinkled. "And a bath."

She pulled the shutters closed to prevent the sun, which would soon be rising, from waking him. As he drifted off to sleep, he barely felt the tender kiss planted on his forehead.

It was nearly noon when Nate awakened, still a little woozy from the vaccination but feeling much better. Seeing his mother at the stove, he asked, "Where's Father?"

"He's in Maryland at the sawmill, buying wood for the coffins of British officers."

That evening, as the grandfather clock in the downstairs hall struck eight times, the two of them eavesdropped once again.

Captain André was in the midst of a story. "We took her from a savage. I was training her as a gift for Lord Howe when she escaped."

"And delayed your promotion, eh, André?" said another officer. "Lord Howe loves falconry. For a gift as magnificent as the bird you've described, you would have gained great favor."

"It's not over yet," declared André. "She's been spotted at Germantown and at Valley Forge. She must be trying to find that savage who, I'm informed, is now aiding the rebels. We'll just wait and bag the both of them. If he does what I expect him to and recaptures her, it will be like picking daisies. Gentlemen," André concluded, "I *will* have that bird!"

Not *our* snow hawk, determined Nate, making a mental note to warn Running Fox.

Rachel knocked softly on the bedchamber door. Nate moved quickly away from the chimney, and Mother pretended to stir up the embers.

In her sleeping bonnet and flannel nightgown, Rachel excitedly asked, "Show me that fancy button again."

"Why?" demanded Nate.

"I cannot get it out of my mind, and I think I know why."

Reluctantly Nate handed it over.

Rachel examined it, exclaiming, "Aha! Just as I thought! When I let Captain André in tonight, I took note of his fancy waistcoat. It has real gold buttons! With a most unusual design," she mused, "exactly like this one."

Nate scowled. "Surely other officers—"

He never finished. Mother quietly said, "The bottom button of the captain's waistcoat was missing."

Nate stared at her. How did she come to notice such minute details? "André must have been in charge of the raid which burned the mill outside Valley Forge," he exclaimed, "and killed the miller and his wife!"

Rachel was shocked. "Why would he do such a terrible thing?"

"Because General Washington had stored some of our army's food there. Now, thanks to your captain, our men are near starving. And he's in our house, eating luxuries!"

Mother stared at Nate. "Charles is starving?"

"He gets one firecake a day and broth. No meat."

"And you?" she asked.

"I was fed these last two days by a farm lady whose son I rescued from an accident."

"Why were you there?" Rachel demanded.

Nate didn't trust her. "I wanted to see Charles."

Her eyes narrowed. "There's more to it than that, isn't there." It was a statement, not a question.

Their conversation was interrupted by the sound of the dining room door sliding open and men being dismissed. The heavy front door clunked shut, and the house was quiet.

André and his men were gone.

Lydia turned sternly on her daughter. "Remember, child, anyone who lets it be known our Charles is in Valley Forge betrays us all to the hangman."

Rachel rubbed her delicate neck uneasily. "I think I have to trim candles downstairs."

When her daughter's footsteps faded away, Lydia Donovan asked Nate, "Tell me more about this woman who feeds you."

"Sarah Walker is the mother of Tad, the boy who was given an assignment with me. She said to tell you that their farmhouse is my 'home away from home,' and she's helping the rest of the army, too."

"Then God bless Sarah Walker!" Mother cried. "And may the divine hand of Providence keep her, and us, safe."

Nate knew that he'd soon need special help from somewhere. Would it come from prayer? Or just luck?

27

TURTLE SOUP

The sound of seagulls fighting over a scrap of fish told Nate he was approaching Philadelphia's waterfront. He could already smell the pine tar and hemp of ships not yet in view. Then he rounded a corner and saw ships everywhere! All usable dock space was taken with vessels unloading, while others lay at anchor in the Delaware River, waiting their turn. With sails tightly furled, their masts were a barren forest.

Red-coated guards watched over everything, as crews of British sailors loaded the freight wagons that were shuttling between wharves and warehouses. The waterfront was a beehive of activity with dockhands everywhere, leaving Nate to wonder which was the master shipwright?

Running Fox had taught him that if he did not know what to do, the best thing was to sit and wait. So he sat down on a piling and watched his reflection in the murky river water.

After a while Nate realized that the British sailors and guards were too busy to notice him. But the nausea and fever he had felt before was coming back. He'd best get the job done and get home.

How could he tell which was his man?

Then he noticed a man working under the hull of a fishing boat that had been hauled out of the water and put up on blocks. Cautiously he approached and quietly said, "Cold day, isn't it?"

The man, removing barnacles from the boat's hull with a mallet and chisel, ignored him.

Nate said loudly, "It's so cold, I passed a *turtle* with its head pulled in."

The man laid his mallet down and looked up at Nate. "What did you say?"

"I just wondered if you've seen any turtles lately?"

The man climbed out from under the boat. He stared at Nate, sizing him up.

Nate returned his gaze. Beneath a greasy wool cap, the man's face was youthful but weathered. His torn, patched jacket fit snugly over a sweater riddled with moth holes. But oddly, Nate noticed, his hands were not gnarled and calloused from years of outdoor work. This man was not what he appeared to be.

He was not responding, either. Thinking he must have made a mistake, Nate was on the verge of leaving, when the dockhand murmured, "Only turtles I've seen lately were in my turtle soup."

The lad spun back around. "Hot or cold?"

"Cold," answered the man heartily.

Nate smiled; "cold" meant it was safe for them to talk.

Carefully looking around, the dockhand nodded for Nate to follow him to a nearby boathouse. When they were inside, the man asked, "You from McLane?"

Nate nodded.

The shipwright stuck out his hand. "David Bushnell."

"Nate Donovan."

Bushnell shook his hand with a strong grip. "Let me show you a different turtle." He pulled a set of engineer's drawings from their hiding place underneath a barrel and spread them on a table. "I designed the turtle three years ago when I was a student at Yale. It works."

Nate was looking at drawings of a man sitting on a plank inside a wooden, barrel-like vessel, propelled by a paddle mechanism and steered by a rudder.

"It takes a lot of strength to paddle against river currents," Bushnell went on, "and a lot of nerve to submerge and stay under, breathing through this tube." He traced the tube that extended out of the contraption's hull up to the surface.

"We harassed the British flagship in New York's harbor with this. And my underwater explosive device gave them a scare. They couldn't understand the strange fire from the deep with no army firing at them from shore." He chuckled. "That was one confounded admiral!"

Nate smiled, imagining the reaction of the fleet commander.

"Next time," Bushnell concluded, "we'll attach bombs to the bottom of their ships. I'm figuring out a way to screw through the copper sheathing over the hulls of their warships. And I'm redesigning an improved turtle right here under their noses."

Nate was intrigued. "How will you ever build it?"

"In sections. No one will see it assembled until the night we put the pieces together."

"Hope I'm around," said Nate eagerly.

"It will be a memorable night!" He looked at Nate. "So, what brings you here?"

Nate relayed the message about the British ship that would soon be arriving with its precious cargo of clothes.

"Well done, lad," Bushnell commended him when he'd finished.

A fresh wave of nausea swept over Nate, making him so dizzy that he had to sit down on the barrel, to keep from falling down.

Bushnell looked at him. "You're sick, aren't you, boy. Very sick."

"Yes, sir," Nate responded weakly. "I was vaccinated for pox yesterday; I'd better get home."

Bushnell agreed. "Sometimes the vaccination's as bad as the pox. The British tried it on the Hessians, and a plague broke out. Died so fast, they had to bury them in mass graves."

Nate received this information glumly.

But Bushnell wasn't finished. "As for me? I'll take my chances. Nobody's going to stick *my* arm."

He looked at Nate with fresh concern. "We've got to get you home, boy, before you pass out."

Outside, David Bushnell steadied him and gave him a shoulder to lean on, all the way to Little Dock and Second Street. Before parting, the ship-wright said, "You've got grit, lad. But it's the grace of God you'll be needing, to get past that guard in front of your house. I can't let him see me here, so you must walk up the drive, as straight as possible, you hear?"

Nate nodded his swimming head. "I'll sneak into my father's wood shop behind the house."

David Bushnell watched behind a stone wall until Nate reached his father's shop.

Barely able to push open the door, Nate collapsed at his father's feet.

28

BREAKFAST WITH THE GENERAL

Nate woke up with a clear head in his father's bed. Swinging his feet out onto the floor, he managed to stand up, but he felt weak. Shakily he pulled on his britches, which were clean now, along with the rest of his clothes.

The door opened. "Well, look who's awake!" It was Rachel. "You pass out in Father's wood shop, he puts you in his own bed with this mysterious blister on your shoulder, and Mother worries sick over you tossing in delirium—for *three days!*"

She stood in front of him, arms akimbo. "Now you get straight back in that bed! You're not going anywhere!"

"Oh, yes, I am!"

"We'll just see about that!" She turned and left the room, crying, *"Mother!"*

Just then he heard the voice of Captain André downstairs, asking, "Is it contagious?"

"It might be," he heard his mother reply. "It shows all the signs of being the pox."

"Good God!" André exploded. "Sergeant, you'll have to move out of the boy's room. I want him quarantined there. Off-limits to everyone! I'd quarantine the whole house if I didn't need it!"

Good for Mother for covering for him! And without lying. Dare he put the family at risk and leave the house against André's orders? What if he came upstairs to check on him?

Nate weighed the risk. He stood up, and the longer he stood, the more normal he began to feel. Slowly he walked over to the china washbasin on his parents' nightstand and splashed his face with the cold water.

Then he noticed the tray of soup and bread Rachel had brought him. After he ate, he felt even more like himself.

He had to get out of the house without being seen. But how? His eyes turned to the balcony door and the tree beyond it. Was he strong enough?

His mother's footsteps coming up the stairs made up his mind for him. She would never let him leave after being so sick. Not a second to lose! Grabbing his jacket, he managed to pull open the balcony door, and quickly climbed out onto the tree and started down. Nate was thankful that the guard who was normally outside was inside, clearing his gear out of his bedroom.

Soon he was hurrying through the snow. At the edge of the yard, he looked back and saw his Mother's face at the upstairs window. He hoped she would somehow understand. But even if she didn't, she would cover for him.

When Christopher Ludwig saw Nate come in, he ushered him into the back room and locked the front door, hanging up the "Closed" sign. As Nate had hoped, Captain McLane was there.

Quickly, he gave Nate his next assignment. "Tell the General the new turtle is almost ready to swim."

"I'll do that, sir," Nate responded, "but I'm not sure I can manage the trip alone. I've been sick for four days from the vaccination Dr. Waldo gave me."

Captain McLane clapped him on the shoulder. "You're over it now, lad, or you wouldn't be here. There are soldiers in Valley Forge sicker than you, and they're up, building their own cabins. In times like these, you have to do what you have to do."

Then the captain had compassion on him. "But I'll send Running Fox with you."

A market wagon was carrying empty flour sacks back to Frankford Mill in the direction of Rising Sun Tavern. Running Fox got them a ride in back.

As they approached the British pickets, Nate dreaded facing the guards again. Would he be searched?

Running Fox hopped out. "Don't want them to see us together." As the wagon went on down the road, he hung back, holding dried herbs for the market in his hand.

The wagon slowed to a halt. Nate was relieved to see that the guards were not the same ones who'd confronted him the other night. The farmer handed them his pass. Seeing the flour sacks, they waved his entire load, and Nate, through.

Running Fox crossed a few minutes later, as they waited around a bend for him. Indians, having citizenship in neither the Colonies nor England, could come and go as they pleased.

When the wagon took the fork in the road toward Frankford Mill, they jumped out, thanked the farmer, and headed down Nice Town Lane as fast as Nate could manage. Sunlight was fading fast.

At the tavern Aunt Neuss was aghast to see Nate so pale. She hurried him and Fox into her private quarters, past the napping twins. "What ails you, lad? You ought to be in bed."

"Is the colonel here?"

She shook her head. "He's at Valley Forge."

"Then we must go there." Nate stooped to kiss the sleeping twins, Andrew and Molly, before they left.

Soon after, they hurried through Sally's field to Manatawana Spring and then through the woods till they came to Devil's Pool. Fox searched around in the cattail reeds under Foulke's Mill for the Leverings' boat. It wasn't there, so the Indian went off to get his canoe.

Nate waited nervously, listening to the forest sounds. A whippoorwill called. Was it a bird? Or a person? Then he remembered that the whippoor-will called like that only in the spring. It was a person. But was it Fox?

Shortly, Running Fox appeared carrying his canoe upside down over his shoulders. "Why didn't you answer?" he asked.

"Can't whistle like that."

"I'll teach you."

The Indian put the canoe in the water, and Nate carefully eased himself into the bow. Quickly Fox took his seat in the stern and began paddling up the Schuylkill.

As they neared Valley Forge, campfires burned among the new log huts that stretched in neat rows as far as the eye could see. And they found that General Washington had finally moved into the small stone house he'd rented for his headquarters.

"Mr. Potts' house," Running Fox informed Nate. "Cousin of Jacob and Odus."

The front door stood wide open, as soldiers carried in the General's belongings.

No sooner had Nate thanked Fox for bringing him than the Indian disappeared.

A familiar figure was carrying a crate of papers up the front steps— Colonel Cadwalader. "Glad you've arrived, Nate. We're just now getting His Excellency settled. Here, take these and set them in his office." He indicated a room to the right on the main floor. "I'll go upstairs and let him know you're here."

Nate brought the crate into the General's office, just as Billy Lee, General Washington's personal servant, came down the stairs and informed Nate that he would not be joining the 2nd Pennsylvania that night. He would be the General's guest, sleeping on a cot near the fire in the kitchen house.

The following morning Nate awoke to see Billy's ebony face. "You're expected at the General's table."

As he quickly dressed, he stared at Billy, the fanciest dressed servant he'd ever seen. He was wearing fine silk clothes with a crisp white scarf tied neatly around the neck. His starched muslin apron was immaculate. And all of it totally out of place in a rough camp like this.

Nate enjoyed watching him scurry about the kitchen, getting everything ready for the General's breakfast, which appeared to be porridge and little else.

"What you gawkin' at, Master Nate? Get on in there! The General's wait'n on ya."

Hurrying into the main house, Nate found a seat next to Colonel Cadwalader, who whispered, "Remember what I told you about listening and not speaking."

Nate nodded; he'd not forgotten his first instructions back at Rising Sun Tavern.

Looking around the table, he noted the ironed linen napkins and freshly polished silverware. Such an elegant setting for such a meager breakfast! But the General never complained; he ate as if it were a grand feast!

Nate did the same.

He recognized everyone there except for the young man with flaming red hair sitting next to General Washington. His uniform was strange, neither American nor British.

Nate listened as Colonel Hamilton briefed General Washington on the latest news from Congress.

As soon as he had finished, Washington turned to the officers with a smile. "Gentlemen, I presume you have all met the Marquis de Lafayette, who has graciously joined our cause. We are honored and pleased to have him with us."

The red-haired young officer replied, "*Merci, mon General!* We French believe General Washington will win America's freedom from the British. We are standing with you in this struggle!"

General Washington smiled broadly. "Most encouraging, my dear Lafayette. We cannot hope to win without the aid of France."

He looked around the table. "Is there any other business?" No one spoke. "Then, gentlemen, we are dismissed."

As they rose to leave, he asked Nate, "How are you feeling this morning, lad?"

"Fine, thank you, Your Excellency."

"Did you have any after effects from the vaccination?"

Nate hesitated. "I was sick for three days. But I'm better now!" he insisted.

The tall man eyed him thoughtfully. "I think Dr. Shippen ought to have a look at it, just to be sure."

Under a watery morning sun, the last wisps of morning mist rose off the Schuylkill River as Nate made his way to the medical tent. Smoke curled up from the log huts, where all men not on work details or guard duty were desperately trying to keep warm.

Nate saw that the men standing guard were wearing pieces of unmatched clothing, and realized that hut-mates must be sharing their garments with whomever had to be outside in the cold. The men inside must be nearly naked!

As he entered the tent, he saw Tad sitting on a camp stool, and Dr. Rush kneeling beside him, preparing to remove the boy's stitches. Tad must have hobbled here on homemade crutches.

"Tad!" he cried, delighted to see his friend.

But when he came closer, Tad looked him straight in the eye and whacked him in the shin with his crutch.

29

STRICKEN ANGEL

Nate jumped backward, rubbing his shin. "Ow! That really hurt! What'd you do that for?" he demanded of his friend.

"Just 'cause I felt like it!"

After Dr. Rush checked Nate's vaccination, he proceeded to take out the stitches from Tad's swollen and red leg. His friend ignored Nate completely, as if engrossed in the medical procedure.

What was going on? Why was Tad being so ornery?

When he was finished, Dr. Rush warned Tad that he'd better soak the leg in hot salt water three times a day and stay off it for another month.

"A month?"

"It's either that, or I'll have to bleed you with leeches."

"Augh! That's even worse!"

Smiling at having made his point, the doctor bandaged him and left.

"Anything I can do for you?" Nate asked Tad.

"When Cousin Wayne returns, we'll be taking more barrels of dirty blankets home for Mama to wash. If you want, you can help me do some *real* work around here."

"You're working here?"

"Much as I'm able."

"I'm ready when you are," Nate volunteered.

Tad poked a crutch out and pushed a nearby barrel of blankets toward Nate, accidentally tipping it over. Nate's stomach heaved at the smell, as he set it back up, replacing the lid tightly.

"You can load these in our wagon; Cousin Wayne left it hitched outside. And bring in the clean blankets Mama washed this week."

Nate worked alone for some time, wondering what was eating at Tad.

When General Wayne returned, he asked Nate to drive Tad back to the Walker house in the wagon so the recovering boy could get some rest.

Once Nate had pulled away from the hospital, Tad let out the anger he'd been holding in all morning, "Ya got no idea what Dr. Rush means to everyone around here. Weren't for him, a whole lot more men would be dying! Pox and putrid fever's killed more than a thousand already this winter. Cousin Wayne told Mama that the doc hasn't slept in days. Folks like him hold this army together, not our fancy commander sitting in that pretty house over there!" Tad shook a crutch at the Potts' house behind them.

"You sure have that wrong!" retorted Nate. "He got less to eat this morning than you did! None of your mother's hot-cross buns on *his* plate!"

Tad said nothing.

"What in tarnation's gotten into you, Tad?"

Tad didn't answer.

"Well, you're still my friend forever, even if you *are* as prickly as a porcupine!"

Tad sighed. "Maybe I'm just tired of being left out of everything."

"Like spying?" Nate guessed. "Well, don't worry, partner; you'll get plenty of other chances. Captain McLane still speaks well of the job we did for him, scouting out the farmers around here."

Tad smiled at that. "Hey, sorry I hit you."

"Forget it," Nate chirped, slapping the reins over the horses' backs.

They passed the burned-out mill, which reminded Nate to tell Tad about the button. "Remember that button the snow hawk found? Guess what? It belongs to Captain André, the British spy!"

Everything was all patched up between them by the time Nate rolled the barrels into Sarah Walker's kitchen.

Tad called his mother.

No answer.

"That's odd," he muttered, waving a crutch at the simmering soup kettle on the fireplace crane.

Nate saw homemade bread cooling in the Dutch oven. Half-churned butter was souring in the corner.

Tad was worried. "Mother never ignores her supper cooking. Something's wrong."

"What can I do?"

"Go outside and call for her. Maybe she's gathering eggs at the chicken coop. I'll look for her in the house."

Nate headed toward the barn. Army blankets were hanging on the clothesline, but her wash bucket was spilled over on its side. Passing the icehouse, he heard something. Children sobbing? He jerked open the door. "Sarah Walker?"

"Mama's in here!" wailed a child.

Nate yelled for Tad.

Sarah Walker was draped over an ice block from the river. She'd laid her whole body on it without a coat. The boys clung to her, weeping.

"Mama's on fire!" little Lewis cried.

Nate felt her forehead; it was indeed aflame with fever. He lifted her to her feet. "Mrs. Walker? It's Nate. What's wrong?"

"Sick . . . all day," she managed, before fainting in his arms.

Nate got the two oldest boys to help him carry her into the house.

Tad greeted them at the door with a horrified expression. "It's the fever, isn't it?"

Nate nodded. "She's burning up." They laid Sarah Walker on her bed.

"Nate," Tad begged, "find my father! Hurry!"

Where? Nate jumped in the wagon and was driving it fast toward camp when Joseph Walker came riding toward him in his carriage with Chaplain Duffield and Running Fox.

"It's your wife, sir," Nate shouted. "She's sick! It's bad!"

"Worse than this morning?" Mr. Walker called back.

"Fever's got her. Passed out."

"It's pox!" Walker cried, putting the whip to his team.

In the farmhouse Nate gazed helplessly at Sarah Walker as she was wracked by convulsions.

Chaplain Duffield pulled the children from her bedside. "You must quarantine them all," he said to Joseph Walker, "and hope for the best."

Nate's heart was wrenched as he watched their father pry small fingers from their mother's skirt. The house filled with anguished screams of *"No-o-o!"*

As he ushered them away, Nate mopped Mrs. Walker's brow.

"Father," Tad called out, "would Dr. Rush come?"

"He might, son," Mr. Walker replied from the kitchen. "But I can't ask him to leave all those sick soldiers for one civilian. Chaplain Duffield's here; we can certainly ask him to pray."

"Pah!" cried Tad dismissively, storming to the kitchen on his crutches as fast as he could hobble.

Nate followed him.

Tad sank down on the floor next to his mother's mending chair and could no longer hold in the grief and despair. Sobbing, he cried, "Tell Dr. Rush I won't be coming back right away. Don't want him thinkin' I deserted."

Nate put a hand on his shoulder. "Sure, Tad. But maybe she'll recover." He tried to sound hopeful.

Shaking his head, Tad shrugged off his friend's hand. "I've seen this thing at camp. I know better."

Suddenly he cried out, "My God! I've killed my mother!" He sobbed convulsively. "I brought her those blankets, full of fever! Just like that Injun said! I did it! I killed her!"

"No, Tad!" his friend exclaimed. "Somebody had to wash them, and she wanted to do it. It was her idea, not yours."

Tad pushed him away. "Ya better be running along now," he mumbled, half to himself.

Nate got up, doubting that Tad had heard a word he'd said. With a heavy heart, he slipped out, fearing that he might never see Sarah Walker alive again.

30

THE DOOR TO THE HEART

As Nate left the Walker farmhouse, he found Running Fox outside waiting for him. Together they trudged through the snow, arriving at Valley Forge shortly before sundown. The snow hawk had spotted them from the mill and now soared gloriously above them, gleaming in the last rays of the sun while they were already in shadow.

Swooping toward Running Fox, she screeched. Fox lifted his head and screeched back, then nodded for Nate to try.

Nate looked up, wishing he, too, could fly away from the sorrows of life. But instead of attempting to answer her, he mournfully ignored her. She flew away.

"Not good," Running Fox warned him. "She wants to be your friend, but you don't call to her."

"She'll be back," the boy responded listlessly.

"You don't call her," the Indian said again. "Not good."

"Not good. . . not good. . . ." Nate repeated miserably. "Is *anything* in this wretched place good? Tell me!"

Running Fox said nothing more. When they arrived at Valley Forge, Nate realized he was looking at an entire camp besieged with disease and suffering—just what he'd left behind at the Walker household. Two men staggered by, holding each other up, seeking a latrine.

Running Fox suddenly pushed him to one side. "Dead horse!"

Nate had nearly tripped over the carcass. The poor beast lay where it had fallen, starved to death. Someone had carved it up for meat, and now its exposed entrails swarmed with maggots.

Nate gagged.

Fox said sadly, "No food for horses. Horses too weak to pull wagon to bring food for horses and men. Many die."

Nate was in despair. The situation was hopeless, and could only grow more hopeless.

It was suppertime, and from hut and campfire came the rattling of tin cups and a sullen chant he'd never heard before: "No meat! No meat!" Standing in the doorways of huts with mud floors that never dried out, others chanted back, "No bread! No soldier!"

"Many men hungry," murmured Fox, and then added, "Many men angry."

Outside the hospital tent they found Dr. Rush sitting under a tree, bone weary. Running Fox sat down with him, cross-legged. Nate did the same, leaning against the trunk of the tree.

Hearing the news of Tad Walker's mother, Dr. Rush sighed. "What will we ever do without her? She's an angel of mercy I cannot replace."

Chaplain Duffield rode up and dismounted. "I've prayed for Sarah Walker's healing, but God may choose to take her home to heaven." He, too, sat down. "How much we need people like her, a true saint."

That was more than Nate could bear; his eyes filled with tears.

"I must go back in," said Dr. Rush, getting to his feet and returning to his duties.

Duffield laid his hand on Nate's shoulder. "These are hard days, son." The three of them watched the sun setting, while the chaplain continued. "But God has not deserted us. He understands all our troubles, all our pain."

Slowly Nate nodded.

"Each of us goes through a terrible dark time—sometimes more than one. These men," he made a gesture that included all of the camp, "are going through such a time together." The chaplain paused. "God always forgives and rescues those who seek Him with their whole heart."

Nate looked at Fox, who nodded. "True for my father. True for me."

"One thing more," said Duffield in conclusion, "the door to your heart has no handle on the outside. Only on the inside. God will not force His way in. You must open it to Him."

At that moment Dr. Waldo looked out of the hospital tent. "Chaplain? We need you. A dying man wants you to pray for him."

As Duffield got up and went into the tent, Fox said kindly to Nate, "Much to think about. I go to Oneidas." And with that, he, too, departed.

Wandering off alone in the woods, Nate looked up at the new moon, high in the night sky. It was haloed by a ring of pale haze, just like the first time he'd trekked into the swamp with Running Fox. The air was crisp and still. He took a deep breath.

Something moved above him. A winged silhouette glided across the moon.

Watching it, he rejoiced. The snow hawk! She was back! "I'm sorry I ignored you earlier," he whispered. Treading silently in his moccasins he trailed her deeper into the woods, taking care not to snap a twig lest he startle her into leaving.

She circled above the tall pines ahead. Does she want me to follow? Like that night at the broken tree?

Nate crept stealthily forward. He could make out something ahead. In a clearing amid tall oaks and pines was a horse. It was standing still, breath coming in puffs from its nostrils, its reins hanging down to the ground.

Nate stopped, his eye caught by a glimmer of metal. It was the hilt of a saber, worn by a man in the middle of the clearing. He had broad shoulders and was down on one knee. His head was bowed, a tricornered hat in one hand. An officer.

Nate became aware of the absolute silence of the scene. All nature seemed to be holding its breath.

Intrigued, Nate shifted to his left to see the kneeling man's face. And suddenly he felt embarrassed, like an intruder. It was General George Washington, praying in the snow.

For a long time Nate stood motionless, spellbound. Then the snow hawk circled lower, catching his eye. It was time for him to leave.

Quietly, as Running Fox had taught him, he slipped away. The snow hawk abruptly changed course, flying toward the camp. He followed her. The bird led him to the Oneida campsite, where brush dwellings had been built around several campfires. She flew off, and Nate found Fox.

His Indian friend pointed in the direction of the hospital tent. "Now Tad's sick, too."

Nate looked at him, shocked. "I thought his leg was healing!"

Fox shook his head. "Not leg. Fever. Pox."

Nate ran to the hospital, feeling as though he was caught in a nightmare from which he could not awaken.

There lay Tad, unconscious and sweating, on a soiled cot with no blanket. Sitting next to him was General Wayne. "The fever started in him an hour ago," the General told Nate. "Came to him, same as Sarah. When I got home, Joseph begged me to bring him here. He couldn't leave Sarah or the children. He has nobody to help him. The neighbors are too scared of the pox."

A weary Dr. Rush examined Tad, still unconscious.

General Wayne moved back to give him room. "Joseph Walker asks you to look in on Sarah, too, if you can. She's too weak to move. He's got six boys with him."

Dr. Rush asked, "Do any of them have this?"

"Not sure. If they weren't handling those sickbed blankets she was washing, maybe not. But Tad was."

"It's highly contagious," Dr. Rush lamented, "and it sounds like it may be too late. But I'll have a look at her anyway; it's the least I can do after all she's done for us. Dr. Waldo will cover for me."

"I'll take you," offered a grateful General Wayne.

Dr. Rush took his black leather bag, loaded it with quinine, a blood-letting kit, and a bottle of live leeches. "We'll bleed her to take the fever down." And they departed on their errand of mercy.

Tad regained consciousness shortly after they left. Seeing Nate, he smiled weakly.

Running Fox, who had come with Nate, gazed down at Tad. "Drink tea," he recommended. Tad sipped the tea slowly, then drifted off to a more peaceful sleep.

Nate looked at Dr. Waldo. "Why didn't you vaccinate him? Especially since you had him working in here!"

Dr. Waldo drew a deep breath. "I did. It may have been too late."

31

ONEIDA CORN

Desperately tired, Nate walked to the headquarters kitchen house. If he could just get some sleep on his cot, maybe tomorrow would be better. But there was a late-night war council going on in the General's office in the Potts' house, with orderlies coming in and out of the kitchen.

"Sorry, Master Nate," apologized Billy Lee. "We got no room for you here tonight. Best go to your brother's hut, and see if you can bunk there." And he handed Nate his bedroll.

Nate was almost asleep standing up when he arrived at Charles' hut. Fortunately, one of the hard wooden bunks lining the small log hut was not being used. He had scarcely lain down before he was fast asleep.

The next six days were spent carrying out Captain McLane's assignment, visiting local farmers and learning about their harvests and livestock. On the morning of the seventh day, the drumbeats of reveille woke him. Nate sat up, shivering under a thin blanket. He could hardly feel his fingers or his toes. The open bunk had been farthest from the fireplace and nearest the door's breezy cracks, and it was way below freezing out!

There were voices outside the hut. One of them was Charles'. "Nate!" he called inside. "You're wanted at headquarters."

Nate rubbed his eyes and searched for his moccasins among the snoring and coughing men. Outside, his brother gave him his scarf to keep him warm. As Nate wound it around his neck, Charles reached in a pocket and produced a carved wooden spoon. "Here, this is for Sally."

"*You* made this? When?"

"Whenever I could. When I was missing her, and when it was snowing so hard I couldn't go out of my hut."

Nate tried to give it back, but Charles said, "No, you keep it. Give it to her when you see her, or give it to Rachel, so Sally won't stay mad that I didn't tell her good-bye, like you said."

In the half-light of early dawn, Nate could just make out its carved inscription: *Sally Winston & Charles Donovan, Always & forever.* It was a betrothal spoon!

Shaking his head, Nate tossed it back to his brother, like a hot coal. "Rachel doesn't see her anymore."

"But *you* might," Charles insisted, stuffing the spoon into Nate's backpack.

"Don't plan to," muttered Nate, as he ran off to headquarters, leaving Charles to wonder.

At the Potts' house, General Washington appeared fresh, as if he'd been up for hours. Taking a seat on the windowsill near the office fireplace, Nate watched as the Commander in Chief greeted his generals and key members of his spy network. They seated themselves at the green felt-covered table, on which were silver inkwells, quill pens, and paper for note-taking.

Captain McLane had been summoned from Philadelphia. Also present were Major Tallmadge, Major Clark from New York, and Chaplain Duffield. As far as Nate could tell, the only persons missing were Colonel Cadwalader and Running Fox.

Soon he saw his Indian friend coming up the front steps, taking all three in a single bound. Behind him something moved through the morning mist. Nate made out a large number of Oneidas, balancing baskets on their heads.

A few minutes after General Washington opened the meeting, a plump but elegant, gray-haired woman came through the door with a basket on her arm, followed by Billy.

The matron's blue eyes twinkled as she offered gingerbread to each of the assembly. Billy poured hot hickory-nut coffee.

Taking a cookie, General Nathaniel Green exclaimed, "Sir, the presence of your wife is the best thing that's happened to us since we arrived!"

To a man the assembly rose and exclaimed, "*Hear, hear!*"

The General beamed. "Well, my dear, it seems that once again you have charmed all the men in your presence."

Martha Washington curtsied to him and them all and returned to the kitchen house.

General Washington laughed, but soon sobered. "Enjoy her hospitality while you can, gentlemen; I'm afraid this is the last of it. Our cupboards are as bare as the commissary's."

Captain McLane agreed. "General Wayne's foraging parties return empty-handed, while local farmers continue to eat well. Nate here and

Tad Walker found their silos full and their cows and horses hidden in the woods."

"Where *is* General Wayne?" asked the Commander in Chief.

General Green answered. "His foraging party got snowbound several days from here and could not risk marching back in their worn-out shoes, especially if we get another heavy snow. It's well below freezing this morning."

General Washington sighed. "I am now convinced beyond a doubt that unless some great change suddenly takes place, this army must inevitably be reduced to one of three conditions: starving, dissolving, or dispersing in order to obtain food in the best manner they can."

He looked around the room. "Gentlemen, our only hope now rests with Him who has helped us hitherto."

Heads nodded. All understood the gravity of their situation.

Then the General's expression brightened. "But He may be once again acting upon our behalf." He held up a folded dispatch. "In response to an urgent private appeal, we have just received word from my friend, Governor Jonathan Trumbull, that Connecticut will be sending fifty wagons filled with meat, and—" Resounding cheers kept him from finishing.

Captain McLane spoke up. "Your Excellency, as welcome as this news is, it's going to take a long time for the governor to make good on his pledge. He'll have to find enough farmers willing to sell their cattle, and look at the troubles we've had with the farmers here!"

At that, everyone sobered.

Then Running Fox, listening at the door, raised his hand.

General Washington waved him in.

"Oneidas bring corn. And Polly Cooper." Fox summoned an old squaw, who had been waiting outside. "She cooks for tribe. She cook for soldiers, too?"

"How much corn?" asked General Greene, who'd been put in charge of their supplies.

"Seventy bushels."

"*What?*"

Fox quickly cautioned them. "If starving soldiers eat corn raw, bellies swell. They die quick. Polly will cook."

General Washington nodded and smiled at Polly. She returned his approval with a toothless grin that crinkled her brown cheeks into deep weathered creases.

"Gentlemen, Polly will cook for the army," General Washington confirmed. "Store the corn in Joseph Walker's barn. We'll ration it, and General Wayne's men may guard it."

"Sir," Chaplain Duffield interjected, "you should know that the Walkers are presently in great distress."

General Washington gestured for him to continue.

"Mrs. Walker fell ill of the pox, washing the contagious laundry from the hospitals. She's been bedridden for a week with the fever."

She was still alive! Nate listened eagerly.

"Death threatens. I fear pneumonia may be settling into her lungs. Likewise, her son Tad suffers in the infirmary from the pox."

"Her eldest son?"

Duffield nodded. "Dr. Rush fears the pox could bring gangrene to his wounded leg. Even if they live, they could be laid up for a month or more."

General Washington rubbed his jaw. "Convey my condolences to Mr. Walker. Apologize for the imposition, but remind him of our dire situation and need for his barn."

Another idea came to him. "Let Polly do her cooking there. She can tend the Walker children, and while she's cooking for us, she can cook for them as well. Provide her some fifty-gallon kettles."

As the meeting adjourned and the officers filed out, the General asked Nate, "How is your mother excusing your absence to the British?"

"They quarantined me because of the fever," Nate explained. "I hope that Captain André thinks I'm still in bed."

"I pray that you are not found out, lad!"

Someone tromped up the front steps and knocked. Nate heard Billy open it. It was Colonel Cadwalader.

"Sorry I'm late, sir. We encountered thieves on the road, dressed like Continentals. Captured some; the rest got away. But I bring bad news from Rising Sun Tavern. The pox is there, too. Mrs. Nuess has her hands full and needs someone to look after Lydia Donovan's tots."

Alarmed, Nate jumped up from the windowsill.

"Lad," said the General, "first, go home and break that quarantine. Then go to the tavern and look after your siblings. While you're there, consider yourself on assignment from me. Listen carefully to the guests as they come and go, and see what you can learn."

Nate rode double-back with Colonel Cadwalader all the way to Philadelphia, through fields and woods, avoiding the roads. The colonel was well familiar with Little Dock Creek and walked his horse along the bank till they got near the British picket line. There he let Nate off and whispered, "Crawl up the creek till you're near them. I'll ride up onto the road and draw their attention. You stay in the creek and sneak past them in the dark!"

Nate did as he was told. The colonel rode up the bank and onto the road, his horse's hooves pounding on the road as he galloped away. The guards shouted at him to halt, then fired when he wouldn't.

In the confusion Nate waded up the creek bed through the icy water until he was safely past the outpost.

Half an hour later, he stealthily climbed the tree and slipped through his parents' balcony door. Just as he was tiptoeing to his room, he heard Captain André downstairs. "Madam, I have been away for a week! I want to make sure that boy is still in his room! You will take me up there now and open his door for me that I might see him for myself!"

André stomped up the stairs after her.

When Lydia Donovan opened Nate's door, she was immensely relieved to see her son in bed, the covers around his chin.

"Is he still feverish?" asked André.

"He has been free of fever for several days."

"Then what is he doing in bed?"

"I wanted him to regain his strength. After all, Captain, it was *you* who confined him to his room, under quarantine. Only you can lift it, and only now have you returned."

32

SILVER-BELLIED MIRACLE

Lydia Donovan convinced her husband William to let Nate stay a month at Rising Sun Tavern to care for the sick twins. Neither of them could go, for fear of leaving Rachel alone in the house with André.

Father drove Nate there. He still had no knowledge of Nate's adventures, having been away in Maryland getting coffin wood during his son's absence. It was a quiet ride.

To their intense relief, they found that while the twins and Aunt Nuess had severe colds, none of them was infected with the pox. Nate remained to nurse them. In his spare time he scouted the countryside, until after several weeks he figured he'd found every hidden cow there was to find. As for Sally, he decided that if he saw her, he'd give her Charles' greetings, but he'd leave the betrothal spoon in the bottom of his backpack.

On each weekly trip to Valley Forge to make his report, the snow hawk had greeted him in the skies. But so had buzzards, who were still feeding on the unburied horse carcasses. The army was weakening. Scarcely a man could breathe without coughing, nor was there a full belly. The corn was nearly gone, and the number of deserters was growing.

Nate never knew where he would be sleeping. One Saturday he again spent the night in the kitchen house at headquarters, and in the morning after breakfast, Billy told him that an emergency meeting had been called. This was highly unusual for a Sunday, since the General was insistent that the Sabbath be observed, and that all officers and men attend worship.

As Nate approached the open office door, he heard the quiet voice of the Commander in Chief. He was praying.

"We have only enough flour for five more days. Then there won't even be firecake in this camp. I've done all I can do. . . ." His words trailed off and left Nate wondering whether an open heart toward God would really make the difference that Chaplain Duffield had said it would.

Just then Captain McLane arrived with Running Fox, and the other officers filed in behind them. McLane reported that Trumbull's wagons were finally on their way.

"When may we expect them?" asked the General.

Major Tallmadge spoke up. "The wagons crossed the Hudson River three days ago, but the roads between there and here are so badly rutted that they are next to impassable. We've only a week to fix them before the meat rots. If we fail, the teamsters will have to abandon much of their cargo of beef to keep their wagons from breaking down on the ruts."

Captain McLane voiced what they were all thinking. "Our men are now too weak from lack of food to do any sustained hard labor. Worse, the British undoubtedly know the wagons are coming and will do everything in their power to capture them."

Running Fox spoke up. "Oneidas will help."

The General listened with respect. "Your corn saved this army from desperate hunger," he said to Running Fox. "What do you propose?"

"We help with roads."

General Washington said, "We will be deeply in your debt. And we will not forget your service to our country."

Cadwalader now added, "As for the British intercepting the wagon train, sir, I recommend dispatching Major Lee and his cavalry to find it and escort it in. He should take enough men to beat off any British attempt."

"All very well and good," said Colonel Hamilton, "but what are we going to eat until they get here?"

"Shad run come early," Running Fox commented quietly.

Colonel Hamilton scoffed. "Sir, there *is* an annual spawning run of these fish each spring. But it is not expected until March. This is February."

Nate fidgeted. He wanted to defend Fox, but dared not interrupt.

General Washington, however, noticed. "Nate, have you something to add?"

Nate stood to attention. "Only that Running Fox knows animals, sir. I've never known him to be wrong about any of them. And it's *late* February, *almost* March."

"Your Excellency," Hamilton protested, "we can't rely on miracles of nature. We've got to plan something more practical!"

"The fact that this army still *exists* is a miracle, Colonel Hamilton," observed the General wryly. "But I am certainly open to other solutions. Do you have one?"

"No, sir," said the colonel, falling silent.

The General turned back to Running Fox. "How may we take advantage of this act of Divine Providence?"

"Be ready. When shad come, we catch them."

"How?" asked several around the room, with disbelief.

"With hands," replied Fox simply, "shovels, baskets, nets."

"If they come," said Major Lee pensively, "we can ride our horses into the river to trap them, to give our men a chance to harvest them. I've seen other fish runs. We won't have long; hopefully it will be long enough."

"Well, then, gentlemen," instructed their commander, "if and when it happens, be ready. Meeting dismissed."

Standing up, he stretched to his full six-foot-three height. "Nate, walk with me to the hospital. I want to see how Sarah Walker's boy is doing."

On their way a familiar voice hailed them. "Hark, the long dark night is breaking!"

Was that a code? Looking into the rising sun, Nate thought he recognized a familiar silhouette.

It was Chaplain Duffield, and as he rode toward them, he was laughing. "As the Good Book says, 'Weeping may endure for a night, but joy comes in the morning!'"

"Chaplain, have you good news?" asked the General.

"Indeed I do, sir! Look!"

Nate looked where he was pointing and saw a great commotion. From all over the camp, officers and men were abandoning their tasks and running to the river.

Captain McLane galloped up, saluting.

"Captain," demanded the General, "what, pray tell, is happening at the river?"

"Use my glass, sir." The captain handed him his field telescope. "It's the miracle we've been hoping for! The shad are running! Just like Running Fox said."

"Come, Nate!" called the General, striding toward the river. "It's not every day we get to see the hand of Divine Providence at work!"

As Nate scrambled after him, a column of Light Horse Harry's cavalry came galloping up, shaking the ground. They split into two files, one stretching out into the river above the men gathering on the bank, while the other did the same below them.

As Major Lee had planned, the horses trapped the fish. Laughing and shouting to one another, men waded in with nets and shovels and baskets, scooping up the silver-bellied fish and throwing them onshore. The men were positively gleeful, happier than they'd been for months. Even the ambulatory patients from the hospital were there, joining in the fun.

And there was Tad, waving at him.

Nate waved back.

General Washington turned to Duffield and smiled. "Tell me, Chaplain, do you think we'll have full attendance at church this morning?"

"I should be very much surprised if we don't!"

The General nodded. "We need to have a day of thanksgiving. I shall draft the proclamation, to be read to every regiment, giving thanks to Almighty God for His unfailing mercy."

That evening around the campfires, the men enjoyed their first meat in weeks—fish roasted on spits with the last of Polly Cooper's corn cakes.

Running Fox and Tad joined Nate at his brother's fire. Fox turned to Tad. "Tomorrow, I'll take you to see your mother. Doctor says you go home. Leg good."

Then he turned to Nate and cocked his head mischievously. "Tomorrow I catch the snow hawk."

33

FLOWN AWAY

At dawn Nate and Fox helped Tad walk home. He wearied quickly, and they had to stop frequently to let him rest. Once again the Schuylkill shimmered with shad, though far fewer than the day before. And there, soaring above them, was the snow hawk.

"America!" Nate gasped, watching her dive, talons extended, into the river, rising up with two shad.

"Catch bird now," said Fox, as he nimbly ran up a bluff with a fishnet over his shoulder. Silently positioning himself, he waited for her next dive.

Down she came, and quick as an arrow Fox cast the net. Nate watched it sail through the air, settling over the snow hawk. Gallantly she struggled for freedom, leaping up, thrashing her wings, unable to fly.

Fox jumped down and wrapped her up in the net, avoiding her razor-sharp beak and talons. Deftly reaching inside the net, he bound her feet with leather thongs. Then, stroking her and smoothing her feathers, he calmed her till it was safe to remove the net.

Nate admired her up close, studying her bright yellow eyes and speckled face. "She is so beautiful!" he gasped.

"We can hide her in our barn," Tad offered weakly, as Nate helped him hobble along toward his farm. Fox carried the snow hawk.

When they reached the farmhouse, Tad went in to find his mother while Nate and Fox took the bird to the barn.

Inside the barn Nate saw the last few bushels of Oneida corn. Fox tethered the bird to a long rope tied to a post, and then untied her feet and pitched a dead shad to her. She caught it and flew up to a roof rafter, where she perched to eat it.

Only then did Nate remember the threat of Captain André. "Running Fox?" he said hesitantly. "Maybe we shouldn't have taken her."

Throwing her another shad, Fox responded, "British won't steal her again."

"But that's just it!" Nate worried. "I heard Captain André say that you would catch her for him. All he would have to do is kill you and take her. He wants to get rid of you in the worst way."

Fox considered that. "André won't catch me. If hawk isn't flying, he will give up."

As Fox locked the barn door, Nate could see his logic: if there were no more sightings . . .

But now, he had another idea, a way of finally getting back at André.

As they walked toward the house, Joseph Walker called to Nate. "Tad needs you now!"

Passing through the kitchen, Nate saw Polly Cooper unfolding and measuring yards of muslin. It was a shroud to wind the dead!

Respectfully entering the darkened room behind Polly, he saw Tad kneel by his mother's bed and clasp her pocked and swollen hand.

On the other side of her bed, Joseph Walker was telling Cousin Wayne, "She's been waiting for Tad all day."

Sarah grasped Tad's hand with her own. "Now you're here, Tad," she gasped. "I leave you in God's hands. I'm flown away."

And with that she breathed her last.

Tad buried his head on her arm and sobbed.

Rain pelted Sarah Walker's cherrywood casket as Nate joined Joseph Walker, General Wayne, Tad, Dr. Rush, and the oldest boy, Lewis, carrying her body past more than a thousand mourners. The sad news had traveled fast. There were multitudes of soldiers whom she had nursed and fed, as well as neighbors whom she had loved.

Chaplain Duffield conducted the burial service, after which no one departed until the last shovel of dirt fell upon her grave.

After the funeral, as the mourners comforted one another, Nate looked for Tad, but he was nowhere to be seen. Finally he found him in the hayloft, staring at their snow hawk. He was crying.

Nate approached cautiously. "You two need each other."

Tad nodded. Nate put an arm around his shoulder and said, "I'm sorry, Tad. I wish I could do something to help you, but I'm afraid that I have to go. Take good care of our bird."

Back at headquarters, Captain McLane briefed Running Fox and Nate. "Since Colonel Cadwalader has headed north with Major Lee and his cavalry to meet the wagon train, we need you, Nate, to be our man at Rising Sun Tavern."

He turned to Fox. "Make sure he gets there safely, then come back to show the Oneidas where they can be of the most help on the roads."

Late in the afternoon, as they neared the tavern, Fox spied a British patrol making camp for the night. Silently pointing to them, he motioned for Nate to follow him. They jumped off the road and landed in a snowdrift behind a fallen tree. To his horror, Nate found himself face-to-face with a frozen Continental soldier. Half buried in the snow, his dead eyes stared glassily at the sky.

Nate gave a strangled cry, which the Redcoats heard. Jumping up from their campfire, they came running.

Before Nate and Fox could flee, they were surrounded by muskets leveled at their chests.

Nate's heart raced. "Long live King George!" he cried, and indicating his plain gray clothes, he added, "Quaker. From Philadelphia."

"Tories," said Fox smiling.

The sergeant in charge apologized and offered them a bite of supper. Nate sat down cautiously. One of the soldiers passed him a long-handled fork with strips of roasted meat.

Warily, Nate watched the figures seated around the fire. The sergeant was staring back at him, his eyes narrowing in suspicion.

All at once, he snarled, "He's a spy!"

"How do you know?" asked one of the soldiers.

"Look at his leggings. He didn't get that mud in town! Philadelphia's cobblestones aren't muddy today, but Valley Forge's roads are hub deep in mud! He's been up to his knees in it." He glared at Nate. "Haven't ya, boy?"

"*No!*"

The sergeant sneered and nodded. "You're one of Washington's errand boys!"

Before Nate could reply, the soldiers grabbed him and Fox, jerking them both to their feet.

"Get 'em in the wagon," ordered the sergeant. "The redskin won't be much fun to hang; they never kick and scream. But the boy, he'll be the youngest spy we've ever strung up. He'll be bawlin' for his momma."

Twisting their arms behind their backs, the British threw them against the wagon.

Running Fox shot Nate a glance that said, *Be ready*.

As one of the two soldiers guarding Fox momentarily turned to lower the wagon's tailgate, the Indian made his move. Quicker than a striking snake, he elbowed the guard in the belly, then swung the heel of his palm into his face.

Falling to his knees, the soldier screamed, holding a bloody broken nose.

"Run!" shouted Fox, kicking the other soldier's feet out from under him and heading for the forest.

Nate pulled away from the only soldier guarding him, leaving his backpack in the guard's grasp. He ran after Fox as hard as he could, hearing shouts and then musket fire and a ball sizzle past his ear.

Fox leaped over logs like a deer. He was nearly out of range when a well-aimed shot found its mark. Fox went down, rolling under a fallen cedar.

Stunned, Nate froze in his tracks, paralyzed. Fox was hit! An instant later he felt the butt of a musket slam into his back, throwing him on the ground.

"Get up, you dirty little spy!" the sergeant yelled at him. Two soldiers hauled him up and dragged him to the wagon while the others went to retrieve his Indian friend.

Another blow between his shoulders sent him reeling into the wagon bed. Nate looked back for Running Fox, as his hands were being tied behind his back. He winced to see the Redcoats haul his friend out from under the cedar by his long hair. Assuming him to be dead, they dropped him face-down in a puddle and joined the rest of the patrol. The wagon jolted forward.

"Oh, God," murmured Nate under his breath, "don't let us leave Fox!"

Abruptly one of the soldiers, looking back, called, "Sergeant, wait! That one's moving!"

The sergeant hauled back on the reins. All eyes were on the Indian, who had rolled over on his side.

"Go get him," ordered the sergeant. "Two hangings are always better than one."

Two Redcoats carried the Indian to the wagon and threw him in the back. Nate, holding his friend, did his best to stop the flow of blood from the wound in his scalp, where the ball had creased it.

As Fox uttered a low moan, Nate wondered if they would hang them tomorrow. Or tonight.

34

IN THE LIONS' DEN

Ahead loomed the grim brick walls of Walnut Street Prison. The wagon stopped at the massive wrought-iron gates while the sergeant explained their prisoners to the Hessian guards. Then the iron gates swung slowly open. As the wagon entered the prison courtyard, the sound of the horses' hooves on the cobblestones echoed hollowly. From windows high above, gaunt-faced prisoners stared down at them.

The wagon came to a halt in front of the gallows. Nate looked up at the platform with its two empty nooses waiting for their next victims. Remembering the hangings in the churchyard, he swallowed hard.

Scared and lonely, Nate thought of his mother. How he wished he was home in their warm kitchen. But gradually he realized that if the British found out who he was, the lives of *all* his family would be in danger. Whatever they did to him, he must not reveal his true identity.

Hessian guards pulled Nate and Fox out of the wagon and dragged them up two dark flights of stairs. They threw Nate in the first cell they came to. The guard with the ring of iron keys laughed as he slammed the cell door shut. "Don't vorry, boy," he taunted Nate in broken English, "you vill freeze to death before ve can stretch your neck."

Down the hall he could hear the guards beating Fox.

Nate was shaking uncontrollably, and not just from the cold. Had he risked his life for this? How could he have been so foolish, to think that one man, one boy, could make any difference?

The sour stench of urine took his breath away. He heard rats scurrying across the floor. Didn't they gnaw on sleeping prisoners at night?

Stumbling in the dark, Nate collapsed against a wall. Gradually his eyes adjusted to the faint lamplight that came in under the cell door. He became aware that he was not alone. He had two cell mates. One lay still; the other, a ragged man, bent over him. Nate moved away, using his hands like a blind man, feeling his way along the frosty walls.

"He's gone," said the stranger matter-of-factly. "Take his coat and pants and put them on. Now, before you get too chilled."

Nate hesitated.

"Do as I say," the man insisted, "or you'll die!"

Reluctantly Nate stripped the corpse of its foul-smelling clothes. The britches reeked of dried vomit and urine, like an old latrine. Nate gagged, but did as he was told.

"Good," said the stranger. "That's how I survived in Sugar House Prison."

"Why were you there?" asked Nate, fastening the britches over his own.

"For spying. But I escaped, and was traveling to see General Washington when a raiding party recaptured me. They'll be sending me back to Sugar House soon."

"How do you know?"

"They heard me speak German. Those Hessians up in New York need me to translate for them."

Nate's eyes widened. "There was a spy coming to us from New York. . . . You're not Hyam—"

"Solomon," the man answered humbly.

As the night wore on, the old man with the German accent kept Nate talking, and in the process revealed that he himself was a merchant banker who'd done much to help finance the Patriot cause.

Finally Nate interrupted him. "I'm cold and tired, and I just want to go to sleep."

The banker refused to let him. "Have you any idea how many men die in here from the cold and from defeat? I've seen it, lad! They just give up, turn their faces to the wall, and wait for death to take them. But that's not going happen to you! Or to me, lad! So tell me about your childhood."

When Nate started to fall asleep in mid-sentence, Hyam pulled him to his feet and marched him around the cell. "Good for the circulation."

Hyam yawned. "Now it's my turn. My family in Poland are all Jewish merchants. Europeans loved the goods we imported from East India, but the rats from our ships spread plague. The Jews were blamed, so our family fled to America."

As if to illustrate his story, three rats ran along the wall. Nate's skin crawled.

Hyam Solomon ignored them. "America is the place where a man can serve God according to his own conscience. I'm fighting to save her from tyrants."

Nate nodded. "The 'new promised land,' my mother calls it."

"Aye, the 'New Israel.'" Hyam paused, a faraway look in his eye. "Since the Romans drove us from our homeland in Israel in ancient times, every Jew still dreams, 'Next year in Jerusalem.' Someday . . ."

He turned to Nate. "You still cold?"

"I'm warmer than when I came." The added layer of the dead man's clothing had worked.

"And your feet?"

"My toes are . . ." He reached down and felt them through the moccasins. "I can barely feel them."

"Then you are going to get up and walk every hour."

"Why?"

"It's the only way I know to keep your feet from freezing."

Hyam kept him walking. And talking. "Where'd you get those moccasins?"

"My Indian friend got them for me from a shoemaker in Germantown."

Hyam Solomon sighed. "I need eight thousand pairs of boots."

"What?"

"Our army can't march without boots."

Nate nodded, thinking of his brother's cracked pair. He was curious now about this man who was working so hard to save his life. "Will you ever go back to Europe?"

"Perhaps. But my real dream is to set my feet on Jerusalem's ancient stones." All at once he chuckled. "But unless God enables me to put boots on our army's feet, none of us will have the freedom to set our feet where we wish. That is why," he muttered vehemently, "I must escape!"

Hyam Solomon's resolve lifted Nate's spirit. "If we do escape, General Washington wants to know how bad things are in here."

"We starve," said Hyam, shrugging and sitting down.

"Don't they feed us?"

"Not much. The British can barely feed their own army, never mind prisoners. But once a week there's an old woman who brings stale bread."

Nate longed for one morsel.

"What's your name, lad?"

"Nate."

"Are you religious, Nate?"

"Huh?"

"You believe in God?"

Nobody had ever asked him that before. "My parents do."

"What about you?" Hyam persisted.

"Why's it so important?"

"Because He's the only one who can deliver us."

"Well," Nate shot back, "He doesn't seem to have helped you much!"

"Ah, but He has."

"How?"

"I'm not hanged."

"Not *yet*," snapped Nate bitterly.

Hyam got up himself and started walking around. "You know the story of Daniel in the lions' den? The Persian king threw Daniel in there, but his faith in God protected him. If we will trust Him like Daniel did, no king, Persian or British, can stop the Almighty from delivering us."

"What makes you so sure?"

"God looks for a man who believes totally in Him and tries his utmost to obey Him. He won't forsake such a man. Daniel's prayers closed the lions' mouths. Mine?" Hyam chuckled. "Mine delay the hangman's noose. General Washington's prayers will win this war."

Nate thought of the night the snow hawk had led him to the clearing in the forest where he had seen the General on one knee in the snow, head bowed in prayer. And the time he had overheard him, pleading with God.

"What about you, young fellow? Can you trust God like them?"

Nate had no answer.

"You want to stay in here?" Hyam asked softly.

"No!"

The older man put an arm around the lad's shoulders. "If you want your Creator to light your path, you must ask Him."

Nate pulled away. "I can't believe this! You're talking like a Quaker!"

Hyam laughed. "And you're still resisting!"

When Nate did not reply, the banker looked him in the eye. "You saw the nooses out there on the gallows. When the hangman settles one around your neck, issues of life, death, and eternity become very clear."

Nate realized he'd better give some serious thought to his new friend's words.

Above them daylight was beginning to come through the single windowpane the guards had left uncovered. They could now see crystals of snow blowing in around the window frame.

Nate yawned.

"Sleep on it. I'll wake you to walk," Hyam promised.

Dropping off immediately, Nate slept soundly until he began to dream. The air was filled with snow, and he and his father were delivering a coffin. The sleigh's right front spring was creaking, and William Donovan was scolding him. "Did I not tell thee to grease that spring? Nothing ruins a solemn funeral procession worse than a sound like that!"

As he came out of his dream, Nate could still hear the creaking spring. He strained to listen. It was real! He wasn't dreaming! There could only be one such sound in all of Philadelphia! And it was coming from the courtyard below them! Could it be . . . ?

35

CHEATING THE HANGMAN

Nate heard the Hessian jailor turning a key in the lock. "New dead vons every day in dis place. Take your pick. Start with the von in here. He died yesterday." He opened the cell door. Someone dragged a rough wooden box into the cell. As the jailor shut the door again, he added, "Shout ven you're ready to leave." His footsteps died away down the hall.

"Father!" Nate whispered, recognizing the newcomer in the half-light. He ran to him and flung his arms around him.

William Donovan stared at him in disbelief. "What in the name of heaven?"

"Nate!" whispered Hyam, rapidly sizing up the situation. "I have a plan! Take the place of this poor soul who won't mind waiting another day for his burial."

Nate winced. "You mean, get in the coffin?"

"Trust me. A short ride in a coffin's nothing to fear."

"But—"

"Get in!" Hyam hissed. Looking up to heaven, he whispered, "This time, you've made it easy."

As Nate climbed into the coffin, Hyam urged his father, "Take your son. Come back for the dead one tomorrow. The guards aren't keeping track of the bodies."

William Donovan nodded.

Nate raised his head and looked at the banker. "If this works for me, it will work for you. As soon as we can, we'll leave a body here and take you, instead."

"We'll see," said William, pushing his son down and putting the lid on the coffin. From his leather apron, he withdrew a mallet and a dozen nails. Quickly he nailed the coffin shut, the blows resounding in the enclosed room. Then he called for the jailor.

The cell door opened, and William Donovan dragged the coffin out. Nate could hear Hyam Solomon carrying on a conversation with the corpse, as if he were still alive.

As the coffin scraped along the hall toward the stairs, Nate thought he heard a birdcall. A whippoorwill? Running Fox! He was still alive!

The sound of Goodness and Mercy's hooves in the snow, mingled with the squeak of the right front spring, reassured Nate. After they passed through the prison gates, he began to believe they were actually going to get away.

And then the sleigh stopped.

He strained to listen. *Tap, tap, tap*—what was that? The tip of a cane tapping the cobblestones beneath the falling snow? His mind raced.

"One minute is all you asked," he heard a woman's voice saying. "One minute is all you get."

Where had he heard that voice before?

"It's all I need, Anna Foulke," said Father tautly. "Tell Sally I may not reopen the school in May."

"You may tell her soon enough yourself. Now be on your way. I've an errand inside the prison."

"In there?"

"Someone's got to feed those poor wretches. I've hired a baker. The British won't trouble me. They know the extent of my investments in their East India Company." She cackled. "It's good to have friends on both sides. Never know how this war will turn out."

"My sentiments exactly," Father assured her.

So *she* was the old woman at Ludwig's bakery—Sally's Aunt Foulke!

They were moving again, with Nate being jolted inside the pitch-black coffin, as they lurched over potholes. Unable to move, Nate panicked, beating his head against the lid. Sealed!

Desperate for air, he passed out, haunted by the memory of the clods of earth falling on Sarah Walker's coffin.

When Nate came to, he was disoriented—no light, no air! *Where* was he? How long had he been here?

No air! *No air!*

Then it came to him: he was in a coffin on the funeral sleigh!

But it wasn't moving. Everything was dead quiet.

Nate listened for Father, their horses . . .

Nothing.

Alarmed, he started thrashing until Father sharply rapped on the lid.

Nate lay still. Where were they?

Doors opened and closed. Shutters banged shut. Were they in their carriage house?

The coffin was dragged from the sleigh. Creaking wood protested against a crowbar. Light swept through the cracks. The lid came open!

Nate sucked deep breaths of fresh air as Father hauled him out.

Despite the foul-smelling dead man's clothes, William Donovan hugged the son he thought he'd lost forever.

And the son who had lost respect for him, now realized what a truly brave man his father was.

They waited in the woodshed for nightfall, so Nate could sneak into the house unobserved by the British sentries.

Meanwhile he ate some of the apples his father stocked for the horses.

Every sound from the direction of Second Street worried him. Would the prison guards discover the switch in the bodies? Would they arrest his father tomorrow?

When darkness blanketed the yard, William Donovan whispered, "It's time."

Bent double, they crept behind a hedgerow to the old elm tree by the side of the house.

Father said, "Meet me at the balcony door. If I go in the front door, no one will pay attention to the backyard."

Nate saw two Redcoats posted by the kitchen door; one of Captain André's staff meetings must be in progress. In the darkness he made it to the elm and started to climb.

As William Donovan admitted Nate into the master bedroom, his mother was overjoyed. "Nate!" she exclaimed softly, keeping her voice down. "Thank goodness! Captain André was questioning us. He was ready to demand your return, to make us prove you hadn't run off to the army. I've exhausted my excuses."

Rushing to hug him, she stopped in mid-stride, wrinkling her nose. "Ugh! What have you gotten into?"

Nate looked at her. "Prison."

"*What!*" She frowned. "We'll hear about that, after you take off those reeking clothes! Where's the tub?"

Quietly Father pulled the copper tub from beneath their high rope bed. Mother and Rachel tiptoed down and back up the stairs with pitchers of hot bathwater. His sister grimaced. "*Eyew!* What pig trough did you fall into?"

Ignoring her, Nate ducked behind a quilt Mother had strung from the bed canopy to the window. As he removed his garments, she retrieved each one with a broom handle and deposited them on the tiny balcony outside the window.

"Tomorrow," whispered Father, "I'll burn them in my workshop."

Behind the quilt, Nate climbed into the tub. His mother handed him a bar of lye soap over the quilt. "Use this."

Nate saw her gingerly pick up the moccasins next to the tub, and start for the window.

"No! Not those," he declared. "Running Fox gave them to me."

"Who's Running Fox?"

"An Indian. He saved my life."

"He did *what?*"

She waited for an explanation, but Nate just shook his head. "Better you don't know."

"Why?"

"Then the British could never make you tell it," Nate said quietly.

She was silent, apparently grateful for his concern.

"Where is this Indian?"

"Still in prison." Then under his breath, Nate added, "For now."

But his mother heard him. "Nathaniel," she said sternly, "surely you're not thinking of rescuing him?"

"Wish I could," he admitted. But he stopped short of revealing the plan that had been forming in his mind.

36

SHATTERED CRYSTAL

When he was out of the tub, Mother returned with fresh clothing and *food!* A roasted chicken leg, a mug of hot cider, even a slice of apple pie!

Eating hungrily, he told her everything that had happened. She was particularly sad to hear of the death of Sarah Walker, who had been so caring to her son.

Then she beckoned to him. "There's something important going on down there. We need to hear what they're saying." As there was a fire going in their bedroom hearth, she led the way down the back stairs to the larder. Following her, Nate grinned; she enjoyed their eavesdropping, though she'd never admit it.

"I've done some listening while you were away," his mother whispered. "Captain André's planning something big."

Listening through a glass, they heard André boasting, "Lord Howe's farewell gala will be the most elaborate celebration Philadelphia has ever seen! He returns to England in May, and General Clinton leads us north to New York in June."

Nate's mouth fell open. Wait till General Washington hears that!

"And we'll have our home back!" Mother murmured. "And Andrew and Molly, too!" In her joy she hugged Nate, who lost his grip on the glass. It shattered on the hard-wood floor.

The voices in the dining room stopped.

Lydia whispered to Nate, "Quick! Spread your pallet on the floor and get on it!"

He did so, as she reached for the extra blanket on the top shelf of the larder, next to the crystal glasses.

Light footsteps came tripping down the front stairs. Rachel came into the kitchen. "What broke?"

"That's what I'd like to know," declared Captain André in the doorway.

Lydia stood by the open larder door, holding the blanket.

André walked briskly to the larder and picked up a piece of glass from the floor.

"Are you in the habit of secretly drinking liquor at night in here, madam?"

Lydia said nothing.

"Or could it be . . ."

Seeing the glasses on the top shelf, he took one down. "That someone has discovered," holding the glass against the wall, he put his ear to it, "how to listen to what they should not be hearing?"

"Captain André," replied Lydia Donovan calmly but firmly, "I came down to see if my son needed an extra blanket. While I was getting this from the top shelf in there," she held the blanket out to him, "I knocked off a glass."

At that moment Rachel stepped up. "Whatever is there to listen to, anyway, dear Captain?" She smiled at him coyly. "Your military matters are of no interest to us plain and simple folk."

For once, Nate was grateful for his sister; somehow she'd managed to say the right thing.

"Plain? Simple?" Lowering the glass, André gazed at Rachel, once again infatuated. "My lady, those words can never describe you!"

He turned to Lydia Donovan. "It may have happened as you say, Madam. But I am increasingly of the opinion that nothing about this family is as it appears. None of you is either plain *or* simple!"

Other officers now appeared at the door. Frustrated, André concluded, "You've been told to remain in bed during our meetings. One more incident like this, and we will have to find other, harsher accommodations for you. Am I understood?"

The three Donovans meekly nodded.

André turned on his heel and ushered the other officers back into the dining room, sliding shut the heavy doors behind them.

Rachel started to help clean up the glass, until Mother whispered, "I'll finish this. You go back up to bed."

They listened to her footsteps going upstairs and the door to her bedroom shut. Putting the shards of glass in the dust box, Lydia Donovan motioned to Nate to resume. Slipping out of his pallet, he crept with her back into the larder.

Mother handed him another glass. "Don't drop it!" she whispered, taking one herself.

Captain André was still speaking. "Frankly, I'm glad we're leaving. These walls seem to have ears. Indeed, I fear we may be meeting in a nest of spies."

Now Colonel Percy spoke. "We may have evidence to that effect, Captain. Yesterday a patrol captured two rebels we suspect may be part of Washington's spy ring, a boy and an Indian. In the boy's rucksack was a carved spoon with two names on it: Sally Winston and Charles Donovan. If that Donovan is related to this family . . ."

"I shall make it my business to find out," replied André. "Our plain and simple Donovans may be plain and simple traitors to the Crown!"

Stunned, Nate glanced at his mother. He could tell she was deeply worried, but she kept listening.

"Back to the business at hand," declared André. "Lord Howe's farewell gala. Not even the royal court will celebrate the rite of spring with as much pageantry as we will in Philadelphia. Our *Mischianza* will be the most brilliant project of my career! A costume ball to end all balls!"

"And earn you the promotion you've been hoping for, eh, André?" Percy wryly observed.

Not if I can help it, thought Nate.

The elaborate plans for the ball were discussed in detail. Finally, André asked, "Colonel, is there any word on the recovery of my bird? Presenting her to Lord Howe would be the crowning moment of the *Mischianza!*"

"*If* we can find her," replied Percy. "There's been no further sighting of her."

Nate smiled. That meant she was still safe in Tad's barn. His smile broadened as the final details of a plan came to his mind, a plan that would ruin André's crowning moment!

André was speaking. "That Indian we took her from . . . chances are, the bird will be not far from him."

"Sir," a young officer hesitantly interrupted, "we may have him. The Indian we captured yesterday sounds similar to the one you described—tall, long gray hair, Oneida."

"Where is he, Mr. Wrentham?" demanded André.

"Walnut Street Prison, sir. Along with the boy."

Nate suddenly felt clammy sweat under his arms.

"The prison guards will enjoy persuading the Indian and the boy to give us the names of their little family of spies," André sneered, adding with an evil chuckle, "Then we can hang them all together. Mr. Wrentham, you may put out a reward for my bird at ten gold sovereigns."

"Ten sovereigns!" exclaimed Percy. "For that I'll go looking for her myself!"

37

THE GOD OF ABRAHAM BE PRAISED!

With the coming of spring, Captain André's plans for the *Mischianza* grew. At each new development Lydia would encode a summary of it, and Nate would wait for an opportunity to take the news to Valley Forge. He had to be extremely careful now; André was watching him like a hawk. He never stopped thinking about Running Fox and Hyam Solomon in Walnut Street Prison. Were they still alive? Were they being tortured?

One afternoon in Ludwig's bakery, Nate found Captain McLane.

"Nate! You're not hanged? How'd you get out of Walnut Street? Besides Running Fox and Hyam Solomon, we have twenty-five other good men in that wretched hole. We *need* those men!"

"My father was picking up corpses," the lad answered. "He came to our cell. It was Mr. Solomon's idea to have Father take me out in the coffin instead of the dead man."

"Brilliant! We can—" He noted Nate's expression. "What's the problem?"

"It's my father. It's against his Quaker principles to assist the Patriots."

"Lad, you *must* convince your father to smuggle him out!"

Nate sighed. "I've tried. He's grateful Mr. Solomon helped me, but he refuses to get involved."

McLane frowned. "Nate, once they figure out who Running Fox is, they're going to start torturing him to learn what they can of our network."

Nate squirmed. "I'll ask Father again."

McLane put an arm around his shoulders. "We're at war. Lives depend on us." He started to leave. "I'll be at the shipyard; we're meeting there daily. If you can get Hyam Solomon or Running Fox, bring them straight to us." He paused. "If we don't get them out—all of them—before the British leave Philadelphia, they'll almost certainly hang them. They have a nasty habit of killing prisoners of war rather than taking them along as extra baggage."

Nate found his father in his wood shop, nailing together two pine-board coffins.

"When do you pick up more bodies?"

"This afternoon," mumbled Father through a mouthful of nails.

"If you think the snow is over for this winter," Nate volunteered, "I'll help change the runners for cartwheels on the coffin sleigh."

"Spring's here. Already did that."

Nate's bid to gain favor had failed. Now what? Just ask straight out. "Can you smuggle Hyam Solomon out?"

William Donovan stiffened. He laid his hammer down and took the nails out of his mouth. "Nate, I've said this before, and I'll not say it again: I'm a Quaker. We don't take sides."

"Father," the boy pleaded, "we're his only hope! You got *me* out."

"But I was not expecting to find you there. I went there on business; I was not planning a rescue. My conscience is clear."

"Regardless of your conscience," declared a voice behind them, "our son's life was more important."

They turned to see Lydia Donovan standing in the door in her traveling cloak and holding her black bag. "Is Colonel Dorfman's coffin ready? He lingers, but it won't be for long. I shall need the wagon."

William Donovan shook his head. "Before you collect the colonel, I must go to the prison. They've sent word that two more convicts have died, in cells 4 and 21. I have the first box almost ready."

"Father," cried Nate. "Cell 21 was my cell. Hyam Solomon's in there! We could rescue him the same way we rescued me!"

William Donovan said nothing.

Nate turned to his mother. "Mother, we can't just let him die there!"

Before she could respond, her husband slowly stated, "Mrs. Donovan, I am not about to risk our livelihood, or my principles."

"Well, they're not my principles," replied Lydia, eyes flashing. "I shall rescue him myself!"

Her husband's silence stretched the tension in the woodshop.

Lydia Donovan murmured, "Lord, help me not to lie to anyone."

Finally her husband sighed. "Son, hitch up the horses. Bring the wagon to load the first coffin—I'm almost done with it. You shall go with her."

"I can't," Nate objected. "The guards will recognize me."

"Then I shall go alone," said Mother firmly. She dipped a bucket into the horse trough, and picked up a currying brush and a bar of saddle soap.

Seeing the soap, Nate chuckled; Hyam might survive prison, but would he survive Mother's scrubbing?

Father loaded the pine coffin he had just finished into the wagon, while Mother went back into the house. When she reemerged with a bundle, William Donovan handed her the reins.

"Be careful, dear wife," he murmured, resting a hand on her forearm. "I disapprove, but I will pray the Almighty will protect the two of you. He knows how important you both are to me. Besides," he looked up at her with a smile, "I would never be able to get along without your cooking."

Nate was surprised to see tears in his eyes, which he'd never seen before. He glanced at his mother and was even more surprised to see them in her eyes, as well.

"Don't worry about me," she said tenderly, slapping the reins on the backs of Goodness and Mercy. "I'll be home in time to make supper."

"Meet me at Potter's Field," Mother said to Nate as she drove off.

Watching the coffin wagon rattle down the drive, he admired her more than ever.

Crouching behind the tall privet hedge that bordered Potter's Field at Seventh and Walnut Streets, Nate saw a dozen open graves awaiting caskets, while many mounds of fresh earth indicated recent burials. The whole place seemed to reek of death.

Beyond the field rose the jail's massive walls. What was taking Mother so long?

At last the coffin wagon pulled up behind the hedge next to him, hidden from the view of the prison guards.

Lydia Donovan smiled and nodded in the direction of the coffin. "I've got him!"

"How did you get the coffin down the stairs?"

"The guards wouldn't help. An Indian prisoner carries the bodies for them."

Nate stared at her. "Running Fox?"

She nodded. "He sent you a message: 'Sharp eyes, keen nose, good ears. See you in the den.'"

Nate grinned. "He's expecting me to rescue him, too."

His mother shook her head. "We dare not attempt this method again. It is truly a miracle that we've gotten away with it twice."

Nate's heart sank. "What about Fox?"

Before his mother could respond, a loud thumping from the coffin interrupted them. Remembering how desperate he'd felt in there, Nate hurried to pry off the top.

Soon a pungent Hyam Solomon emerged and took a deep breath. "Freedom! The God of Abraham be praised!"

Lydia Donovan pointed to the bucket.

Hyam's face lit up. *"Ach, Mikva!* Soap? This is heaven!"

She turned her back, while Hyam stripped off his foul-smelling garments and scrubbed himself with the brush and soap—quickly, because it was so cold they could see their breath.

When he was ready, Nate handed him the bundle of his father's clothes. When the banker was dressed, Nate grinned; Father's broad-brimmed hat looked great on Hyam and neatly hid his Jewish frontlets.

Mother laughed out loud. "Behold, the perfect Quaker gentleman!" she exclaimed. "No one will suspect!"

A lookout in front of the shipwright's boathouse kept watch for any approaching British soldiers. As he and Hyam approached, Nate hugged himself as if freezing and loudly lamented, "What I wouldn't give for a bowl of Mother's hot turtle soup!"

"It's better cold," declared the lookout, waving them in.

Puzzled stares from the spy family met the "old Quaker gentleman." Bushnell was feeding a log into the fire in the cast-iron stove while Ludwig, Tallmadge, and McLane warmed themselves.

Then Tallmadge spoke up. "You know our newest and youngest member, Nate Donovan," he said to the others, "but none of you have met our esteemed colleague from New York, Hyam Solomon."

Removing his Quaker hat, Hyam bowed to their hushed applause. Then taking a seat near the stove, he sighed, "Ah! Many thanks! Prison was very cold."

Major Tallmadge continued: "Gentlemen, Nate has brought news confirming our suspicions that the British will be departing soon. They've found the City of Brotherly Love of little use to them and will be soon returning to New York. We wish them *bon voyage!*"

Everyone smiled as Tallmadge went on. "Moreover, Lord Howe's request to be relieved of his command has been granted, and Captain André plans a citywide farewell party for him, which he calls the *Mischianza.*"

"Mischi-*what?*" asked Ludwig.

"Never mind," replied the major, turning to Nate. "According to your report, André wants this ball to be memorable! Well, we propose to make it so! Captain McLane, I believe you have something in mind?"

McLane nodded with a smile. "Something that should be of particular interest to Mr. Solomon."

He nodded to David Bushnell, who announced, "I've invented some underwater explosive devices—torpedoes, I call them. We tested the prototypes in New York's harbor."

"*Ach!*" Hyam Solomon chuckled at the memory. "The British fleet dodged explosions with no enemy firing. They started shooting at phantoms! A great show it was! Alas, there was no lasting damage."

"This time," Bushnell grinned, "we need to change that!"

McLane spoke up. "We've received intelligence that within a fortnight a whaling ship will arrive in this harbor. Its cargo will include barrels of whale oil. I propose that we seize five of them and set fire to them behind the main British pavilion tent soon after midnight, during *Mischianza*.

"Why so late?" asked Major Tallmadge.

"To be certain the revelers will be so drunk they'll be of little threat to us," responded McLane. "You ever seen barrels of whale oil on fire?" He glanced around the room. "*Ka-boom!*" he shouted, and all present laughed.

Captain McLane grew serious again. "Gentlemen, our mission is to break into Walnut Street Prison and free the prisoners. With barrels of whale oil blowing up in the midst of the *Mischianza* up on the hill, while at the same time torpedoes are detonating in the harbor below, we should have all the chaos and confusion we need!"

Nate realized he had something to offer. "We've caught the snow hawk that Captain André was training for falconry. He was hoping to recapture her himself, to present her to General Howe as a crowning farewell gift. But he doesn't know we already have her."

Captain McLane was not impressed. "So?"

"Captain André has planned a parade of exotic animals. At the end we will present the snow hawk to Lord Howe. But just as he is about to accept her, we will release her! The crowd will watch her escape—the perfect symbol of America escaping British control."

Now McLane *was* impressed! And Hyam Solomon was delighted! "Then let us name her that—America!"

"Running Fox already has," noted Nate wryly.

38

NATE AND THE GENERAL

By mid-March the days were warmer, the trees around Philadelphia were budding, and the threat of snow was now remote. Night after night, Nate and his mother listened at the wall as the British General staff planned the *Mischianza*. Captain André seemed obsessed with the project, which was to be a surprise for Lord Howe.

Whenever André sent Nate to the bakery for fresh gingerbread, the lad would carry a coded message of the latest, increasingly elaborate plans. But as the days stretched into weeks and the May 18th date for the *Mischianza* drew nearer, Nate felt an increasing urgency to get their own surprise ready. Somehow he had to get the snow hawk closer to Philadelphia.

One afternoon he raised this concern with McLane, but before the captain could reply, Mr. Ludwig spoke up. "The bakers are setting up a bakery at Valley Forge. I've arranged to meet them there in two days with supplies. If the lad can get past the picket line, I can pick him up on the Germantown Road a mile beyond. I'll take him to the camp and bring him and his bird back with me."

"It could work," McLane mused. "But we'll have to get a pass for you, Nate. With André's suspicions as high as they are, we can't risk having him find out you're missing." He thought for a moment. "Your little brother and sister staying with your Aunt . . ." he speculated. "Your mother will be concerned for them. . . . She'll want you to pay them another visit."

"What if I run into any of the Redcoats who caught me and Running Fox?"

"Their road patrols won't be standing picket duty," the captain replied. "The British are very methodical; once a duty's been assigned, it's never changed."

They set his meeting with Ludwig for nine o'clock Friday morning.

When Nate related the plan to his mother, who was spinning flax at her wheel, Lydia Donovan said, "Let me present it to Captain André."

That afternoon, as the captain came calling, ostensibly to inform them that he would need their dining room that evening, but obviously in hopes of encountering Rachel, she confronted him. "Captain André, it has now been three months since I have seen my little children. I have spring clothing for them. I request that you permit me to visit them."

As Lydia Donovan had anticipated, the captain shook his head. "Out of the question, madam! I need your presence here to ensure that this house maintains its excellent hospitality. But I will permit your son to deliver their clothing and to spend one day with them. He may have a forty-eight-hour pass. No longer."

Two days later, as Nate was making ready to depart with the twins' clothing, his mother reminded him to tell Charles of the spoon that was now in enemy hands. "It's strange they haven't questioned us."

Rachel, who had apparently been eavesdropping outside the parlor door, now entered. Picking up her needlework sampler, she matter-of-factly observed, "They probably thought it was Charles who was their prisoner. Died in jail."

Nate stared at her, open-mouthed. They'd never confided in her!

Rachel smiled. "Don't worry; I won't tell."

Nate searched her eyes and fervently hoped Captain André had stolen only her fantasies, not her heart.

Bumping along in Ludwig's wagon from Rising Sun Tavern, where he'd delivered the twins' clothes, to Valley Forge, Nate realized how much he missed Tad's mother. How strange it would be to visit the camp without her!

When they arrived, he heard men cheering as the bakers unloaded flour, extra ovens, and paddles at the commissary. "Huzzah! No more firecake!"

On his way to headquarters to make his report to General Washington about conditions in Walnut Street Prison, Nate saw improvements everywhere. Fresh latrines had been dug, and the bloated horse carcasses were finally being buried.

Cheerfully he approached the sentry in front of the stone cottage. "Nate Donovan to see General Washington," he announced.

The sentry did not recognize him. "Your purpose?"

"Personal report. At the General's request," he added.

"He's busy," replied the sentry, unimpressed.

Now what?

Just then, Martha Washington strolled up the walk.

"Nathaniel!" she exclaimed with delight. "You are a sight for sore eyes! Come in and cheer up the General!"

The sentry now spoke up. "Ma'am, the General left orders that he was not to be disturbed."

Mrs. Washington laughed. "Corporal Steele, my husband will be delighted to see this young man! I'll take full responsibility."

The corporal relaxed and smiled. "Very well, ma'am, if you say so."

Walking on into the hall, Martha Washington tapped on her husband's office door and opened it.

"Excuse me, dear, but your youngest spy has returned."

"Nate?" The General looked up. "Come in, lad! Let us have a look at you! We'd heard from Hyam Solomon that you'd escaped from prison. I want to hear all about it!"

Billy appeared with a plate of gingerbread cookies. "General, sir, these are still warm."

He and Martha exited, leaving Nate alone with the General.

Washington stood up. "Let me shake your hand, young man. You kept your promise and visited that prison!"

"Not the way I had planned."

"Have a cookie and tell me the whole story. Leave nothing out."

Nate recounted his adventure, concluding, "I'd be dangling from a noose, if it weren't for Hyam Solomon."

General Washington leaned forward. "I'm informed that your *mother* delivered him out of there. How did she manage *that*?"

Nate began to fill him in, but the General, shaking his head in wonder, stopped him. "Patsy?" he called out the window, using his nickname for his wife. "Can you come in for a moment? I want you to hear this!"

Nate smiled at the obvious affection he had for her. When she'd joined them, he resumed, telling everything, including Hyam's disguise as a "Jewish Quaker."

He told how Running Fox had been captured, too, and how André intended to hang him with the rest of their spy family as soon as he caught them. And he related what Captain McLane had said about time running out.

When he got to the part about his mother driving the coffin wagon into the prison by herself, General Washington slapped his knee. "She did *that*?"

"An answer to my prayers," murmured Martha Washington.

The General agreed. "She deserves a commendation for saving one of America's greatest friends."

Martha nodded thoughtfully. "I'll make a note of that, dear," she said, reaching for a quill pen on the desk next to her. She winked at Nate and murmured, "You've been a tonic for him."

General Washington stood and took his tricornered hat and cloak from their peg. "Come, Nate. Ride with me and tell me about this peculiar British *Mischianza*."

There was a hint of summer in the breeze, as Nate and the General strode across a green lawn now peppered with violets and clover.

When the sentry came to attention, General Washington ordered, "Corporal Steele, bring me Nelson and a mount for Master Donovan."

The corporal soon returned with the two horses, and Nate noticed that his left arm hung helplessly at his side.

As they rode away, General Washington explained. "At Germantown the corporal took a musket ball through the arm. At Brandywine, another to the belly. And still he serves me. These are the true heroes of Valley Forge; they have held this army together. God bless them all, every one!"

Hearing a quaver in the General's voice, Nate glanced in his direction and caught a hint of moisture in his eye.

The two riders passed beneath a lacy canopy of treetops. New buds tinged the rolling woodlands a yellowish green, with dashes of white dogwood blossoms and pink wild cherry.

General Washington led the way up a steep bluff, as Nate filled him in on the details of Captain André's celebration plans.

At the top the General turned his horse. "Well, Nate, I've things I must do, and you need to find Mr. Ludwig and head home. I'm proud of you, son. You survived prison, turned in your report, and kept your word to me."

"It was an honor, sir," said Nate straightening in his saddle, as the tall horseman galloped away.

39

PLANNING *MISCHIANZA* MISCHIEF

Returning the horse to headquarters, Nate found Charles and Chaplain Duffield waiting for him. His brother hugged him. "Look at you! You're alive! You got out of the Walnut! I thought you were bedbug crazy to tell General Washington you could do it—go in and get out. But you *did*! How'd you do it?"

"Getting in wasn't hard; I got caught by a British patrol. But getting out—" he paused. "Father rescued me."

"What?"

Nate told him the story, ending with, "I guess you'd have to say it was Divine Providence."

Chaplain Duffield smiled. "You've passed your trial by fire, son."

"Well," proclaimed Charles, "tell Mother I'll be coming home soon."

"Be careful," Nate warned his brother. "The British found your spoon in my rucksack. They're looking for a Charles Donovan, though they may think it was you who 'died' in that prison. Anyway, we can't be too careful."

Charles nodded. "Perhaps Divine Providence will watch over me, too," he said quietly.

Mr. Ludwig was baking in the Walker farm's big brick oven when Nate came in the kitchen door. He smiled; it smelled just like his Philadelphia bakery!

Seeing him, Tad's siblings hugged his neck with warm gingerbread crumbs all over their faces. And as much as he missed Sarah Walker's greeting, he felt the warmth of her love lingering throughout the house.

But where was Tad?

He found him near the silo. "How's our snow hawk?"

"Keeping me company. Come on, I'll show you."

As Tad led the way to the barn, Nate was glad to see that his leg seemed much better. He still favored it, but not like before. Another week and he'd be good as new.

Perched under the peak of the barn as high as her rope would allow, the snow hawk gazed down at them with yellow eyes. Fierce and aloof, she yearned to be free.

"She doesn't belong here," Tad fretted.

"She'll be free soon enough."

Tad looked at him, curious. "Heard you'd been captured. Same day Mama was buried. Thought you'd died, too. We all did." He fell silent, then murmured, "Sometimes I miss Mama so bad, I want to die myself."

Tad was going through his own fiery trial, Nate thought. Well, maybe there was a way to help him. "Tad, Running Fox got that bird for us." He paused. "We're going to get Fox out of prison, and we need your help." Nate revealed Captain McLane's plan to simultaneously spoil the *Mischianza* and free the prisoners.

"Wouldn't miss it!" Tad pledged.

"Good! You'll present 'America' to Captain André, and just as he's ready to impress Lord Howe—"

"I release her! She escapes André a second time, and we make a total fool of him!"

Shaking hands on it, they prepared an empty corn barrel for her journey. With a hammer and chisel, Nate made airholes and then hauled the bird gently down toward the barrel. As the hawk approached, she resisted, beating at them furiously with her wings.

"I made a leather hood for her," called Tad. "If she can't see, she'll calm down."

Eventually they got the hood on the hawk and settled her into the barrel, where she soon did quiet down.

While the two boys waited for Mr. Ludwig to take them and the snow hawk to Philadelphia, Nate told Tad about prison and how he had taken a dead man's place in the coffin. "Want to know something spooky?" he said at the end. "Hyam Solomon called our bird 'America,' the same name Running Fox gave her."

When Nate and Tad asked Mr. Ludwig if he had any thoughts about where they might keep the bird, he suggested Widow Neuss's barn at Rising Sun Tavern. It was closer to town but still well beyond André's grasp. He would drop them off there before stopping at Frankford Mill.

Tad bade his father farewell, promising to return as soon as they had settled America into her new hiding place. Checking to make sure the barrel containing her was secure in the back, the two boys got into the wagon.

But when they got to Aunt Neuss's place, she did not agree with Mr. Ludwig. "Can't keep her here; too many British spies about."

Nate's spirits fell. "Aunt Neuss, we can't keep her in Philadelphia. André is sure to find her. He's already put up a reward for her—ten gold sovereigns!"

"So, what are you going to do with the money?" someone behind them coolly asked.

Nate and Tad whirled around. It was Colonel Cadwalader.

"You mean, *we* should claim the reward money?" asked Tad.

"Why not?" replied the colonel with a wry grin.

"But how can we?"

"Tell André this, Nate: A farm-boy friend of yours heard about the price on the bird's head and managed to catch her. Learning the captain is frequently at your house, the boy asked you to give him this message: the captain must pay one sovereign as a down payment immediately, and the rest when the boy delivers the bird to him at the *Mischianza*."

"It could work!" exclaimed Nate.

But the colonel shook his head. "Don't be so quick to accept a thing. Always think it through as far as you can. Imagine what your opponent's response is likely to be and your response to his response." He thought a moment. "André's going to ask you if you've actually *seen* the bird. You can assure him you have, that the boy had the bird with him in a barrel."

"What if he asks the boy's name? If he knew it was Tad, he might raid the Walker farm and start hunting Tad."

Instead of providing the answer, the colonel said, "Think it through, Nate."

He did, finally saying, "I don't give him the boy's name because the boy's scared and afraid he won't keep his end of the bargain. But what if he wants proof we have the bird?"

"Think, Nate."

For a long time he said nothing, then, "We could show him one of America's feathers, much as I'd hate to take one from her."

"He'd part with that sovereign in an instant!" exclaimed Tad.

Aunt Nuess asked, "Now, what's a Quaker boy going to do with his half of the reward?"

Nate knew right away. "Two sovereigns will buy Father new springs for his hearse; the rest will go to Hyam Solomon, who saved my life. He said that if he could put shoes on the army's feet, the Almighty would put *his* feet on Jerusalem's ancient stones. I mean to help him."

Ludwig had to get back to the city. "So, where do we put the bird?"

"In my aunt's barn," cooed a voice behind them.

It was Sally! Had she been watching for him? From her house she could see Rising Sun Tavern.

"What about your aunt?" asked Nate.

"She's taken a spell of gout in her foot. Not likely to be checking on anything," Sally replied, her eyes dancing.

"After you get the bird settled," Aunt Neuss said, "Tad can come and check on her, and help around here like he used to."

"Well, let's get going," urged Ludwig, and he took them all and America to the Widow Foulke's. When they arrived, the baker wished them well and went on his way, leaving the two boys to carry the barrel into the barn.

"What'll we feed her?" Nate asked.

"We've got meat in the smokehouse," Sally said. "I'll feed her pieces each day."

Tad, looking at the two of them, heads close together, said, "Reckon I'll get started toward the Rising Sun. With this leg I'm going to need a head start." And before Nate could object, he took off.

Nate turned to Sally. She had that look again, the same one she'd had at the gate the time he'd almost kissed her. He sensed she wanted him to kiss her now, and . . .

"Sally, you in there?"

Nate looked at her as Sally groaned.

"Sally?"

"Yes, Auntie."

"You tell that boy he needs to get on over to the tavern; it's getting dark! You hear me?"

"Yes, ma'am." Turning to Nate, she whispered, "I wish you didn't have to go."

But he was already up and moving toward the barn door. "I've got to see the twins. That's why Captain André gave me the pass." And before she could say anything more, he was on his way.

"I'll take good care of your bird," she called after him and then added softly, "but *you'd* better come back and check on her, too."

40

THE NOOSE DRAWS TIGHTER

Three days after his return to the city, Nate had the opportunity he'd been waiting for. Captain André came calling to see Rachel, who was accompanying her mother on an errand of mercy, nursing a sick neighbor. Nate took a deep breath. "Captain André, a boy from Germantown came by here recently, looking for you. He's recaptured that bird you lost and wants to claim the reward."

Captain André eyed him suspiciously. "Did you see it?"

"Yes, sir."

"Describe it."

"It was some kind of hawk."

"How large?"

"I don't know, exactly; it was in a barrel." Nate paused, as if remembering something. "But it must be awfully big. The boy said that its wings, outstretched, were longer than his arms!"

"How do you know it's *my* bird?" André demanded.

"I don't. But he said to give you this feather." Nate got the long white feather and handed it to him.

André stared at it, and slowly smiled. "This is almost too good to be true. The snow hawk! The crown jewel for Lord Howe's farewell party!"

Wait till that jewel flies away from you and Lord Howe, thought Nate.

"On the night of the *Mischianza,*" André ordered, "he must deliver the bird to me at the main tent, just before midnight. Tell him I'll give him the reward then."

Nate remembered Captain McLane's advice. "I'll tell him, but he won't believe me. He's afraid you'll simply take the bird without paying him."

André glared at Nate. "I'm an officer and a gentleman! He has my word on it!"

Nate shook his head. "I'm afraid he doesn't trust the word of British officers. He said you must give him a written note of promise *and* one of the gold sovereigns on good faith."

"Outrageous! Where is that boy?"

"I don't know," Nate replied truthfully, unsure of Tad's exact whereabouts. "He said for you to give the note and the sovereign to me, and he'd find me."

André scowled, obviously not caring for this at all but unable to think of an alternative.

Going to the parlor desk, Nate opened it and withdrew a piece of paper, the inkwell, and a quill pen.

Before taking it, André asked, "Why should I trust you?"

Nate hesitated. Don't act scared, he told himself. Just be firm. "Because if you do *not* trust me, how will you get the bird back?"

André glowered at him with steel-gray eyes. "Very well. That bird is a rare prize. I lost it once; I'll not lose it again!"

He took the paper and quill and began to write. When he finished, he signed it with a flourish and handed it to Nate, along with a sovereign. "Mark me well, boy," he declared menacingly. "If I find you are lying to me, this entire family will pay!"

As Nate replaced the ink and quill pen, he accidentally opened Mother's secret compartment. And André was staring right at it! In plain view were Lydia Donovan's two gold coins, the secret letters, and the little silver key to the family Bible that contained her written prayers for George Washington and Charles!

Did he realize what he was looking at? Nate started to panic. But just then Rachel came waltzing into the room, and the captain, beaming, turned to greet her.

Quickly Nate closed the secret compartment. Had André noticed?

It was the day of the *Mischianza*. For the past three weeks, whenever Nate had been sent by Captain André to Ludwig's bakery, he would pass on to Captain McLane what he and his mother had been hearing through the wall. Lately the British officers were talking only about their feverish preparations for the *Mischianza*.

He had also handed André's note, the gold sovereign, and his missing gold button to McLane for delivery to Tad. Then he informed Captain André that all arrangements for the transfer of the hawk had been made.

Meanwhile Colonel Cadwalader had slipped into the city in disguise. At the bakery he briefed Nate and Captain McLane on the Patriots' preparations for the evening. The barrels of whale oil were ready, and the Levering brothers were standing by to help put them in place. David Bushnell had hidden his torpedoes in the shipwright's boathouse. And Ludwig, now on his way from Frankford Mill, would soon arrive with Tad, Sally, and the snow hawk.

"Sally's coming?"

"Yes," the Colonel replied. "She's been invited to the *Mischianza*, as has every young lady for miles around."

"You *want* her to go?"

"I do, indeed. I want every pair of eyes in there I can get." Cadwalader wore a grave expression as he concluded the briefing. "The British are packing up to leave for New York. They've got their mind on the *Mischianza* and won't be looking out for us. The last thing they want right now is more prisoners; in fact, they'll soon regard the ones they have as excess baggage. If we don't free them *tonight*, they could well hang tomorrow."

Nate walked home, deeply worried about Running Fox. Would they be able to get his friend out? He looked up at the gray sky as he went in the kitchen door. Duffield would ask God for assistance. Maybe he'd better, too.

From the front hall, he heard subdued voices. Another staff meeting had just adjourned; they were occurring night and day now. Two officers had apparently paused on their way out. He recognized their voices, André's and Colonel Percy's.

"We've learned that the spoon in the rucksack," Percy was saying, "connects the girl with the egg basket to this house!"

"She does see the boy who lives here sometimes," André replied, "but his name is Nate, not Charles."

"I think we're going to find there *is* a Charles connected with this family," insisted Percy.

"I've never heard them mention one," André answered defensively.

"It would seem, Captain, that Lydia Donovan has a sister whose cousin is serving in His Majesty's Royal Navy—a flag officer, Commodore Barrington. Aboard his ship in the harbor this morning, he informed me that the Donovans' elder son, Charles, left their household last fall. It is thought that he joined the rebel army."

There was silence. Then André spoke with an uncertainty in his voice that Nate had never heard before. "They're Quakers! If what you say is true, his Meeting would have disowned him!"

Percy was unimpressed. "Has it not occurred to you that the rest of the family might be in sympathy with his beliefs? That they might indeed have had their ears to the wall, as you suspected?"

"Colonel, I *have* investigated that possibility and found no conclusive evidence!"

"Perhaps it was there all along, Captain, but your infatuation with their daughter caused you to overlook it."

André was, for once, at a loss for words.

Percy wasn't. "Do you realize," he exclaimed, "you may have endangered the King's army?"

Now the captain found his tongue. "With all due respect, Colonel, tonight Lord Howe will see what a loyal officer I am! The *Mischianza* will be a splendid success, one that he will remember for the rest of his life! It was planned by *me*, in *this* house, under the *tightest* security. *Nothing* will go wrong!"

The front door slammed as they exited.

An hour later Captain André, having regained his composure, came calling. Dismayed at the door being opened once again by Nate, he perked up as Rachel came tripping down the stairs.

"Good afternoon, Captain André. The weather could not be better for our ball this evening!"

Nate frowned at her, but the two were oblivious to him.

"Rachel, my dear," said the captain, beaming, "your gown is ready to be picked up at the dressmaker's. If any alterations are needed, have them put on my account."

Nate's mouth fell open. She was going to the *Mischianza*! On André's arm! Against Mother's express warning about him!

André bowed, clicking his heels together. "Until this evening, when you will be the fairest of the fair!"

Rachel sighed and almost swooned as he left.

Her brother was appalled. "Rachel! In the name of all that's holy, what are you *doing?*"

In the arms of an imaginary partner, she waltzed around him, twirling her skirt to a full bell. Then she reached out and closed his open mouth. "Really, dear brother, that look is quite unbecoming."

"Rachel! You are ninnyhammer *crazy!* The moment André gets you alone and starts asking questions, you're going to get us all hanged!"

She tossed her head. "Oh, don't be a dolt! He only wants a pretty girl to dance with. Me! I shall be the most envied lady in Philadelphia!" She ducked under his arm and ascended the stairs, her nose in the air, until she encountered her mother, coming down.

"Turn around, young lady, and march yourself right back down. We're going to talk."

Nate watched, unnoticed.

"Donovans do *not* attend pagan festivals! They do *not* wear ball gowns! They do *not* carry on with the enemy! *Especially* when our troops are suffering and dying!"

"But Mother," Rachel pleaded, "Captain André begged me to go! He's bought me a beautiful gown of the finest blue silk! I've never had anything like it, and it didn't cost Father a shilling!"

Mother glared at her, unmoved. "No gown! You are not going!"

Furious, Rachel shot back, "What if the British *win* this war, Mother? Would not marrying one of their officers be a most excellent move?"

"Not for a Quaker! Meeting would disown you!"

"What? For dancing?" Rachel's green eyes flashed. "Why not Charles, for fighting? Or you and Nate, for spying?"

Lydia Donovan's jaw clenched, and she raised her hand as if to slap her daughter. Nate held his breath; he'd never seen Mother so angry.

Shaking, Mother restrained herself, her love for her daughter overcoming her anger. "Rachel," she said, her voice breaking, "you are smitten with him. But hear me: *He shall crush your heart!*"

Rachel burst into tears. "Let me choose for myself; it's only fair! He truly cares for me! He has promised to write me from New York!"

Mother grew silent.

If Mother forbids her to leave the house, Nate thought, *she'll sneak out and go anyway.*

As if his mother had had the same thought, she calmly said, "Very well. I will allow it, but only on this condition: You shall be escorted not by Captain André but by your brother!"

"Oh, no, Mother!" cried Rachel. "He'll ruin *everything!*"

For once, Nate agreed with her. Escorting her would ruin his plans. How could he join McLane's raid on the prison?

"Besides," continued Rachel, "Sally Winston's been invited, too. She's coming into the city for it, and we've arranged to go together!"

"What will Father say?" Nate asked her.

"Captain André has requested the pleasure of my company," his sister scornfully replied. "Actually, it's more like an order, and Father never resists his orders. The captain has, in fact, hired all available carriages and drivers to take officers and their ladies to and from the ball. And Father is among them with our good carriage. He'll be busy; he won't even have to know." And with that she flounced up the stairs.

41

MISCHIANZA!

Philadelphia had been buzzing for days. At a time when many cupboards were almost bare, Tories and Patriots alike condemned the vast sums of money the British were spending on the ball. Magnificent tents now lined nearby Fifth Street, awaiting the evening's gala.

At Mother's request Nate accompanied his sister to the dressmaker's shop four blocks away. He was annoyed at having to wait outside while she required one final fitting. He was more annoyed when he had to help carry the gown all the way home and up the stairs to her room.

Before she could ask him to do anything else, he bolted out the front door and went to Ludwig's bakery, where Tad and Sally were waiting for him.

"Nate!" Sally exclaimed joyfully, running to him and throwing her arms around him.

Surprised, and delighted, Nate hugged her back.

Closing her eyes and tilting her head up, she waited expectantly for a kiss.

But Nate, aware of Tad and the baker watching them, blurted out, "Um, it's sure good to see you, Sally," and pulled gently away from her grasp. "Hello, Mr. Ludwig and Tad," he said, shaking hands with them. "Where's America?"

"She's in her barrel in back," Tad said.

"Is she alright?"

"Just fine," responded Tad with a grin. "Rarin' to get free."

"Won't be long now," Nate assured him.

He turned to the baker. "The presentation is scheduled for midnight tonight, so we'll be back to pick her up at 10:30. Can we borrow your wheelbarrow to take her?"

"Yes. The others will be here, too."

Nate looked at him. "What others?"

"The raiders. We're leaving from here just after midnight."

Nate nodded. "We'd best get home. Captain André's carriage will be picking us up at eight." To Sally, he added, "Rachel's expecting you to go with her. And since Mother wants me to escort her; you, Tad, get to take Sally."

When they reached the Donovan household, Rachel was in her new blue silk ball gown and looking breathtaking, Nate had to admit.

"Sally!" she cried, as the two girls hugged each other.

Nate said, "Rachel, this is Tad Walker."

Rachel, sizing up the boy standing behind Nate, smiled broadly and curtsied. "Why, Mister Walker, it is *indeed* a pleasure to make your acquaintance."

Tad stammered, his face turning red, and Nate felt like throwing up. Was there *no* man his sister would not flirt with?

Lydia Donovan appeared and announced, "You all need to eat something. Come into the dining room."

When they were seated, she brought them each a bowl of vegetable soup and a thick slice of fresh-baked bread. The boys ate ravenously. The girls took a spoonful of soup and a bite of bread and then stopped, much too excited to eat. Sally went up to put on the Quaker wedding gown Aunt Foulke had loaned her, and Rachel went to help her.

As soon as the girls had left the dining room, Lydia turned to her son. "Promise me that you'll watch out for your sister tonight, Nathaniel. I'm very worried about her."

"I will, Mother," Nate assured her. But how? He was committed to take part in the prison raid.

Promptly at eight the carriage arrived, its black lacquer and brass handles and spokes gleaming. The girls swept down the front steps, their long hair arranged in tall pompadours, decorated with golden silk ribbons. The boys followed behind in their Sunday best.

The carriage driver called to Rachel. "My instructions were to pick up two ladies, ma'am. Didn't say anything about two young gentlemen."

"He's my brother," Rachel sweetly replied, indicating Nate. "My mother has said he must escort me to the ball. And his friend is escorting my friend."

The carriage man shrugged and held open the door for them, murmuring, "Good for your mother."

It was a warm evening for May, and a gentle breeze carried the scent of lilacs through the open windows of the carriage.

As they approached the *Mischianza*, Rachel and Sally took out their blue butterfly masks and hid their faces behind them.

Over the grand tent flew dozens of gaily colored silk pennants while a row of torches illuminated the driveway for arriving carriages. At the tent's entrance, guests promenaded in under an archway of flowers and then through a double-facing column of British Grenadiers standing at attention in full-dress uniforms, wearing their great bearskin hats.

As their carriage arrived at the entrance, two Redcoats stepped forward to open the doors and offer the ladies a hand down. The girls were presented to the majordomo, who checked their invitations against the guest list and bellowed at the top of his lungs, "Miss Rachel Donovan and Miss Sarah Winston!"

Hearing their names, Captain André came forward. He was dressed like a Turkish sultan, with a turban, and a broad red sash across his chest. Waving good-bye to the boys, the elegant young ladies raised their masks and swept in, Rachel taking the captain's right arm and Sally his left.

As the boys walked away, Tad whispered to Nate, "How are you going to keep your promise to your mother?"

"I don't know, but we've got to get in there somehow."

They had reached the end of the drive when Tad got an idea. "We could go to the kitchen tent and tell them we're from Ludwig's bakery."

Nate pursed his lips. "Let's try it! André has certainly bought enough gingerbread from them, and he sent me to Ludwig's to put in a huge order for tonight."

"We could be sent from the bakery to help them set it out."

"Perfect!"

In the gathering darkness they circled around the grand tent to come up on one of the kitchen tents in back. As they approached, a sentry challenged them. They explained that they'd been sent by the bakery, and the soldier directed them to an adjacent tent. "You'll need to get into costume. All the help is to be in livery tonight."

At the next tent Tad said to the guard, "We're here from the bakery. Where do we get our costumes?"

"Go on in. You'll see the men's dressing area on the right. Find two sets of livery that fit and report to the steward."

Behind a canvas screen Nate and Tad pulled on white stockings, cream breeches, and green waistcoats. When they found the steward and informed him they were from the bakery, he said, "You're late! And where are your masks?"

"Masks?"

"Look, boy, we have to wear these ridiculous outfits *and* masks, by order of Captain André! You'll find them back there," he indicated the dressing area. "When you've got them on, come back here."

When they returned, the steward pointed to a table piled high with gingerbread cakes. "Each of you take a tray of those and circulate among the guests. Then come back and get more."

As they entered the grand tent, Nate and Tad were taken aback. The tent itself was two stories tall and enclosed nearly an acre of lawn. Fairy-tale castles and towers rested on large wheeled platforms, illuminated by brightly burning candles in lanterns, sconces, and chandeliers. The tent's canvas walls were painted to resemble Sienna marble and held dozens of full-length mirrors that reflected the light and made the interior space seem even more grand. At the peak of the great tent was suspended a massive crest and shield, featuring a silhouette of His Britannic Majesty, George III.

Nate murmured to Tad through his mask, "You go to the left; I'll go right. If you find Rachel first, come get me."

They separated, and Nate began to look for his sister, offering gingerbread cakes as he went.

There were at least a thousand guests packed inside, men in powdered wigs and embroidered slippers with long white silk stockings squiring ladies wearing full silk gowns of every color. Nate was amazed at their elaborate high hairdos, flaxen wigs laced with ribbons and glittering jeweled pins.

He heard violins playing a Mozart minuet and saw precise lines of gentlemen and ladies facing each other, dipping and swaying in a graceful, elegant formation.

Suddenly Nate recognized one of the ladies in the dance—Sally! How did she ever learn to do that? She seemed to be having a wonderful time, and he was jealous of the young officer with whom she was dancing.

And then he spotted André. He was watching the dancers, with Rachel giggling and leaning tipsily on his arm.

As the minuet came to an end, gloved hands applauded, and André led Rachel toward the punch bowl. Nate, grateful for his mask and livery, and taking care to avoid their direct gaze, circled around behind them. Cautiously he drew close enough to hear what they were saying.

"Captain . . ."

André smiled and patted her hand on his arm. "I think we know each other well enough for you to call me John."

"John, I really wonder if I should have any more punch. I feel a little woozy."

"Nonsense, my dear! You'll be fine. A night like this deserves champagne."

The knuckles of Nate's hands whitened on the tray he was carrying. Rachel had never had any spirits in her life! And André was obviously trying to ply her with drink. Nate wanted to slam the tray over André's head!

But if he did, everything would be ruined. Taking a deep breath, he decided to wait and watch. He stayed close behind as the captain guided his sister to the punch.

They were almost at the punch bowl, when a tall, broad, authoritative figure stepped in front of them. "Rachel? Rachel Donovan? Is that you behind that mask?"

42

AMERICA FLIES FREE!

Rachel was shocked! "Cousin Barrington?" she stammered.
Commodore Barrington was genuinely glad to see her. "How *are* you, young lady! And how is your dear mother?"

"Your cousin is just fine, sir!" Rachel replied. "I cannot believe that you're here. My goodness, I haven't seen you in ages!"

The commodore chuckled. "It was six years ago, before this dreadful war. And you were in pigtails, a far cry from the lovely young lady you've become!"

Rachel smiled, recovering her poise. "Allow me to introduce my escort, Captain André."

The two officers bowed to each other. "I believe we have a friend in common," Barrington said. "Colonel Charles Percy."

André looked surprised.

"He visited my flagship this morning." He turned to Rachel. "How is the rest of your family?"

"Just fine, cousin." She turned to André. "John, perhaps I *will* have that glass of punch now."

Nate realized she was desperately trying to end the conversation.

But the Commodore persisted. "Have you heard from your brother Charles?"

Rachel paled and said nothing.

André turned to her, still smiling though his eyes were narrowing. "Why, Rachel. You never mentioned you had a brother named Charles. In fact, none of you Donovans did."

"You never asked," she replied lamely.

Captain André held her gaze. "It would seem that I have been mistaken about you, my dear. And indeed, about your whole family."

They were interrupted by the long, clear fanfare of twenty herald trumpets, held aloft by pages in brightly-colored pantaloons. The guests fell silent, the last of their conversation dying away.

Captain André, the master of the *Mischianza*, addressed the young lady by his side. "You must come with me for now, my dear. Everyone is waiting."

And with Rachel on his arm, he led a procession of guests toward the south side of the grand tent. Nate followed them as closely as he dared. The mask and livery hid his identity, but André knew him too well. As they approached the wall of the tent, other servants in livery rolled up a canvas flap that had covered the entrance to another tent, a long, narrow canopy with no sides.

Guests gasped. It was a jousting course! Knights in costume armor were actually going to charge at each other with fake lances. On the far side of the course was a grandstand with enough seats to accommodate them all. In the center of it was a box cordoned off with gold rope, reserved for Lord Howe and his special guests.

Framing the entrance to the jousting tent was a high-stepped archway covered with red roses. The master of the *Mischianza* now led an increasingly reluctant Rachel up the steps. At the top of the arch, with all eyes on them, he turned to face the sea of upturned faces.

"Ladies and gentlemen," he proclaimed, "the tournament is about to begin! Now, who shall wear the colors of this fair damsel?" Captain André elevated her hand, showing her off to the crowd.

"Will it be one of these bold knights?" André indicated the two mounted and helmeted warriors, visible through the entrance. "Or," he scanned the audience, "is there a Sir Charles among us?"

The guests looked at each other, puzzled. What did he mean?

Nate, standing at the foot of the archway, knew. He felt a knot of fear in his stomach. André was about to expose his sister! And their whole family!

He looked around and was relieved to see that both Tad and Sally had worked their way close to the archway.

Captain André continued. "Ladies and gentlemen, I give you Rachel Donovan!" There was a smattering of applause. "Now Donovan is a fine, upstanding Quaker name in William Penn's fair city, unless . . . they be rebels!"

He turned to Rachel. "Tell me, mademoiselle, hide you any rebels?"

Rachel choked but forced herself to smile. She blurted out, "Oh, no, sir! We left them all in Ireland!"

The audience roared with delight, and Nate breathed more easily.

But André was not finished with her yet.

"Nay, friends! She lies!"

Rachel froze. "What are you *doing?*" she whispered.

André looked at her with contempt. "Did you *really* believe," he said scornfully, making little effort to keep his voice down, "a simple provincial bumpkin would ever grace a British officer's table?"

"But you said . . ."

"Did you *really* think that I would marry the likes of you?" He laughed at the folly of it.

As Rachel's fantasy world came crashing down, she turned pale and then green. Suddenly her stomach heaved convulsively. She swallowed hard, fighting to keep it down. But it was no use. With a great retching groan, she vomited out all of the evening's punch and gingerbread—most of it on André.

The guests were aghast.

André was enraged, his face turning the color that his scarlet sash had been before Rachel redecorated it.

"Get out of my sight, you disgusting creature!" he hissed at Rachel.

Reeling, she turned to go down the steps, even as Sally started up them to help her.

"I'll deal with you—all of you in that nest of rebels—tomorrow," he spat after her.

"You two!" he cried, gesturing to two servants (Nate and Tad!) at the foot of the archway steps. *"Get her out of here!"*

Sobbing hysterically, Rachel needed both Sally and Nate to support her. Tad led the way, clearing a path through the crowd to the entrance.

At the driveway Nate raised his hand to signal for the next carriage, which looked familiar. So did the driver; it was William Donovan!

"Oh, thank God!" muttered Nate under his breath. As their carriage drew up to the entrance, he ran around to the outside and whispered up to the driver. "Father, it's us! Rachel's sick. We've got to get out of here *now!*"

With Sally's help, Tad lifted Rachel into the carriage, then joined Nate and William Donovan on the driver's bench, all of them in matching livery.

On the way home Nate told his father everything that had happened. "And so," he concluded, "we all have to get out of the city. *Tonight!* Tell Mother to get herself and Rachel ready to leave right away. If we wait till morning, André will have us all arrested and most likely hanged as spies."

Tad spoke up. "Better let us off here, sir."

"What? Why?" demanded William Donovan.

"Father," said Nate, "there's something more we must do. If we told you what it is, we'd be putting you in even more peril."

His father groaned and reined Goodness and Mercy to a halt. "I never should have permitted thee and thy mother to become involved in spying." He shook his head. "But my family's safety is all that matters now. When wilt thou return?"

Nate thought before jumping down. "In a few hours, well before dawn. But we'll have to leave then."

"And how are we to pass through the picket line?"

Nate shook his head. "Maybe God will show us."

It was past eleven by the time Nate and Tad retrieved the snow hawk from the bakery, and wheeled her barrel to the kitchen tent area of the *Mischianza*. Nate asked another liveried servant where the parade of animals was being formed, and was directed to a tent next to the jousting course.

There a grand procession of wheeled cages was being readied. They contained animals that Nate had never seen before—bears, elk, cougars, and wolves. There was even a tropical snake, a green python from the Rum Islands, so long it would take four men to carry it.

There was a man with a list who was apparently in charge of forming the parade. Nate and Tad went up to him and explained what was in the barrel.

"Well, it's high time! Captain André has had us looking everywhere for you and your bird!" He called to his assistant. "Roger! Go find the captain and tell him that his precious bird has arrived!"

Nate whispered to Tad. "I can't let him see me." He looked around. "I'll wait over there behind that cage. Deal with him exactly as we planned. Just be sure to get the rest of the sovereigns."

"What if he wants to see her?"

"Give him only a peek, until you actually take her out of the barrel inside. I'll be in the crowd. The moment she flies free, run down the hill toward the docks. I'll be right behind you."

The captain, having changed into his full-dress uniform, was coming toward them. Nate slipped away and watched as Tad first presented André with his promissory note and then showed him the bird. The captain produced a small purse and handed it to Tad. Giving him his instructions, he directed Tad to the end of the procession. He was obviously saving the best for last.

Tad took the bird to his place at the back. As André went in to join Lord Howe and the guests of honor, Nate slipped into the back of the jousting tent and went around behind the grandstand.

One by one the animal cages were rolled past the reviewing stand, to the *ohhs* and *ahhs* of the guests.

Walking behind the last cage of animals, Tad approached the reviewing stand. He had taken the snow hawk out of her barrel, and she was riding on his arm. She was wearing her belled leather hood, and each of her legs was secured with a stout leather strap, wrapped several times around Tad's wrist.

In front of the stand, he stopped, and as if on cue, the bird stretched wide her great wings. A gasp of awe rose from the guests. And then a ripple of applause.

Captain André stood and addressed Lord Howe, in a voice that all could hear. "Paris, the City of Lights, may boast of her fireworks. But you, sir, have made Philadelphia even brighter with your inspirational leadership!"

"Hear, hear!" cried junior and senior officers, with their ladies enthusiastically applauding.

Lord Howe, noticeably pleased, gave a slight bow to the captain. And returned his fascinated gaze to the bird.

André resumed his presentation. Signaling for a drumroll, he proclaimed, "Sir, may this gift always remind you of America. I myself have personally begun the training of this magnificent creature, which I now give to you, for your favorite sport of falconry."

The captain motioned to Tad to turn over the bird to him so that he might let the General have a closer look.

This was the moment they had been waiting for. Nate came out from behind the grandstand, to be as near as possible.

Carefully Tad started to unwind the leather strap from his wrist. He was about to transfer the bird to André when, almost as an afterthought, he reached into a pocket and produced a gold uniform button. "Oh, Captain, I believe this is yours."

As André took the button, Tad added, "It was found at the mill near Valley Forge, the one you and your men burned down . . . with the miller and his wife in it."

Shock spread through all who heard.

André froze.

Tad instantly released the two thongs attached to the snow hawk's legs and whipped off her hood. *"Go!"* he urged her, lifting his arm.

She needed no further encouragement. Seeing the night sky immediately beyond the reviewing stand, she made for it, stretching her great wings. With four powerful beats she cleared the canopy and climbed into the night sky toward the nearly full moon.

Jumping off the reviewing stand, Tad bolted out of the tent, with Nate right behind him.

43

CRACKING THE WALNUT

When Nate and Tad reached the waterfront, they paused to catch their breath in the shadow of a warehouse. "What in tarnation?" muttered Tad, looking out at the harbor.

Dancing like fireflies, lights bobbed up and down everywhere. The boys squinted to make out what they were seeing. Couples from the *Mischianza* were enjoying romantic excursions around the harbor in Venetian gondolas, each of which had a lantern suspended from its front and back.

Behind them, up on the hill, they could hear that the music and dancing had resumed. "They're not coming after us," breathed Nate with relief, "but we've still got work to do."

The moon was bright; and, careful to remain in the shadows, he led Tad along the waterfront to the shipwright's boathouse, to meet the rest of the raiding party. Soon they were joined by other silhouettes, moving silently and quickly.

Nate grinned to see the Levering brothers, who had obviously evaded André's dragnet. Captain McLane had assigned ten men to help the Leverings roll the five barrels of whale oil up the hill behind the *Mischianza* tents, two blocks north of where they were meeting.

Dressed in black, one of the men was whispering with a local wine merchant who was supplying the *Mischianza*. And now Nate realized the cleverness of the captain's plan. More wine barrels would be needed, as the evening wore on, but mixed in with them would be five of a decidedly different vintage—whale oil!

The men in black stuffed each of the special barrels with a wick soaked in flammable camphor, threaded through the cork hole. "When they're all in place," the captain whispered to the Leverings, "light the wicks and clear out fast!"

The Leverings and their crew left to begin their mission. Watching them disappear into the night, Nate could hear the faint strains of Mozart on the breeze. He glanced up at the moon and wished it weren't so bright. Six blocks to the west he could plainly see the ominous outline of Walnut Street Prison.

Captain McLane indicated that Nate and Tad should follow him to the boathouse. There he rapped softly twice and then again. The door opened, and they entered. Around the chart table, illuminated only by the moonlight coming in the window, stood Colonel Cadwalader, Major Tallmadge, and twelve other men. They had rubbed lantern soot on their faces, and the newcomers quickly did the same. The raiding party was complete.

In a low voice McLane gave them their final instructions. "Going through this one more time: we'll take out the outside guards first. Silently," and he drew his hand across his throat.

Colonel Cadwalader turned to Nate. "Lad, you stick with me. I'll do the dirty work for both of us."

McLane told Tad the same thing and went on. "We know that normally there would be four guards outside and eight inside, with a second shift off duty in their barracks. But it's safe to assume they've had to send several up the hill to do guard duty at the *Mischianza*."

He looked around the circle. "As soon as we leave here, we will get into position at the prison. When the church clock strikes one, it will be our signal to move. We'll have to work fast. I've arranged with the Leverings and Bushnell to start each of their fireworks at the count of two hundred after they hear the clock."

He smiled grimly. "The explosions on the hill and the torpedoes in the harbor should draw the remaining guards outside. After we take care of them, we'll get their keys. During all the confusion, we'll empty the Walnut and take our men up Little Dock Creek."

Cadwalader chuckled. "Nate, you remember when I drew the picket guards' attention with my horse?" The lad nodded. "Well, we have a bigger surprise for them tonight, eh, Captain?"

McLane smiled. "A squad of light cavalry will be waiting for us near the picket line outpost. As soon as we get there, they'll charge the guards at that outpost and other nearby outposts to convince the British that they're under attack. They'll be dropping homemade bombs—iron pots filled with gunpowder and nails." He laughed. "That ought to send them running every which way, and will allow our men to get through."

He grew serious again. "We need to remember one thing: Any prisoners we don't get out of there tonight will be swinging from the gallows in the morning."

As they were leaving the boathouse, Captain McLane gave a hunting knife to each of the raiding party's two youngest members. "We'll be using these, instead of guns. Our best friends tonight are 'silence' and 'surprise.'"

Taking the cold steel blade, Nate dreaded the thought of having to use it. He remembered Duffield saying that in God's eyes self-defense was not the same as murder, but still . . .

He gripped the knife handle tightly as they slipped silently through the deserted streets, crouching low and staying in the shadows.

Coming to the open space of Potter's Field, they dropped on their stomachs and crawled through the grass and around the grave mounds toward Sixth Street. Up ahead loomed the fortress of Walnut Prison.

In the guardhouse next to the massive iron gate to the courtyard, two sentries were visible in the light of their lantern.

McLane crawled up beside Cadwalader and whispered, "We're in luck! There's only two."

"I don't like this," Cadwalader whispered back. "There should be more. Where are the others? Inside?"

McLane now hand-signaled the raiding party to split into two groups. He and Cadwalader would lead one group, with Nate and Tad sticking close to them, as instructed. Tallmadge would lead the other group around the back of the prison to approach the gate from the opposite direction.

The circling maneuver took them nearly half an hour.

Cadwalader pointed to himself and then to the tall guard. Captain McLane nodded and indicated he would take the smaller one. The two officers were tensed, ready to spring into action. Nate and Tad were right behind them.

Minutes passed. Nate could hear the sound of his heart beating as he waited.

Finally, on the still night air came the sound of a single chime.

Instantly McLane and Cadwalader sprang into the guardhouse and silenced the guards before they could utter a sound. Nate and Tad followed closely behind McLane, as he took the key to the iron gate and quickly opened it to let both groups of raiders in.

As they ran across the courtyard toward the main door to the prison, it opened, and a guard came out to join his comrades at the guardhouse. Seeing the raiders, he started to raise his musket.

Cadwalader stopped, flipped his knife in his hand, and gripping its blade, threw it at the guard's chest. It sank in to the hilt, and before he could fire his musket, the guard dropped to the ground with a strangled cry.

The raiders pressed themselves against the wall of the prison, on either side of the front door, and waited. Nate imagined the Leverings counting—*198, 199, 200.*

Up on the hill, the sky above the *Mischianza* tents suddenly lit up. A pillar of fire streaked heavenward, followed a second later by a deafening *ka-boom!* Four more flashes instantly followed and then *ka-boom-boom-boom-boom!*

Nate stifled a laugh. In the debris blown aloft, he saw the great shield with the likeness of King George spiraling slowly upward.

The flashes died away, but the night was now lit by the blaze of burning tents and rent by the screams of women and the cries of animals escaping. To add to the turmoil, the Levering brothers had opened all the cages. As they ran free into the night, bears roared, wolves howled, and cougars screamed.

Nate smiled with grim satisfaction. But there was more! Now, down in the harbor, torpedoes began exploding against the hulls of British warships. The Royal Navy, assuming they were under attack, soon began returning fire from their heavy guns at their unseen attackers.

In the gondolas women shrieked, and their escorts shouted.

Chaos reigned supreme!

The main prison door flew open, and five Hessians rushed out to see what was happening. The raiders jumped them and cut them down, grabbing the two rings of keys that would open the cells.

"Move fast, men!" cried McLane. "The Redcoats will figure out what's happening, and will be here any minute. Ben," he said to Tallmadge, throwing him a set of keys, "take the first floor! We'll take the second."

He and Cadwalader ran up the stairs, followed by Nate and Tad and the rest of their group. One by one McLane unlocked the cells, and Cadwalader shouted, "We're Continentals, boys! Here to take you home!"

Weak cheers greeted them as the prisoners realized that their prayers were being answered. The raiders helped each prisoner toward the stairs. Some had to be half carried.

But where was Running Fox? Had they killed him? Nate remembered that Fox's cell had been on the second floor, but he and Tad were almost at the end of the corridor; there were only two cells left.

"Check the one on the right," he said to Tad. "I'll take this one."

There was almost no light in the cell from the hall lantern, halfway down the corridor. But he could make out a crumpled figure on the floor in buckskin! With streaks of gray in his matted long hair. It was Running Fox.

"Oh, thank God! Tad!" he called out. "I've found him!"

As he had seen his mother do, Nate put his hand on Fox's neck and felt a faint pulse. The Indian gave a barely audible groan.

"He's *alive!*" cried Nate joyfully, and picking Fox up under his arms, he started to drag his friend out into the corridor.

Suddenly, down on the first floor, a shot rang out. "Got him!" someone yelled.

"Who fired?" called down Cadwalader from the head of the stairs. It was supposed to be a silent operation.

"Had to, sir. There was a floor guard at the far end of the hall. He was hiding back there; we couldn't see him."

Cadwalader peered into the shadows at the far end of the second floor corridor. All he could see was a stool. An empty stool.

Frowning, the colonel started down the hall.

Nate pulled his friend's limp form halfway out into the corridor.

"Nate!" cried Cadwalader, starting to run in their direction, "look out!"

Nate turned to see a young Hessian guard emerging from the dense shadow in the corner. Not much older than Nate, he was obviously frightened, but he had a musket which he was raising to fire.

In that instant Nate realized he'd have to kill him or be killed!

The young guard pointed his musket at Nate's face, its barrel shaking.

Stab him in the stomach! Nate commanded himself, but he was frozen.

"*Do it, Nate!*" yelled Cadwalader, pistol out, racing down the corridor.

Nate was shaking, too. He couldn't!

44

THE LAST TRAP

As the scared young Hessian's finger tightened on the trigger, Nate wondered if it would be the last thing he would ever see.

Crunk!

Blam!

Even as the guard crumpled to the floor, Nate felt a puff of air on his cheek. That was how close the musket ball had come, as it passed him and ricocheted harmlessly off the ceiling.

And there stood Tad, grinning, a three-legged stool clutched in his hand. "Now, we're even!" he said, with a laugh. "You saved my life; I just paid you back!"

Colonel Cadwalader looked down at the Hessian coming to his senses, extended his pistol, then thought better of it. "Throw him in there and lock it," he ordered Tad, indicating the last cell that had the key ring in it. "And hurry! We've got to get out of here!"

Nate and Tad carried Running Fox down the stairs and out into the courtyard, where McLane had gathered everyone. Each escapee who could not make it on his own was assigned a raider or two to help him.

Now, through the courtyard gate came thirteen figures on the run. It was the whale-oil gang! "Boys, you shoulda seen it!" cried Odus Levering. "Things blowin' up all over the place! Ole King George's shield a-flyin' through the air like a pie plate!"

They roared with laughter.

"We got them all out," McLane informed the Leverings. "Are the canoes and boats ready?"

"Aye, sir," replied Jacob. "Three canoes and two flatboats."

"Then let's get moving!"

As the men went out through the prison gate, McLane drew Nate aside. "Your entire family's in grave danger now, lad. They need to get out of the city *immediately*!"

185

"Yes, sir," Nate nodded. "But how?"

From his jacket, the captain drew an official-looking folded document with a red ribbon around it.

"Here. This is a safe-conduct pass I've been saving, in case I ever needed it."

Nate took it and looked at it, mystified. "What's a safe-conduct pass?"

"Signed by André in his own hand, it will pass its bearer and those with him through any picket line."

Nate was astounded. "How did you ever—"

McLane chuckled. "It's a forgery but a very good one, if I do say so. I copied André's handwriting and signature from the promissory note he wrote to Tad. It's even sealed!"

At Nate's unspoken query, McLane grinned. "Remember that gold button off his uniform? I borrowed it from Tad, long enough to use the raised impression."

Nate looked at him, concerned. "But you were going to use it yourself."

"Your family needs it more than I do. Besides, I've got to help Tad take Running Fox up the creek with the rest."

"I—we—can never thank you enough!" Nate exclaimed, sticking out his hand.

McLane shook it. "See you at Valley Forge."

Dashing up the driveway of 177 Second Street, Nate found his father putting luggage into the back of the carriage. William Donovan glared at him. "I hope thou art satisfied, young man! Thou hast forced us to flee for our lives like common criminals!"

Nate hung his head and said nothing.

"Go in the house and help thy mother get everyone ready. And get out of that ridiculous costume!"

Until that moment, Nate had forgotten he was still in livery. The white knee-stockings were mud brown now, and the green silk waistcoat was torn in several places.

Inside, Mother and Sally were trying to comfort a still-weeping Rachel. The girls had changed into traveling clothes, and Nate ran upstairs to do the same. Throwing some clothes in a bag, he hurried back down. "We've got to leave right away!"

As Sally helped Rachel out the front door, Mother went quickly to her secretary desk. Opening its secret compartment, she took up the two letters and gold coins and put them in the bodice of her dress.

Before they joined the others, Nate whispered to his mother, "We broke into Walnut Street Prison and got our men out! Every last mother's son of them! Running Fox, too! He's still alive!"

"Praise be to God!" she exclaimed softly.

Nate held the carriage door open while Mother and Sally helped Rachel get in. Just before entering, she turned to her brother and smiled weakly. "Thank you," was all she said. But it was enough.

He climbed up next to his father, who was staring straight ahead. "Since thou hast reduced us to fugitives, whither shall we flee?"

"The only place we'll be safe, Father. Valley Forge."

"Out Little Dock then?"

"No, we'd better take the Germantown Road."

"It's an hour longer."

"Tonight, for us, it's safer. We have a safe-conduct pass." He gave it to his father, explaining how he got it.

His father urged Goodness and Mercy on their way. As they pulled out onto Second Street, Nate looked back at their home. Would they ever see it again?

As they approached the Germantown Road, to their left—in the direction of the British picket lines—there was a series of muffled explosions followed by wild shouts and the rattle of musket fire. William Donovan threw a sidelong glance at his son, a sour expression on his face. "Friends of thine, I suppose."

"Um, yes," mumbled Nate, struggling to hide his grin.

In a few minutes the picket outpost on their road hove into view. A sentry holding a lantern stepped out of the guardhouse and held up his hand for them to halt. William Donovan brought the carriage to a standstill and handed the sentry the pass. He took it into the guardhouse, where he and another sentry examined it in the light of their lanterns.

Through the window Nate could see them discussing it. What was taking so long? Now they called to their sergeant.

Lydia Donovan, observing this from the carriage window, began to pray. "Father in heaven, You have watched over our family until now and guarded our steps. Please, help us now. Deliver us from this last trap of the enemy."

Nate, up on the bench beside his father, mouthed a fervent amen. He didn't know what made him turn around and look behind them. But in the moonlight he could make out a lone horseman, riding furiously in their direction. He was about a mile away, which meant he'd be there in about three minutes.

Mother saw him, too. "Heavenly Father, if You have ever heard our prayers, hear them now!"

The sergeant came out. "This pass seems to be in order. I know the captain's hand. But we've never seen a seal like this one." He handed it back.

The onrushing rider was now almost within hailing distance.

"The Yankee Doodles have been stirring up quite a bit of trouble along the line tonight," the sergeant said with a smile. "But you folks wouldn't know anything about that, would you?" He looked carefully at William Donovan.

"No, I'm afraid I don't," said Father truthfully, his face set like flint.

The rider coming behind them was shouting now. Nate could hear him, but the sergeant hadn't noticed yet.

"Very well, you may pass. Safe journey."

"We thank thee, sergeant," responded Father, slapping the reins.

As they drove away, Nate whispered, "Father, hurry! They're after us!"

Father hesitated, then took the buggy whip from its holder and cracked it over his team. "*Haagh*, Goodness! *Haagh*, Mercy!" he cried, and the horses leaped forward into a gallop.

Behind them the rider reared to a halt at the outpost and jumped off his horse, pointing in their direction.

As the lights of the outpost receded behind them, Mother's prayers turned to praise, "Oh, Father! Thank You!"

45

SAFE HAVEN

The rising sun, looking exactly like the one painted on the tavern's signboard, bathed it in a warm glow as William Donovan turned the carriage into the yard. Inside the carriage all his passengers were asleep.

"Better wake them up," he said to his son and realized that Nate, too, had nodded off. Turning, he knocked on the roof of the carriage and called, "We're here!"

The occupants stirred, and Nate jumped down to rap on the inn's door. In a moment it was opened by a sleepy Aunt Neuss, wearing a nightcap and a soup-stained robe over her nightdress. "Nate? What in heaven's name?" Then she saw the carriage behind him.

"Aunt Neuss, we've stirred up a hornets' nest. They'll be coming down the road soon, looking for us and you, too, I'm afraid. They mean to hang us all!"

"Well, you all come inside for some hot tea, and tell me all about it."

Nate put a kettle on, while Aunt Neuss went upstairs to fetch the twins. In a few moments she returned with Andrew and Molly, rubbing sleep out of their eyes.

"Mama, Mama!" they cried, running to their mother, whom they'd not seen in half a year.

Tears streamed down Lydia Donovan's face as she hugged them to her. Even Rachel's eyes were brimming. Molly and Andrew snuggled up in their mother's lap, clinging to her, as if by letting go they might lose her again.

Nate quickly told Aunt Neuss about the snow hawk, the surprise at the *Mischianza*, and the prison break. "André knows we're part of the spy ring. He'll be after our whole family! He knows the twins are here, so this place will soon be swarming with Redcoats!"

He looked at his great aunt. "You're now in as much danger as any of us, so please, come with us now. The only place we'll all be safe is at Valley Forge."

Scowling, the old woman started to shake her head.

Lydia Donovan added, "He's right, dear Aunt; you must come! It's only until the British leave the city. But now we must make Godspeed!" And she led the way upstairs, to pack up the children.

While they were waiting for the women, Nate and his father went out to care for the horses, giving them a drink and some oats.

"They did well last night, didn't they," Father said as they rubbed down Goodness and Mercy.

"They surely did, Father! They surely did."

It was afternoon when they passed Gulph Rock and sighted the log huts of Valley Forge. With a twinge, Nate recalled that it was here with Running Fox that he first saw the snow hawk. Would he ever see her again?

Perched on a boulder by the side of the road was a familiar figure, waving at them.

"Tad!" shouted Nate, jumping down and running to him.

"Been waitin' for ya.' Figured you'd be along 'bout now. Cousin Wayne says you're stayin' with us."

"How's Running Fox?"

"The Hessians messed him up pretty bad. But he didn't give us away. He's in the barn—wouldn't stay in the house."

Nate's brow furrowed. "There's eight of us."

"Nah, that's nothin'! We used to take in boarders. Besides, Mama would want it that way."

Hearing this, Lydia Donovan emerged from the carriage. "From what Nate has told me, Tad, I owe your mother a great debt of gratitude. She looked after Nate, as if he were her own."

"No more than you'd have done for me, ma'am."

Lydia got back in the carriage while Nate and Tad joined William Donovan on the driver's box.

"Turn left, down that track, Mr. Donovan," Tad instructed, and the carriage started to bounce over the field. Ahead of them, two men were walking.

Nate shielded his eyes from the sun. "That's not. . . ."

"It is," confirmed Father. "Charles!"

The younger man turned and, recognizing the carriage, came running. "Father!" he cried, even as William Donovan reined up, jumped down, and put his arm around his elder son's shoulder.

The rest of the Donovans now tumbled out of the carriage to greet him, followed by Sally.

Charles hugged his mother, whose eyes were filled with tears. Then it was Rachel's turn and the twins and Nate and Aunt Neuss.

And then Sally. But when he hugged her, she did not return his hug. Instead, she glanced sideways at Nate. Did Charles notice?

Apparently not. He was looking at his family, surprised. "What are you all doing here?"

Nate explained.

"This is splendid!" exclaimed Charles. "How long can you stay?"

"We'll be here," his father declared, "till the Continentals chase the British out of our houses!"

Nate stared at his father. But William Donovan wasn't finished. "I never thought I'd be visiting the Patriot camp, but I must admit, if what this army has done to build such character into my boys is any sign of what our new nation may expect, then good is going to come out of this war after all!"

Chaplain Duffield had joined them. "Mr. Donovan," he declared, "if all American families had young men like yours, ready to serve in the army, our independence would indeed be secure!"

Nate watched his father, who was standing still, gazing at the man whom he'd so bitterly judged for breaking up his family. Slowly a smile appeared on William Donovan's face.

The chaplain turned to Nate. "Corporal Donovan and I are on our way to look in on Running Fox. Come with us."

While the others went in the house, Nate hurried to the barn to see his friend. Running Fox was lying on a bed of straw. He weakly raised his left arm in greeting.

His face was terribly bruised, the eyes swollen almost shut. One side of his mouth hung down. A splint held his right arm straight.

At the sight of him, Nate fought the urge to weep. Would his friend ever recover?

46

WITH GRATEFUL THANKS

The first Saturday in June, General Washington invited Nate to join him on his rounds at Valley Forge for the last time. The General and his staff anticipated that the British would be departing Philadelphia in a matter of days. The moment they did, the Continental Army would break camp and follow, looking for an opportunity to attack.

Nate, riding Mercy, watched the tall horseman gracefully mount Nelson, his big gray. As the two of them rode through camp, at every regiment's campsite men stood and cheered their commander. "God bless ya, General, sir! We're gonna lick 'em!"

General Washington leaned toward Nate. "These men have endured and survived a terrible ordeal. They're ready to go anywhere now and do anything I ask of them. Outgunned, outnumbered, it will make no difference to them. Mark my words: the 'Valley Forge veterans' will be the backbone of this army."

Nate didn't want to ask, but he had to. "Sir, are we as good as the British?"

"We'll see, soon enough." The General smiled. "But I do believe our enemy is in for quite a surprise!"

That evening the Walker house came to life again for the first time since the soul of Sarah Walker had flown away. On the wide porch every column and rail was decorated with fan-folder swags of red, white, and blue.

As the sun set and the sky outside turned lavender and then purple, inside the candles in the silver candelabra and brass wall sconces were lit. In their dress uniforms General Washington's staff officers entered the elegantly decorated dining room and stood behind their chairs.

Joining them were some special guests that General Washington had invited—"the family," as he called his spy network in Philadelphia. In uniform were Colonel Cadwalader, Majors Tallmadge and Clark, and Captains McLane and Bushnell, who had received a commission in the army's corps of engineers. The civilians included Hyam Solomon, seated in the place of honor at the General's right, and several men and women Nate did not recognize. Across from Polly Cooper was Running Fox, nearly recovered from his wounds and looking decidedly uncomfortable in the company of all these people. Tad, Charles, Nate, Sally, and Rachel sat at the end with the Donovan family and Aunt Neuss.

When all were assembled, General Washington asked Chaplain Duffield to say the blessing. Soon, with a scraping of chairs, the guests began enjoying a festive meal of spring lamb, roasted potatoes, and fresh greens, with decorative loaves of sourdough bread, courtesy of Ludwig's bakers.

Tink, tink—after his guests had enjoyed their blackberry flummery and hickory coffee, the General rose and gently tapped his spoon against his pewter goblet.

"First of all, I would like to give special thanks to my staff officers. Gentlemen, you have served me faithfully and well through a winter we will never forget. When the army made camp here last December, we did not know if there would *be* an army, come spring, or a United States of America."

He looked out the window at the emerging stars. "But with the help of Divine Providence, we have survived. Our prayers were answered. And in this forge we have been hammered into an army of steel, capable of winning this war."

Nate joined the others in standing and applauding until the General raised his hand.

"Only Patsy and a few of my aides know how much I have wanted to do what is coming next." He paused and looked around the table. "The world will never know, and the annals of military history will never record, the deeds of these courageous few, who in their quiet way have served their country heroically. I refer, of course, to our spy family. And tonight, on behalf of all American Patriots, it is my privilege and pleasure to honor them."

Nate's brow furrowed, but the Commander in Chief soon explained. "Someday this war will end. When it does, healing must occur between us and our neighbors who sided with the enemy. This family's secrets must remain secret."

All looked at him solemnly. He nodded to Colonel Hamilton, who came forward with a few small, polished wooden boxes. "In each of these is a silver medallion, which can never be worn. Each is inscribed, and I will now read what is written there."

Hamilton opened the first box and handed it to him. To read the fine lettering on the silver surface, the General put on his half spectacles.

To Skuhanaksa, Running Fox, our prized spy, scout, and courier. Without his aid and that of his fellow Oneidas, the Continental Army could not have lasted the winter. With the grateful thanks of these United States.

If Fox was uncomfortable before, his discomfort now became acute, as the General motioned for him to come forward. As the reluctant Indian did so, all applauded, and Nate and Tad cheered. Fox bowed slightly, took his award, and fled from the house in embarrassment. But as he left, Nate noted a smile playing at the corners of his torn lips.

"The next medallion will, no doubt, come as a surprise to some of you." His eyes twinkled as Hamilton handed him the box.

"This goes to one of the first members of our family who helped establish our network, and who informed me of Lord Howe's intent to occupy Society Hill, almost before he had thought of it himself."

To Nate's shock, he realized that the General was looking directly at his mother!

"Madam, you were the most cunning and brilliant of them all! For outstanding service we award this medallion to you, a true American heroine."

To Lydia Donovan, for courage in the face of extreme peril with her home occupied by the enemy, and for the daring rescue of an American prisoner of war. On behalf of a grateful nation.

Nate's jaw dropped open. Mother knew General Washington? Before *any* of them?

Lydia went forward and smiled broadly as she took the box.

"Be sure to let me know, Madam, if your expenses have exceeded the sum of the two gold coins I gave you."

As she resumed her place at the table, her children stared at her in awe.

"Momma!" cried Rachel, "Why didn't you tell us?"

"Why do you think!" hissed Nate sharply.

There were other awards, and then General Washington cleared his throat. "The last award goes to another member of the Donovan family, a true son of the revolution, who has become a personal friend. Nate Donovan is still too young to be a soldier, yet his ears saved our army at White Marsh and confounded their army at *Mischianza.*"

To Nathaniel Donovan, for unwavering courage in the presence of the enemy and for valor in the rescue of American prisoners of war. With the grateful thanks of these United States.

As Nate shook the Commander in Chief's hand and received his award, he had never felt so proud in his life.

The General now addressed William Donovan. "Sir, our gratitude cannot be expressed enough for the service your family has rendered to our cause. I trust you are as proud of them as we are."

William Donovan stood. "General Washington, I will be honest. We are Quakers. Until recently, despite the involvement of certain members of my family, I could not bring myself to support your cause."

He hesitated. The room was silent. "Yet I cannot help but compare the virtuous leadership I see in you and your officers to the corrupt and oppressive immorality of the British leadership, who would forcibly return us to the yoke of the Crown."

As one, the guests stood to their feet, in silent recognition of the devout principles of this good and simple man.

General Washington smiled. "Before we adjourn, we have one more presentation, though not a medallion this time. Perhaps an early birthday present." He turned to Cadwalader. "Colonel?"

Colonel Cadwalader now came forward, carrying a bundle wrapped in homespun. He handed it to Nate. "Open it, lad."

Nate did. It was a new, buff-and-blue uniform of a Continental soldier!

Nate was speechless, but his eyes, growing moist, spoke for him.

"Mr. Donovan," declared General Washington, "normally your younger son would have to wait until his sixteenth birthday to wear this uniform. Unless, of course, you wanted to grant him special permission now."

Nate looked at his father pleadingly.

William Donovan turned to face his son. Slowly a smile spread across his face, and he nodded.

"Thank you, Father!" cried Nate, running upstairs to put it on.

In a moment he returned, looking every inch the Continental soldier! The guests applauded.

"It fits you well, Private Donovan," General Washington observed. "But you may not always be able to wear it. I've assigned you to assist Captain McLane, whom, as you know, is often in civilian clothes."

Martha Washington now spoke up. "Mr. Washington, I believe that concludes our festivities!"

"Indeed it does, Patsy." And to his guests, he announced, "Let us adjourn."

As the guests began to leave, Captain McLane came over to Nate and put a small diary in his hand. "You've earned this, lad, and the trust that goes with it."

Nate looked down. It was a code book, just like the captain's!

Just then he felt a gentle but firm hand on his arm. It was Sally. "Nate," she said sweetly but urgently, "I need to see you outside for a moment. Right now!"

Bewildered, Nate excused himself and followed Sally outside toward the barn.

As soon as they were alone, she flung her arms around his neck and kissed him on the lips.

Shocked, he kissed her back.

Suddenly he was torn away from her and whirled around. It was Charles, who now swung his fist at his brother. Nate ducked but caught a glancing blow on his left cheek. He stepped backward, rubbing his face.

"She's mine!" snapped Charles. "And you know it!"

Sally stepped between them. "Friends," she said, obviously enjoying the moment, "you mustn't fight over me! My heart will find its own way. When it does, neither fist nor cannon shall shake it."

And with that, Sally gracefully twirled her satin gown and flitted away, snubbing them both.

Looking blankly at her and then each other, the two brothers burst out laughing. Charles grinned. "Brother, I think she has been playing with both of us! Indeed, we mustn't let a woman come between us."

And with that he put his arm around Nate, and the two went back in the house.

47

THE CRIMSON CROSS

The British evacuated Philadelphia, and the Continental Army was in hot pursuit, looking for an opportunity to attack. The Donovan family was heading home. To escort them, Private Nathaniel Donovan had been granted a special forty-eight-hour pass by his new superior officer, Captain McLane.

On their way they dropped off Sally at her aunt's house. As Nate helped her down from the carriage, she placed a hand on his arm. "If I send you my poems, Private Donovan, will you read them?"

"Um, yes, of course," he stammered.

"And will you write me back?"

"Surely. But you know we will be on the march. There will be little time for letter-writing."

"I will take my chances," she said, looking deep into his eyes.

It was dusk by the time they reached 177 Second Street. A warm summer breeze brought with it the scents from the Delaware River. As Father cared for the horses, Nate carried their baggage inside. He took his parents' bags up to their room and paused to go out on the balcony. He reached out to the old elm. He'd first climbed it as a boy, long before war had come to their city. The last time he'd climbed it, it was a matter of life and death. He wondered how long it would be before he would see it again. However long this war lasted, he now knew what they were fighting for—freedom. And if necessary, he was now ready to give his life to achieve it.

Below he heard a knock and his father opening the front door. "Good evening, Mr. Donovan," said a familiar voice. "I realize you've just arrived home, but I wondered if I might have a word with you."

"Come in, Pastor Duffield." He called to his wife, "Mrs. Donovan? We have company. Might we have some tea in the parlor?"

Nate heard the chaplain say, "Now that the city is ours once again, I've been praying about what I should say tomorrow, in my first sermon back in my pulpit. I felt I should go back to the first legislative act of our colony's founder, William Penn."

"As a Quaker," commented William Donovan, warming to the subject, "I'm familiar with that. It reads: 'To establish laws that shall best preserve true Christian and civil liberty, in order that an example may be set to the nations.'"

"Exactly!" agreed Duffield. "And George Whitefield, America's great traveling preacher, had the same vision. He knew that those liberties—indeed, the future of America—depended on her relationship with God. And so, he preached on freedom, under God, for every man. He preached it from Maine to Georgia . . . *and* from the balcony on this house! I was among those who gathered in your yard to hear him."

This balcony? Nate listened, astonished, as his father responded, "I remember it well."

"Toward the end of Whitefield's life," the pastor went on, "he saw clearly that British rule was approaching tyranny. We often spoke of it. More than once he quoted Galatians 5:1 to me: 'For freedom Christ has set you free; stand fast, therefore, and do not submit again to the yoke of slavery.'"

There was a long silence.

Then William Donovan said in a voice so low that Nate could barely hear him, "I know the verse. Until now, I have not been willing to apply it to America's struggle for freedom." He paused. "I shall have to give this much thought and prayer."

Now Nate heard his mother. "Pastor, have some mint tea."

"Ah, Mrs. Donovan," observed the pastor, "a taste of heaven!" He addressed them both. "My sermon tomorrow will be based on that verse from Galatians. I would be honored, Mr. Donovan, if you and your family would attend. But I do not want to offend your principles."

"I shall be delighted, friend. And there will be no offense taken. But as for my son, since thou hast grown close to him, why dost thou not invite him thyself? He's upstairs."

Having brought the pastor up to the balcony, Father left them alone.

The night was clear. The full moon seemed unusually close.

From his jacket Pastor Duffield pulled out an ancient red leather bag, which Nate recognized. It was the same pouch that Running Fox had rescued from the graveyard.

Duffield opened it and took something out, which he carefully unwrapped. It was a cross, worked in elaborate silver filigree and set with five large red rubies, attached to a silver chain.

Pastor Duffield now hung it around Nate's neck. "This cross—the Crimson Cross—is not to be worn, lad. It is too valuable to be displayed."

Nate fingered the cross, not knowing what to say.

"George Whitefield himself gave that cross to me, Nate, when I was not much older than you. He told me that it came from the Holy Land and that in each generation it was to go to a young person who would give himself or herself to carrying out God's plan for America."

The night was still; it seemed that even the moon and stars were listening.

"Only God can free America from British tyranny; and only by honoring God will America remain free, a place of refuge for all mankind. If she forgets this, she will disgrace her freedom and provoke her God."

Nate met the pastor's gaze. "God forbid *that* should ever happen!" he declared.

"Nathaniel Donovan," said Pastor Duffield solemnly, "you have committed yourself to fight for America's freedom. But only the purest in heart, and those of noble character, will sacrifice themselves that others might live free. To become such a man, you must live the life to which this cross calls you."

Duffield's eyes softened. "One day, when you are old, you must give the cross to the young person whom God points out to you. I've searched a long time for the right one—for you. Cherish it always. Let it remind you of your destiny, God's plan for you to be a guardian of freedom."

Nate lifted it from his chest and held it in front of his face. "I accept that destiny, sir."

"God bless you and keep you, Nathaniel Donovan, in His service always."

Above them there was a movement.

Nate looked up, and his heart leaped in his chest. There against the midnight sky, her great white wings outstretched, was the snow hawk.

"America!" he cried joyously, "you're free!"

HISTORICAL NOTE

While this story is fictitious, it is closely based on truth. There was indeed an Irish Quaker family in Philadelphia, only their name was Darragh, not Donovan. The family's mother, Lydia Darragh, was later discovered to have been one of General Washington's most effective spies. He himself did set up a spy network in occupied Philadelphia, which used the codes and methods described.

While the Quakers spoke in eighteenth-century "plain speech," it is too difficult to read, so we left it in the mouth of only the father, William Donovan. For the same reason, we gave Running Fox fairly fluent English. Incidentally, he was patterned after the respected Christian Indian in Philadelphia known as "Good Peter."

The Reverend George Duffield was the beloved pastor of Old Pine Street Presbyterian Church and served as a chaplain in the Continental Army. Sally Winston, extremely popular among the young men of Philadelphia, never married. The Widow Foulke and Aunt Neuss are fictional, but Foulke's Mill and Rising Sun Tavern were real places, as were the other locations. Little Dock Creek existed, but did not run into the Schuylkill River. Hyam Solomon, the Jewish banker, actually imprisoned only in New York City, was one of the major financiers of the struggle for independence. And proving that truth is stranger than fiction, we did not invent the crude and boisterous Levering brothers.

The British chief of counter-intelligence, Captain John André, was drawn true to life. While in Philadelphia, he commandeered Ben Franklin's house for his own use, and planned the farewell celebration for Lord Howe, known as the *Mischianza*. The amazingly elaborate plans of that event are not exaggerated. André later persuaded Benedict Arnold, whom he had befriended in Philadelphia, to surrender West Point, and was caught and hanged as a spy.

All of the people the reader meets at Valley Forge were real, with the exception of Tad Walker, whose mother's death was indeed greatly mourned by the soldiers of Valley Forge. Colonel Alexander Hamilton served with gallantry, and would later become the nation's first Secretary of the Treasury. Lafayette became a favorite of General Washington, who regarded him as a son. Major Ben Tallmadge was Washington's chief of intelligence, the overall head of the spy ring, which included Colonel John Cadwalader and Captain David McLane.

The Oneida Indians have always been proud of their long trek from central New York State to Valley Forge, bringing bushels of corn, which were cooked by Polly Cooper. Baker Christopher Ludwig helped to feed the Continental Army, and Dr. Benjamin Rush was a medical doctor, a Christian educator, and a signer of the Declaration of Independence. Dr. Albigence Waldo did indeed introduce the vaccination against smallpox into the Continental Army. Headquarters guard Corporal John Steele was an ancestor of author Sheldon Maxwell.

In spite of the lack of solid historical evidence for the often repeated story of the early shad run at Valley Forge, we decided to include it.

As for the action scenes, the massacre at the barn happened as described, but there was no raid on the notorious Walnut Street Prison, nor did the Patriots disrupt the *Mischianza* with whale oil.

We hope the reader had as much fun reading this book as we did writing it.